The Winds

of

Mitamura

Other Books by John Ball

The Van
The Kiwi Target
A Killing in the Market
Rescue Mission
The Fourteenth Point
The First Team
Phase Three Alert
The Murder Children
The Winds of Mitamura
Mark One: The Dummy
Miss One Thousand Spring Blossoms

Virgil Tibbs Mysteries

Five Pieces of Jade
The Eyes of Buddha
Then Came Violence
Singapore

Chief Jack Tallon Crime Novels

Police Chief
Trouble for Tallon
Chief Tallon and the S.O.R.

The Winds
of
Mitamura

John Ball

SPEAKING VOLUMES, LLC
NAPLES, FLORIDA
2014

The Winds of Mitamura

ISBN 978-1-61232-998-7

For Mardie Iglehart

Author's Note

THE PREPARATION of this book was greatly helped by Mr. Yoshitaka Kohrogi, whose expertise concerning the Miyazaki Prefecture of Japan was invaluable.

Sincere thanks are also tendered to Mr. Masaya Fukushima, who contributed materially through his detailed knowledge of Japanese rural life.

The resourcefulness of Dr. Paul Natvig of Milwaukee, Wisconsin, was a major asset in obtaining sometimes very obscure research materials.

Most of all, the author is profoundly indebted to Mr. Dan Reitz — and wife. Eight or nine years ago, while he was in Japan, Dan acquired a bride. With unerring taste he selected a compact package which contained liberal quantities of beauty, brains, and talent — plus an eye for detail that would make a foraging eagle tremble. Through many long days and evenings Dan and Yoshiko went over the entire manuscript literally word by word, supplying hundreds of details as well as providing delightful company. Thank you, Dan. Yoshiko San, *iroiro osewa ni narimashita.*

John Ball

The Winds
of
Mitamura

Chapter One

To the fertile mind of Professor Archer Bancroft the poly-chromatic world and its masses of varied, and sometimes discord-ant humanity provided countless fascinating opportunities for il-luminating social research. As a result, whenever sociologists gathered for formal discussions the name Bancroft came up fre-quently for good reason. Knowledge of his fellow men was both his passion and his profession and to it he had already made many outstanding contributions.

From the earliest days of his college career he had thirsted to do constructive original work and the man who had been his depart-ment chairman had encouraged him. That had been the start; within five years he had gained recognition, by the end of ten, students from many countries were coming to attend his lectures. Big, bluff, and hearty, he dominated the campus, but such was his personality that almost none of his faculty colleagues resented that fact or begrudged him his well-earned celebrity. They all knew he had refused frequent and generous offers to go elsewhere. He had done much to make his own college famous and because of that they had all to some degree benefited.

To Bancroft himself all of this was secondary; the endlessly fascinating study of human cultures and behavior was permanently established in the forefront of his mind and his own ego had long since given way to this determined dedication. As he sat in his office, straining the durability of the chair he had tipped back almost to its limit, he was considering a member of his staff who, it seemed to him, was ripe for greater things.

Dr. Peter Storm, Assistant Professor of Sociology, was so obviously competent that even Bancroft himself could find little in his work to criticize. He had picked the younger man himself from a forest of candidates for the job and was more than satisfied with his choice. In academic preparation Storm was secure and in the classroom he was outstanding, at times even brilliant. He was also thoroughly reliable, something that Bancroft rated very highly indeed. So far his career development had been close to distinguished, but one significant element was still missing. He had yet to publish.

It was time now to attend to that.

Bancroft tipped forward to an upright position and picked up a small object from the top of his desk. It was a miniature Tibetan bronze, barely three inches high, but classic in its beauty and sense of repose. From time to time Bancroft brought a piece from his collection to his office and kept it on his desk, the better to inspire and focus his thoughts. So strong was his empathy, he sometimes had the illusion of communicating with the object itself, or through it with the skilled and talented artist who had created it. He had never been to Tibet, but he had a consuming desire to go someday.

As he held and studied the tiny statuette it seemed to expand its own dimensions to encompass not only the Land of Snows, but also centuries of culture and refinement spread over the thousands of miles that made up the Orient. He was still intent in his contemplation of the seated miniature figure when he sensed that someone was just outside the door of his office. A moment later Peter Storm came in, on time literally to the minute for his appointment.

Bancroft put down the bronze and brought his thoughts back to the time and place of his physical presence. He waved his associate into the chair beside his desk and made it clear that the interview to follow would be a pleasant one.

"Peter," he began as soon as the right moment had matured, "the Wycliffe Foundation has just come through with a grant that I've been after for some time. It's very generous. So how would you feel about taking a semester off from your teaching duties to do a piece of research?"

Storm had a noted ability to get right to the heart of things. "If I understand you correctly, Arch, what you are proposing is that I do something that will look well in print."

Bancroft had to admit to himself that that one had been right over the plate, as a consequence he took a moment to frame his response. "Just for the record," he began, "I've never subscribed to the 'publish or perish' philosophy. But when you do something that might be significant, then there is a certain obligation to put it on the record for the benefit of others who may follow. That's the whole point of the literature, as you well know. I'm aware that you'll soon be up for your tenure and you're going to get it regardless; what I'm more interested in at the moment is putting your talents to work in a wider orbit."

Bancroft picked up the exquisite little statuette once more and handed it silently to his younger associate. Storm took it and turned it over in his hands. When he had examined it for half a minute, he spoke. "I'm not up on Oriental bronze work, so I don't know much about this. It's obviously fine and, judging by the patina, at least a century old. Since I assume that it's from your own collection, those are easy conclusions. Is it Chinese?"

"No, Tibetan; otherwise you were entirely correct." Bancroft put the piece down once more and then began to fit his fingertips together, a sure sign that he was about to translate thoughts into words.

"Peter, how are your Japanese language lessons coming along?"

Storm's shoulders slumped. "Arch, don't ask. I don't know how I ever got involved in the first place. It must be the most fiendish language on the face of the earth. You speak one way if you are talking to an equal, a totally different way if you are addressing a superior, and a third way if you're talking to someone beneath you. Women speak differently from men. And the writing . . ." He shook his head. "Impossible."

"But you have learned something, haven't you?"

"Enough to say 'good morning' and to ask the way to the head. But my hopes of reading the literature are down the tube, and that's what got me started in the first place. Why do you ask?"

Bancroft took his time before he answered. "I've been having some conversations with Doug Weissberg concerning modern-day Japan. There have been drastic changes, particularly during the past five years. You will recall that this country deliberately isolated itself for centuries. All would-be visitors were barred, and no Japanese were allowed to travel abroad except on government business. The national culture that was built on more than a thousand years of tradition was unique — and almost fanatically guarded."

Bancroft clasped his hands behind his head and shaped his thoughts for a moment. "As you well know, right after World War II all that changed," he continued, "and Japan entered the modern world with a rush. Lately that speed has accelerated in almost every area — sociologically, commercially, and in the professions. Japanese engineering, for instance, is now the world's finest in many areas. The young people have all but discarded the old ideas of formal courtesy and manners of speech. Instead they keep up to the minute on all of the latest pop stars and hairdos. The old Japan doesn't seem to interest them in the least."

"In a way, a tragedy," Storm said.

Bancroft nodded his agreement. "Which brings up an idea," he said. "Peter, I've been able, with some help, to locate a small village that seems to be typical of thousands of others throughout Japan. Tourists never go there and there isn't any industry other than agriculture. Now the question is: in such a small, strictly localized village, how much has the contemporary overlay penetrated into the lives of the people? Is the place blanketed by TV sets, or do some of the old ways still prevail? If so, do they have something to contribute to contemporary society? And how long can they hold out — how secure are they as of right now? Lastly and most important: what chance has the indigenous culture of the people to survive in opposition to all of the alien influences that have been and are being brought to bear?"

"I like the last part best," Storm said.

"I knew that you would — it's the heart of the thing, really. And it's not only Japan: important and unique cultures are being threatened all over the world for the same reasons. It's a subject that merits investigation. Would you like to take it on?"

"There must be some competent scholars who speak fluent Japanese."

"I'm sure that there are, but I don't want them. Peter, anyone who knows Japan well enough so that he or she can speak that very difficult language is bound to have a whole set of thoroughly preconceived notions and ideas, and that's just what I want to avoid. I want a fresh outlook; someone able to approach the subject with a completely open mind. A previous knowledge of Japan would be a drawback, something like sending an ambitious presidential candidate to cover a major political convention."

Peter had another reservation. "Arch, a project like that could take months."

Bancroft brushed that one aside. "The literature is already well supplied with in-depth studies of both urban and rural Japan. I'm not proposing another one. What I am suggesting is a specific investigation of one particular thing. With your professional background and competence, a month or six weeks in the field should be all that you would need. Furthermore, the funds are more than adequate and a university-related interpreter can be provided."

He paused realizing that he had been lecturing. Peter understood perfectly and wisely remained quiet.

"Let me put it this way: if I didn't have the Johnson Memorial Lecture to give and that confounded meeting in Boston to chair, I'd be very much interested in doing this one myself."

Storm realized that he would have to declare himself. "I'd like to think about this a little, if you don't mind," he said. "It does sound like an interesting idea and quite frankly I'd like to see Japan and experience some of its culture — if there's any left."

Bancroft checked visually that there was no one hovering outside his office. "Peter, if you have any marriage plans that this might disrupt, tell me now."

Storm shook his head. "When we finally got down to discussing things rationally, we both found out that we were on the verge of a major mistake. So by mutual consent it's off with no recriminations either way. We're still friends."

"I'm sorry, but if it wasn't going to work out, then you're to be congratulated. You understand what I mean."

"Of course."

"Now, Peter, while you are turning this over in your mind, there is one more idea I'd like to have you consider. This is entirely optional with you, but you know the proven value of the male-female research team concept and the added vitality that it frequently provides. Masters and Johnson were pioneers to a degree and so were Hartman and Fithian."

Storm looked at his superior for a moment and then drummed his fingertips on the top of Bancroft's desk. "Arch, if you're suggesting that I take a female research partner with me, and you are, then obviously you have her all picked out and waiting in the wings. Frankly, I would a little rather work alone, but on the other hand, I know that you wouldn't stoop to matchmaking. Who is she?"

Bancroft made no attempt whatever to be coy. "First, let me make it very clear that if you take this project on, you will be running it your way. If you want her, fine, if not, forget it. Her name is Marjorie Saunders and she's a candidate for her master's under Doug Weissberg — he proposed her to me. Twenty-four, single, definitely serious-minded. She's capable of a strictly professional relationship — if you chose to go beyond that, that's your business. She's been majoring in the Orient and speaks some Japanese, although she's never been there."

"Is that your evaluation?" Storm asked.

"No, I haven't met her yet, but I'm about to. She's coming on campus this afternoon, ostensibly to bring me some material from Doug relating to the Boston meeting. She doesn't know that she's under consideration for this project, or that it even exists. Incidentally, Doug tells me that she's excellent at shorthand — that could be very useful in the field."

Storm got to his feet. "Is she flying in?"

"Yes."

"Then obviously you'd like to have me meet her and form an opinion. Since Weissberg proposed her, I would assume that she's all right — but I certainly wouldn't want to go off to Japan with her until I'd had a pretty good look myself first."

Bancroft tipped forward and got up himself. "Definitely not, and let me emphasize that whatever you decide, you are in no way committed to her. I made that very clear before I let Doug send her over."

"When is she due in?"

"Two forty-five. She'll be expecting you. I'll be here when you get back." He glanced once more at the top of his desk and

prepared to leave. He discovered that he felt slightly uncomfortable
— he had intended only to propose the Japan idea to Storm and
to read his reaction to it. Instead, he had allowed his own research
enthusiasm to take over. He had opened the bag all the way much
sooner than he had intended. By doing that he had given his
associate very little choice.

He thought for a moment while there was still time, but he saw
no visible way to backtrack. Storm would know that the whole idea
had largely been created for him, therefore he would take over like
the good professional that he was.

Bancroft turned to lock the door, then in the hallway he addressed his colleague once more. "I'd like to have your general
opinion of the whole idea," he said.

"I'll tell you when I get back," Storm answered.

As he drove toward the airport, Peter Storm began to filter out
some conclusions. He was being prodded into something and that
automatically annoyed him a little. But instead of allowing himself
to become emotional about it, he tried to review factually what he
had been told.

There was no doubt in his mind that Bancroft was trying to help
him. From the first day that he had walked on campus Archer
Bancroft had been in his corner, guiding and advising him without
ever overdoing it or taking advantage of his position as the department chairman.

Now Bancroft was setting him up with a basically interesting
research project so that he would have some significant data to
publish. Peter was not concerned about getting his tenure, but
some of the trustees strongly advocated that as many faculty members as possible should appear at suitable intervals in some form of
print, no matter how obscure. Money had to be raised each year
to keep the college going — that was a fact as realistic as preg-

nancy. One useful tool for impressing potential donors was a list of recent faculty publications even though in some cases the achievements were shadowy — such as appearing as associate editor of a small piece in some local journal.

Peter rolled down the window next to the driver's seat and let the air flow in. All right — he would do it. He had nothing against the idea and he certainly owed it to Bancroft and to the college. It would have suited him better to have picked his own subject and his own time, but if Archer Bancroft, to whom he owed so much, wanted him to go to Japan, then he would oblige and incidentally get the unwritten requirement for tenure off his back.

Satisfied with that, he drove on until he reached the airport and parked his car in an available stall. In the terminal building he went first to the airline counter and checked the board. The flight due in at two forty-five was on schedule.

"Do you have much of a load coming in?" he asked the agent on duty.

"About twenty will be getting off here, sir."

"In that case, will you do me a favor. I'm to meet a Miss Marjorie Saunders, whom I don't know."

The agent wrote the name down. "No problem, sir. As soon as the pax are all off, we'll page her and ask her to come here."

"Thank you, that will be fine."

Since he had a few minutes to wait, Peter walked leisurely to the newsstand and surveyed the publications on display. The men's magazines with the nude centerfolds were stacked relatively high — obviously they sold well. There were some hot-rod media, two or three aviation periodicals, a few women's publications with vapid, unreal models pictured on their covers, and a scattering of miscellaneous titles crowded together.

Two revolving wire stands held soft-cover books. One of the racks was almost entirely filled with obvious sex titles, a few professing at least to be scholarly, the rest frankly titillating fiction with characteristic teasing covers. The other held some semi-classics: Somerset Maugham, Poe's tales of horror, and *The Adventures of Sherlock Holmes.* A distinctive cover, apparently taken from a Japanese block print, caught Peter's eye; the title was *Snow Country.* He remembered having heard of the book and picked it out of the rack to examine it.

According to the notices reprinted on the back cover, it was a genuinely important work. Peter bought it and then found a place where he could sit down. He did not start to read; the plane was due in shortly and he preferred to do some thinking instead.

For several minutes he turned the various facets of the proposed project over in his mind, adjusting himself to the prospects as he saw them. His concentration was not broken until he heard the paging system ask that Miss Marjorie Saunders please report to the ticketing counter.

Peter got to his feet. Because the same aircraft was due to make a return flight within the hour, the counter was somewhat crowded and various pieces of baggage took up room on the floor. Instead of trying to get the busy agent's attention again, he stood to one side and waited. He had been there only briefly when he felt his arm touched.

He turned to face a young woman who spoke to him. "Dr. Storm?"

"Yes."

"It was very kind of you to meet me. I'm Marjorie Saunders."

He sized her up quickly and expertly. Height five feet four, which was good. Face and hair, decidedly attractive. Figure, very superior. Her hips were exactly right, narrow enough to be trim, curved enough to be intensely feminine. Her breasts were obviously excellent in a way that no bra, no matter how well advertised, could simulate.

She was definitely something; far more, in fact, than he could possibly have expected. Only one thing truly surprised him: he had not expected that she would be black.

Chapter Two

THEY COULD HAVE let him know.

Not that it mattered that much, but for a few seconds he was off balance. He had the quick thought that Arch Bancroft had leaned a little backward in order to avoid the semblance of prejudice; a word in advance would have made identification at the airport a little simpler. As these thoughts raced through his brain, Peter added one more — he would have to be particularly careful not to take notice or embarrass her in any way. A moment's carelessness now could seriously prejudice their working together if, indeed, they were to enter into any such partnership.

"Do you have any luggage?" Peter asked.

"No, I'm planning to go back tonight — in fact I have to."

"Then my car is in the lot right outside. Shall I bring it around?"

She looked at him. "I'm not that helpless, Dr. Storm," she answered.

He held the door open for her. As he did so he looked quickly around out of professional interest to see if they were attracting any attention. As far as he could detect, no one appeared to be the least concerned. He filed that slender bit of data away — wondering how long it would hold up.

As soon as they were outside he allowed himself to make a further appraisal of his companion, trying to evaluate her as he would any promising female in the same age bracket. He particularly like the way that she walked, with her head well poised and a quiet pride in her bearing.

He glanced again at her profile. Her features were quite aquiline; her nose in particular was well shaped with no evidence of either spread or flattening. Her eyes were dark, of course, and the bit of eye shadow that she wore was a mistake, in his opinion, but her lashes appeared to be real. When she turned toward him with an animated smile he decided that regardless of her color, he had really lucked out. "I see that you're reading Kawabata," she said.

He had all but forgotten the book in his hand. "I just picked it up at the newsstand," he admitted.

She was pleasantly informal. "Have you had a chance yet to read any of his other things, such as *A Thousand Cranes?*"

"No, I haven't." He sometimes offended people by telling the simple truth like that, but on the other hand he never found himself trapped in a complex web of lies.

"I must confess that he is one of my favorites," she continued. "I don't flip over Indian gurus and things like that, but he certainly was a great master."

Then Peter remembered. "The Nobel Prize," he said.

"Yes, and so well deserved!" She brought her hands together in a moment of mental stimulation. "The opening sentence of *Snow Country* is very simple in English: 'The train came out of the long tunnel into the snow country.' But in Japanese it has an inner rhythm that flows like fine poetry."

As Peter bent over to unlock his car he noticed that her legs were excellent. "I don't understand the language that well," she explained. "Not at all. It was pointed out to me."

Peter put her inside and then walked around to get in himself. As he did so he realized that she had no distorting accent in her speech at all. There was no slurring, none of the southern thickness that characterized so many blacks. As he fastened his seat belt he wondered how much of the general consciousness of Negroes was based solely on skin color and how much came from the speech deviations that characterized so many black people, often intentionally.

He remembered that he was a host and resumed his role. "I understand that you've never met Dr. Bancroft," he said.

"No," she answered. "I'm looking forward very much to the privilege. He must be a tremendous person."

"He is."

Undoubtedly Arch himself hadn't known — he should have guessed that.

For the time being the conversation stopped. He concentrated on his driving, aware that by not making small talk he was giving no offense. He couldn't discuss the Japanese project because as yet she didn't know of it and it was Bancroft's baby to talk about, if he decided to go ahead.

He pulled into the faculty parking lot next to the social sciences hall and escorted her into the building. Bancroft was in his office once more when he arrived at the door; he paused long enough to get a welcoming nod and then showed her in.

As Archer Bancroft got to his feet even Peter's trained eye detected nothing but a suitable greeting for a young lady interested in his own field of specialty. He made her welcome and received the packet she had for him with obvious interest. For a minute or two he reviewed its contents, nodding approval once or twice as he did so. "This is just what I needed," he told her. "It was so kind of you to bring it over."

"It's my pleasure, Dr. Bancroft. I wanted to meet you very much."

"I'm flattered," Bancroft said. "I understand that you're taking your master's; tell me about it." He made it more than a polite question as he leaned forward and evidenced real interest. Peter knew it for a fact and wondered if the girl could tell. Probably not on such short acquaintance, although Archer Bancroft was habitually interested in everything that the world contained.

For almost fifteen minutes the conversation revolved around Marjorie Saunders' interests, and general sociological topics. During most of the time Peter sat quietly, admiring the expert probing job that was being done. Then Bancroft glanced at him while the girl was looking into her purse for a moment. Peter understood and gave the only response that he could, nodding his head just enough for his superior to see.

When the conversation resumed Bancroft brought up the subject of the proposed Japanese study in a casual manner. He sketched in the general idea in broad terms and invited her opinion.

The response she gave him was one of immediate interest. The young woman freely confessed that she had never been to the Far East despite her avowed interest in that part of the world and some grasp of the Japanese language.

Bancroft checked with Peter once more and then probed a little more deeply. When he judged the time to be right he told her that Dr. Storm was considering undertaking the project himself and that if he did so, he might be interested in a suitable female research partner.

At that point Marjorie Saunders became visibly tense and excited, but she still exhibited a restraint that Peter at once appreciated and admired. "Dr. Bancroft," she said, "I know that there must be many candidates for that assignment; probably you've already made some preliminary decisions. But if you'll allow a late entry, please, oh please let me submit what qualifications I have for your consideration!" She regathered herself and tried again. "I realize that I have almost no chance, but consider me, will you please?"

As the meeting broke up Bancroft promised that he would add her name to the list of those interested in the Japanese study. As Peter drove her back to the airport he was braced for a barrage of questions he was not prepared to answer. Mercifully Marjorie Saunders took a different tack; she asked about his teaching work and whether or not the rest of the college community appreciated Bancroft's vast reputation in his field. He was quite comfortable on those topics and the ride was soon over. When he discovered that her flight was not going to depart for almost an hour due to a mechanical delay, he took her into the coffee shop and offered refreshments.

It would have been inhuman of her then not to have talked a little about the project in which she was so interested and she did. During their conversation Peter tried to measure his own reaction, and the visible public's, to his sitting with an ethnically different companion. Insofar as he could tell, if the waitress who was serving them or any of the other patrons who saw them together had any thoughts on the subject, they kept them well hidden. There were no side glances, no looks a fraction longer than they should have been, no business of pointedly turning away. His own reaction was a gradual easing of his awareness as he grew more accustomed to her presence. He had never felt uncomfortable with any of the students at the college who were also black, but he had never been in precisely the same position; he was obviously escorting Marjorie Saunders on a one-for-one basis.

The fact that she was so trim and neat appealed to him strongly. He was well aware of the fact that both her speech and her manner were well above the norm for a young woman of her years, and she was obviously intelligent. Her eyes, he noted, were highly expressive and when he looked into them, all he could think of was female.

When the flight was called he saw her to the departure gate and held her hand for a brief moment. She was warm and inviting. He realized fully that a possible professional association should rule out any possible intimacies, and that was just as well. However, for a reason he could not entirely fathom, he was angry with himself as he drove back to the college.

On his desk there was a note to phone Dr. Bancroft at his home. He put through the call and received an invitation to join the Bancrofts for dinner. He accepted, as he was expected to do, and a half hour later he was seated in the very comfortable living room of his host with a glass in his hand. He knew that he had been summoned for a reason and he had a very good idea what it was.

Bancroft dropped onto the other end of the sofa while his wife was safely out of hearing in the kitchen. "Peter," he began, "when I discussed Miss Saunders with you in my office before you went out to get her, I was unaware of her heritage."

"I know that," Peter said.

"I assumed that you would. As soon as you two had left, I called Doug Weissberg and we had a discussion." He paused long enough to consult his own drink. "Now let me lay it out for you exactly as I see it; if you don't agree with me at any point say so."

"All right, I will."

"Good. Now to begin with, as things are today, ethnic backgrounds are supposed to be ignored. As for myself, I believe in the basic dignity of every human being, but I also realize that utopia has not yet arrived. To pretend that it has, in all respects, would be asinine. The Greeks and the Turks are not currently falling into each others' arms in a paroxysm of brotherly love. The Palestinian terrorists aren't dining on chicken soup and matzoh balls."

"Agreed."

"I told Doug that freedom from prejudice is an admirable quality in anyone, but realistically he should have advised me of Miss Saunders' background. And for a very basic reason that he knows as well as I do: there is a definite hostility toward Negro people in many parts of Japan."

Peter drummed his fingers soundlessly on the padded arm of the davenport. "On principle," he said, "I dislike the idea of ruling anyone out because of creed, color, and so forth. Also, as a person I rather like her. If Doug says that she's qualified, I'll buy his opinion. But if she's going to run into a stone wall in the Orient, then it wouldn't be doing her any favor to take her."

Bancroft turned his body to face him more squarely. "Peter, let me fill you in a little more, based on what Doug just told me during our conversation. Marjorie Saunders isn't what you might call an ordinary black girl, if there is any such thing. For one thing she didn't grow up under anything approaching ghetto conditions: her family is wealthy and they've given her every advantage that they could. She's been to the very best private schools, she's ridden in horse shows, and has had the finest clothes to wear."

"So she's had, as a result, a much higher degree of social acceptance."

"Precisely! Her family has been able to shield her almost completely from most of the frustrations that might otherwise have beset her. It's Doug's feeling that she has had only limited contact, at the most, with the all-black community."

Peter weighed that information in his mind and considered it carefully. "I see two sides to the coin," he said finally. "If she has not had to encounter too much in the way of prejudice in the past, then confronting it in Japan might well throw her."

"True," Bancroft agreed.

"On the other hand, people very often receive the kind of reactions that they invite — as you well know. The fact that she has the kind of background that she does could make a material difference. The Japanese are very sensitive to genuine refinement — I'm well aware of that. She speaks remarkably well and you did notice, I'm sure, that she's quite attractive."

"Indeed I did, Peter. Her father, incidentally, is a surgeon, good enough that he has the American Board and is frequently called in by his colleagues of all backgrounds. The family lives in an impressive mansion in the very best part of town. He belongs to the country club and sits on the board. Doug has met him and it is his impression that Dr. Saunders is an exceptional person in every respect."

"Having met his daughter, I'm not too surprised."

"Incidentally, Marjorie was elected prom queen during her junior year in high school. A white escort took her to the dance."

Peter did react a little to that, but he kept it entirely within himself. He was surprised at that much freedom from prejudice, either way, even a few years back. "That's interesting," he said.

"She belongs to the college Mensa group, so intellectually she's in the top two percent."

Peter got to his feet and walked a few steps before he turned around. "Arch, since she has that kind of a background and is so very much interested in your proposal, I'd be a fool not to want her for a research associate. Also there are some advantages. A little less likelihood of unwarranted gossip, not that I give a damn about that. A good image professionally. A better chance, perhaps, of working objectively together."

Bancroft nodded. "All true. Now what's the rest of it?"

"Just one more item." Peter took his time before he voiced it. "I wish to hell that I knew how the rural Japanese will react to her."

Chapter Three

I N THE UNCEASING CRUSH of mid-morning Tokyo traffic Ted Wakabayashi guided his rotary-engined Mazda with a patient head and an experienced hand. The daily smog that reduced visibility drastically in all directions palled over the city like a standing curse that no living man had the power to lift. The heat was there also, but it was endurable; the choking traffic and the packjam of humanity that gave the Japanese metropolis five times the population density of any American city were the indigestible elements that had to be accepted and endured. There was a certain glamor to Japan, Ted knew, but not a shred of it was to be found in the heart of metropolitan Tokyo on this benighted business day.

A taxi pulled up a hair's breadth away from his own car and he silently cursed the stone-faced driver who had no consideration for any vehicle but his own. Not long ago 90 yen had opened the door of many of the taxis in the city, now it was ¥170 and the meters ran with hotter intensity. Tokyo was just too damn expensive for anybody except, perhaps, the Japanese, who seemed quite suddenly to have cornered most of the money in the world. If they ever got into an economic showdown with the Arabs and their oil wells, it would be one hell of a battle.

He crept a few more feet forward and a little closer to the entrance to the toll freeway that would eventually take him to the airport. He didn't know how much longer he could stand the pressures of Tokyo; he kept thinking of his quiet home in Gardena on the south side of Los Angeles where he had grown up. He did not know what divided emotions a Jew from New York might feel standing on the soil of Israel, but as for himself he was American *in toto* and only the fact that he was bilingual accounted for his presence in Japan at all.

Japanese had been spoken at home during his boyhood for the sake of his parents. Earlier in their lives they had been up to the formidable challenge of emigrating to a then highly unfriendly new world, but they had never been able to contend with its language. The company that he worked for had asked him one day if by any chance he could speak Japanese. Before he had thought he had answered that he could, thus one American engineer had been shipped off to Tokyo to head up an office there. He often wished fervently that he had kept his big mouth shut.

Since he could do little else but think in the midst of the eternal traffic jam, he recalled once again his collegiate days when he had taken his minor under the guidance of Dr. Archer Bancroft. Sociology had not been his prime concern, but Bancroft had made it so infernally interesting he had never forgotten those lectures. Now Bancroft had asked him for a favor and he was more than willing to respond, even though it included driving to the airport at an awkward time of day. Only in the evening could it be expected to be relatively easy.

At last he inched his way to the tollway entrance, drove up the ramp behind a Nissan truck, and took his ticket. Once on the elevated roadway it was a little better and a constant parade of traffic lights no longer impeded all progress.

Bancroft's associate professor was coming in on Korean Air Lines to do a research project. Ted already knew a good deal about it since he had suggested as a good study subject the small village

where his grandparents had lived. It was small and relatively isolated, so for what Bancroft wanted Mitamura was close to ideal. It
wasn't much of a place, but at least it wasn't Tokyo and that in
itself was a blessing.

He thought of attractive Betty Yamada, who worked in one of
the underground shops for which the city was famous. Since she
came and went by subway, she was forced to live more like a mole
than a human being — always breathing sterile conditioned air
while her skin and body tried to find substance in the constant glare
of artificial lights. During the winter months she never saw the sun
except on her day off. It was a helluva way to spend her youth. The
rice paddies of Mitamura weren't much, but at least they had
sunlight and the air carried the breath of life and the scent of
growing things.

He was getting poetic and that was enough of that.

He had never met Dr. Storm; he had graduated before Bancroft's new associate had come on the faculty. If the man turned
out to be a toothy character with a beard, then he was prepared
to welcome him properly, point him in the right direction, and
wish him well. On the other hand if he turned out to be anything
like Bancroft himself, then the *mizu shobai*, Tokyo's vast entertainment industry, had much to offer. As was essential in Japan,
he had an expense allowance that was astronomical by American
standards and Dr. Storm could be considered a valuable contact if
it was put the right way. Any company in Tokyo that scrutinized
entertainment expense accounts too closely would have vast difficulties in recruiting and retaining good key employees.

Bancroft's letter had mentioned a female research partner, but
it had not been clear whether or not she would be coming on the
same flight. If a female did present herself, then he would restudy
the situation, taking into account Storm's relationship with her, if
any, and how good-looking she was. All in due time.

Ted parked his car and checked with Korean Air Lines; the flight was running late. With time on his hands he went to the Pan American Clipper Club, greeted the hostess on duty by her name, and settled down with a Bloody Mary. After reading the *Wall Street Journal* and a copy of the *Los Angeles Times* that some passenger had been kind enough to leave behind, he checked with his office by phone and then went to meet the incoming flight.

Knowing his way around Haneda Airport, he engaged one of the uniformed greeters to pick up Dr. Storm in the arrival area. When the girl returned not too many minutes later she had a man in tow who was a reassurance the moment he came into view. His appearance was just what it should have been. He was moderately tall and well groomed, which meant so much in Japan. His age was right: he was old enough to be accepted as a *sensei*, or teacher, but he was also still young enough to suggest that the richest parts of his life still lay before him. And his face revealed a natural cordiality that implied he would get on well with people.

"Dr. Storm?" Ted came forward with the words. "I'm Ted Wakabayashi; Professor Bancroft asked me to meet you."

Storm's hand was firm and secure. "Thank you for coming, Ted, I was told to expect you."

"Are you alone, doctor?"

Storm set down the small case he was carrying. "No, my research partner is with me. She should be out shortly."

Ted was quick. "If you've already made your own arrangements . . ."

Storm shook his head. "Neither of us has been here before. Did Dr. Bancroft write you about her?"

"He mentioned that she might be with you, that's all."

"Dr. Bancroft picked her for this project because she's very interested in the Far East. She speaks some Japanese."

"She does? That's great, but how did she learn? Is she nisei?"

"No, she's . . . coming right behind you."

Ted turned, saw Marjorie and her happy smile, and gave instant fervent thanks that his ancestors had blessed him with an impassive face to use when he needed it. He needed it now. A *kokujin!* She was the best-looking black girl he had ever seen and she walked like a queen, but good God, in Mitamura . . .

He called up the reserves and with their help kept his composure intact while he was being introduced. When he was over that hurdle he recovered the power of speech. "I have you both in the Imperial Hotel for tonight," he announced. "I made reservations for two to be on the safe side."

Marjorie was delighted. "Oh, good! That's the famous Frank Lloyd Wright building, isn't it?"

"It was, but the old building was torn down some time ago; the land was just too valuable for a three-story hotel."

He excused himself and arranged to have the baggage sent on the airport bus; his small car would never be able to hold it along with three people. By the time he had done that, he had recovered his balance and was himself once more. He could get along with anybody, but he had set this whole thing up in Mitamura where the people had probably never seen a *kokujin* in their lives and they would be scared witless. The children would run and hide. He might as well have invited Macbeth's witches to stop in for tea.

He collected his guests once more and headed in on the expressway toward the central city. Beside him Storm was taking in everything with professional interest. Ted knew what reaction to expect and presently he got it.

"If it weren't for the signs, and driving on the left," Peter said, "this could be any busy American city."

"Japan has modernized in a rush," Ted told him. "They never do anything by halves in this country — it's always all out and gung ho, with no holds barred."

"In the villages too?" Marjorie asked from the rear seat.

"Not as much so, no, but don't try to find the Japan of the Tokugawa Period; it simply doesn't exist any more."

"Which is to be expected," Peter said.

Ted kept his eyes on the road as he spoke. "Feudal Japan is gone, but Japanese life and culture are still very much alive. Some Japanese even feel that all this modernization is only a passing phase and that someday Japan will revert back to what she once was. Personally I doubt it, but you know how long Puritanism hung around in our country, as an example."

"Indeed I do," Peter agreed.

When they reached the hotel, efficiency intruded once more as they were ushered inside, greeted in good English, and processed with mechanical precision. Ted saw his guests to the elevator and made a date to meet them for lunch in half an hour in the second-floor dining room. Then he sat down in the almost too spacious lobby for a few minutes of considered thought.

Peter Storm had told him that this was their first visit to the Far East, so there was a good chance that they would not know about the Japanese sensitivity toward dark skin of any kind. The indigenous population was practically all of one race, but there were often decided differences in pigmentation — the results of a mixed heritage uncounted generations ago. Light skin was highly prized and those of darker cast, although pure Japanese in ethnic terms, suffered a disadvantage. The American Negro G.I.'s had acutely compounded the problem when they left the *ainoko*, their "love children," behind them.

He had suggested the village of Mitamura with its limited population and one small inn and had made all of the advance arrangements. So when he saw his charges off in the morning, his own problem would not be over — it would be only the beginning.

He felt sorry for the girl; it was just too bad that her color was certain to foul up her first Japanese experience. Especially in Mitamura. He had heard certain things and it was very possible that they were true. Of all of the places that she might have gone . . .

He wished intensely that he could do something about it, but it was far too late for that now.

The subject came up at lunch. The meal was going quietly and well in the surroundings of the elegant dining room when Marjorie asked her question. "Ted, there's something I want to know before we leave for the village where we'll be working. Will the fact that I am black make any particular difference in this country?"

He sensed at once that she already knew the answer; what she was really asking was the degree of distrust and hostility that she might have to face. "Both of you will be conspicuous as *gaijin* — foreigners. That will create some difficulties, and you will have a language problem too. On top of that . . . ," he hesitated for the right words, ". . . the Japanese are much too sensitive about skin color, I won't deny that to you. Hopefully, when they get to know you, they will feel very differently."

He knew that he had hurt her. She lowered her head and while no tears came into her eyes, he had an understanding of what she was going through. Indelibly burned into his own mind was the memory of the World War II relocation camp where he and his parents had been confined simply because of their Japanese ancestry. They had thought that they were complete Americans until that second day of infamy. It would haunt him for the rest of his life.

Marjorie recovered herself. "Thank you," she said. "I was afraid that it would be that way, but I wasn't sure."

Peter put down his fork. "Ted," he declared, "I've given serious consideration to abandoning the project here and now. If we can't go into the village simply as two human beings, granted that we will be foreigners, and if we can't win the acceptance of the people there on a basis of reasonable human exchange, I'm going to call it off."

Wakabayashi firmly shook his head. "No. In the first place, simply by going to Mitamura and doing what you have planned, you will automatically improve things a little. And remember that politeness is a major factor in the Japanese culture."

"I don't want to quit," Marjorie said. "I wasn't raised that way. There's no point in trying to run away from what I am and I won't be guilty of it. I'll do my best, and take my chances that I'll get by."

The plates were removed and the dessert was served, an interlude that cooled things down a little. Then Peter spoke. "It's purely coincidental, but it happens that we three together represent the major divisions of mankind. Certainly we get along."

Marjorie looked at him. "If you're willing," she began, "I want to go to Mitamura with you. I have some reasons of my own."

Peter accepted that. "All right," he declared, "We'll go on as planned."

Silently, Ted Wakabayashi implored his ancestors to assure him that he himself had done the right thing.

On the southeastern shore of the island of Kyushu the waters of the Pacific Ocean wash with timeless patience against the prefecture of Miyazaki. Most of the area of this far southern part of Japan is fiercely mountainous, leaving only a small portion that is suitable for agriculture. With what land they do have the farmers of Miyazaki, by means of long and unstinting labor, accomplish some remarkable things. In a good year, when the many plant pests and the frequent typhoons leave them relatively alone, they manage to bring in two complete crops, thanks to chemical fertilizers and other means of enriching the soil. By giving every scrap of arable land meticulous hand care, they raise a variety of significant crops and in their paddy fields they normally succeed in producing more than three tons of rice per acre, a figure twice what is accomplished in China and three times the accepted output in Indonesia.

It is not easy work. It calls for much back-breaking toil by both men and women, but the sometimes intricate growing processes are something they thoroughly understand. Because they do, they accept the necessary labor as part of the process of living and take a proper pride in their annual achievements.

The paddies that they work have for the most part been in steady use for generations. They were once systematically built, beginning at a smoothly excavated base and then continuing upward by layer upon layer of careful construction many feet high. Each paddy was designed to hold an even inch and a half to two inches of water over the top of the muddy soil and to maintain that level by constant irrigation for many weeks, to give growing rice precisely the conditions that it needs to achieve fruitful maturity in the shortest possible time.

Because the systematic cultivation of rice is very close to a precision operation, and because it requires a massive amount of human labor made up of equal parts of skill and patience, the people of Mitamura had long since learned to regulate their lives to conform to its exacting requirements. Precious daylight was seldom wasted and every day of good growing weather was a blessing for which grateful thanks were given.

The rice seedlings were well started when the single telephone in the village rang in the schoolhouse and the *sensei* answered. She listened and understood, aware that she was talking to a man whose family had long been prominent in the village and still had land holdings of nearly four acres. She agreed, with well-concealed hesitation, to make all of the necessary arrangements and to notify those persons who would be concerned. This last was an unnecessary assurance, because there was no possibility that news such as she had just heard could be kept from anyone in the village for any period of time at all.

She feared the result. Everyone was busy and transplanting time was already very close. The idea of a pair of *gaijin* coming to look over their shoulders as they labored, and to interfere with both their essential rest and the few pleasures that they allowed themselves during the heart of the growing season, was appalling. It directly concerned her too, because she would have to explain to her pupils and prepare them. They were all innocent children and none of them had ever seen a *gaijin*, except perhaps in pictures. Some foreigners even had hair the color of rice straw, which was something that no rational person could explain.

There was only one possible thing to be done, and that was to notify the village head, the *yuryokusha*, at once. Because this was an unprecedented emergency, she made a quick arrangement to cover her absence and then set out on foot without further delay. Mitamura was not an average Japanese village and there were certain things that no outsider could be allowed to know.

Chapter Four

WHEN TED WAKABAYASHI picked up his two charges the following morning, he had a hotel hire car waiting. He had deliberately left them alone otherwise on the sound presumption that they were adults and might not have wished for close shepherding throughout the preceding day and evening. The greeting that he received when he came to take them back to the airport made it clear that his guess had been correct.

He saw them through the hotel checkout formalities and supervised the stowing of their baggage as a good host should. Then he climbed into the car after them and nodded an instruction to the driver. "How did you make out yesterday?" he asked as soon as they were in traffic.

Peter Storm looked toward Marjorie, who answered. "It seems as though all my life I couldn't wait to get to Japan."

As she paused to find the right words, Ted helped her out. "You're disappointed," he said.

"Yes," she admitted. "Terribly. After lunch, since it's so close to the hotel, we went for a walk over to the Ginza. The people were Japanese, the signs were in Japanese, but everything else was Chicago all over again. Constant crowds, trains overhead, incessant traffic — all I got out of it was a fearful headache."

"Is it still there?"

"No, it's not so bad this morning. But I could have cried. I wanted so much to see the magic of Japan."

Because he was an American himself Ted understood and sympathized with her. "Tokyo is a mad jumble," he said. "And it's getting worse. But even here there are many of the things you were looking for. You have to dig a little for them, that's all."

He stopped and wondered if he was telling her the truth. There were still many places in Tokyo that preserved some of the old traditions — the Kabuki theater, for instance — but the huge department stores of the Ginza offered little in the way of such glamor except perhaps a kimono department and the girls at the foot of the escalators who were there solely to bow to the customers.

"It will be different when you get down into the lower part of Japan," he offered for encouragement. He knew that he was right in that, because nothing on earth quite matched the compressed high tension of Tokyo that, unfortunately, was the first impression of the country that almost all visitors were subjected to upon arrival. It wasn't his fault, God knew, but it was the way that things were. But New York wasn't the United States either, despite the fact that it had the Statue of Liberty.

"We went to the Kokusai Theater," Peter volunteered. "The hotel got us excellent seats and it was a very spectacular show."

"You didn't go to any of the nightclubs, did you?" Ted asked.

"No, after the show we went back to the hotel; we both needed more rest."

"It's a good thing you did," Ted agreed. "I should have warned you. Some of the clubs can hit you with a hundred-dollar tab before you've got your chair warm. And that's only the beginning."

That was enough on that topic and he left it where it was. As the car entered the tollway he wondered how much he should tell them about the village they were going to visit. They were past the racetrack before he finally made up his mind to say nothing at all. There was no real need; they would find out soon enough on their own and he saw no need to deliver a lecture.

At the airport things were much easier because there were no customs and immigration aisles to be cleared. He saw his guests through the check-in process and verified the fact that their reservations were in order and their boarding passes issued. At that point Storm had the good sense to turn and thank him for all that he had done, thereby freeing him to get back to the city and the work that would be waiting on his desk.

Forty minutes later the flight to Kagoshima was announced. This time the people who responded were almost all Japanese, most of them carrying small items of hand baggage tied up in cloth squares. Some of them were obvious newlyweds; the rest seemed to be rural Japanese who presumably had been in the big city visiting relatives or taking a holiday. When everyone was on board all of the seats were filled, leaving barely enough room for the two stewardesses to move up and down the aisle.

Peter looked in vain for a glimpse of Mount Fuji as the plane turned south from Tokyo; the entire atmosphere was thick with hazy smog and visibility was limited to a few miles. It was another minor, endurable disappointment, hopefully not an omen of still more to come.

The airport at Kagoshima was very much smaller than the one at Tokyo and deplaning was a simple affair. The atmosphere was noticeably different; by means of the displays in the small terminal building Peter determined that while this was a tourist area to some degree, it was almost entirely for Japanese consumption.

He also noted that for the first time Marjorie was the object of considerable attention. None of it was in any way overt, but he could both sense and feel it. He was sure that many of the people in the terminal thought that she was his wife.

He felt his light case being lifted out of his hand; he turned quickly to discover a young man conventionally clad in a dark suit, white shirt, and plain narrow tie who gave him a quick half bow "Welcome to Kagoshima, Dr. Storm," he said. "Japan Travel Bureau. I have your car waiting. I will have your baggage put into place. Please may I have your baggage stubs."

The words were spoken meticulously, the obvious result of careful rehearsal. It was a good try and Peter was grateful for the help.

"I have for you a small car," the young man continued. "Our inquiry shows that the roads to Mitamura are sometimes too thin for a large Toyota. In this way we can assure your arrival."

"That will be fine," Peter responded. "Are you coming with us?"

"No, sir, but your driver knows the way. I am very sorry, sir, he does not speak any English, but he is a very good driver — the best one we have."

"I may be able to manage in Japanese," Peter said.

The young man had not expected that and for a bare moment he hesitated. Then he continued as planned. "It will be a quite long drive, sir, and beside the way there will not be any eating places suitable for you. I suggest that you dine here before departure. The car will be glad to wait."

Peter turned toward Marjorie. "Are you hungry?" he asked.

"No, I had enough on the plane," she answered. "But please have something yourself; I don't mind at all."

"I'm not hungry either." He turned again to the guide. "Perhaps we can start now if the driver is ready," he suggested.

The young man bowed slightly with his heels together and then left immediately in search of their baggage. By the time that Marjorie had returned from a visit to the ladies' room everything was ready. The car seemed very small indeed, but somehow all of their gear had been fitted into the little trunk and beside the driver.

Peter followed Marjorie into the back seat and was relieved to discover that there was a fraction more room than he had expected. They were not crowded together and there was just enough space for his feet and legs.

No more words were necessary; the guide shut the door and waved them on their way as the car pulled out from the curb. Presently it turned and headed northward toward what, to Peter Storm at least, was a part of the great unknown.

It was fitting that on the first day of the rice transplanting season it should rain — it very often did. To the farmers of Mitamura and to their equally hard-working wives it did not make a great deal of difference, for they would be wading in the deep paddy mud all day anyway with their hands and arms immersed most of the time as they set out the young plants in groups of three, exactly seven tenths of a foot apart, in precise rows. Only in this way could they insure maximum production from their limited acreages.

To Kojima Akitoshi it was a beautiful sight, almost a poetic one, and despite the inclement weather he wanted to make sketches if it was at all possible. The facilities of the little inn were limited, but a large straw umbrella was located and made available to him. With it and the rest of his equipment he set out to record what was being done, and with each step that he took he felt a little closer kinship with the soil of his own beloved country.

To him Japan was like a close blood relative, and the country which for centuries had held all genuine artists in the highest regard returned the compliment. Although he did not give lessons, he was universally addressed as *sensei* out of regard for the high nature of his calling. So great was the respect accorded him, none of the local families that had marriageable daughters even for a moment dreamed of a sending a go-between to suggest a possible union. Even in the paddy fields of Mitamura it was known that one of the greatest glories of Japan was her incomparable heritage of art and design, therefore the fact that Kojima Sensei had chosen to honor their village with his attentions was humbly accepted as a great blessing.

Because of the steady downpour, the farmers had put on their straw raincoats, which offered some protection to their backs as they ceaselessly bent over, doing the work that had to be done. It was hard, but at least it was not as cruel as transplanting the mat rush plants in January; the farmers who did that up north had to work all day in water that was icy cold. Rubber boots to some degree protected their feet and legs, but there was nothing that could be done for their hands. Hardened as the flesh was, it customarily swelled to twice its normal size; quite often great cracks would open up that were very painful and sometimes would not heal for many weeks. In Miyazaki it was mercifully warmer and the January paddy water, when they did have to work in it, was not quite so cold.

As the rain continued to come down onto the paddies and the men and women working in them, to Kojima Sensei it seemed as though one of the incomparable block prints of Hiroshige had been reborn in living reality. He did not dare to compare himself to that great master, but with his charcoal and pad he sought to convey in his own way both what he saw and what he felt. To the humble men and women who labored below him in the thick mud there was an unbridgeable gulf of social status and education between them and they could hardly comprehend that they were worthy of his gifted notice.

When they had been riding for more than three hours Peter saw his research companion make her first attempt to use the Japanese language. She leaned forward and touched the driver on the shoulder. When he turned momentarily to give her his attention she said, *"Otearai, kudasai."*

The driver shook his head and continued on his way. Obviously he did not understand, or could not provide what was asked for.

Marjorie tried again. *"Benjo,"* she said.

This time the driver nodded and at the same moment hit the brake. The car pulled to the side of the narrow road and stopped. Cutting the engine the driver quickly got out, ran around the car, and held the door open.

Peter decided to get into the act. *"Uchi,"* he contributed.

When the driver looked at him in bewilderment, Peter pointed ahead. *"Uchi,"* he said again, and indicated his companion. He didn't try to frame a complete sentence; he wasn't at all sure that he could, but he did know the word for "house."

It was not clear at first, then the driver understood. He had occasionally had foreigners before and to a limited degree he understood their peculiarities. The great, wide, wonderful, windswept out-of-doors was not good enough for them. But it was not for him to question, only to oblige. He got back into the car and continued to the next farmhouse. There he stopped, got out once more, and went inside to explain.

Presently an elderly woman who was badly bent over came out to receive her unexpected guests. When she saw Marjorie she stopped dead in her tracks and invoked the protection of the Lord Buddha. She had known that such people existed, but she had never before confronted the reality. As Peter watched, Marjorie picked up her purse and went to meet her. When they were reasonably close, the old Japanese grandmother still rooted to the spot where she had stopped, Marjorie bowed. It was not notably graceful, but her intention was clear. *"Anata no benjo wa kudasai,"* she said carefully. *"Watakusha wa kagen ga warui desu."*

At that moment Peter witnessed a very small miracle. First of all, the elderly woman understood. Secondly, the universality of human need, particularly feminine need, prevailed over all obstacles. With a quick prayer the old woman banished any demons who might have been wandering about in the vicinity, then she gestured Marjorie inside.

As soon as the two women were out of sight, the driver poked Peter's arm and then pointed toward a small clump of trees.

Ten minutes later they were on their way once more. "You speak Japanese very well," Peter said. "How did you learn?"

"I didn't." Marjorie was disconsolate. "I thought that I had a little, from my books and language records. But when we got inside, that lovely old lady asked me a torrent of questions, and I couldn't understand any of them."

"Then how did you know that they were questions?"

"I heard the 'ka' at the end. There was a Japanese girl at school, but she wasn't interested in teaching me. She told me that I could never learn Japanese and to forget it."

He understood how she must feel. First the disappointment with Tokyo, then the bitter knowledge that her color would all but isolate her despite her good intentions. To top it off, the irritating matter of not feeling well when she had to make such a long drive in a very small bouncy car. He wanted to talk to her, but he was unsure what to say. Perhaps silence would be the kindest thing he could offer.

She solved the problem by starting a topic herself. "I hope that Ted has lined up a good interpreter for us. I don't have any confidence at all."

"You'll get it," Peter assured her. "There's a certain mental panic that always comes when you face a totally new situation, but as soon as you decide that you can contend with it, your mind opens up and almost at once you do much better."

"It's so very difficult," Marjorie confessed. "Everything is backwards, and of course there aren't any helpful Latin roots to lean on."

"Try talking to the driver," Peter suggested. "There's no substitute for practice, you know that."

When she did not respond for a few seconds Peter wondered if in some unintended way he had offended her. Because he was a teacher by profession, he sometimes had a tendency to offer instruction when it was not wanted. He knew that and he tried to be careful.

Once again Marjorie herself came to his rescue. "I can't think of anything I can say," she declared.

As she spoke the first of the rain hit the roof of the little car. The driver started the wipers and then hitched forward on his seat the better to watch the road ahead. Presently, as the downpour increased, he slowed to a walk and then turned off onto a single-track unpaved road that appeared to lead off into nowhere.

The wetness made the surface uncertain so that the tiny car had a tendency to slide sideways every few seconds, but the driver kept it under control and maintained a steady forward speed. Before long the track narrowed considerably; it was then that the small size of the car became an essential asset. There were a number of places where Peter was sure that not even a normal-sized compact car would have been able to pass; whoever had laid out the roadway had apparently been thinking in terms of pedestrians and wheelbarrows at some time in the distant past.

He was not sure how long they were on that road; the pounding of the rain, the frequent skidding of the wheels, and the steady abuse that the tires were taking from the uneven surface all tended to keep him somewhat keyed up and blunted his sense of time. Then, as though some celestial cue had been given, the rain eased and the visibility improved enough to reveal the fields and paddies adjacent to the road. Impulsively Marjorie seized his arm. *"Look!"* she said.

He did, and saw before him what could have been a page of

history. He saw the laborers in the paddies bent over in their straw raincoats and despite his very limited knowledge of Japan, he recognized at once that it was a classical scene. It could have been two hundred years ago and there was nothing he could detect to spoil the illusion. Even the pattern of the still-falling rain fitted perfectly into the timeless composition.

Despite himself, he was moved; for the first time he was genuinely aware of the thousands of miles that separated him from his accustomed pattern of life on the other side of the vast Pacific.

He looked again at Marjorie and saw that she was almost transfixed. "It's true," she whispered. "It's real! It's Japan as I dreamed that it might be."

He hadn't realized that she was so strongly romantic; somehow his awareness of her being black had carried with it the implication that she had no such sensitivities. That had been a cruel error and he swore to himself not to repeat it. If the scene affected him as it did, how much more it had to mean to her with her avowed interest in Japan and its traditional culture.

The driver pointed ahead. *"Are ga Mitamura desu,"* he said. Peter understood that easily. Their destination was in sight, just ahead.

Chapter Five

As THE SMALL CAR he was in successfully fought the slippery and uncomfortable road during the last half mile of his journey, Peter Storm looked through the rain-streaked glass at the paddy, which reached almost up to the narrow roadway, and at the patient people who, bent over, were working in the steady downpour. For a few seconds a sense of indignation took hold of him: it was not right that human beings had to do manual labor under such conditions. He did not know whether to blame the circumstances or the animal stubbornness of the people themselves, who literally did not seem to have sense enough to come in out of the rain. He made a mental note to find the answer to that question during his study program.

His attention was diverted when he saw that the car was entering the village proper. Mitamura was very small; he estimated quickly that in normal weather less than a five-minute walk would take him from one extreme end to the other. The houses were compact, square, and had apparently been built in pairs. They were crowded together almost as though they feared that some evil influences might come over them at nightfall. He would have liked to have seen more, but the windows were badly fogged except for the small area he had wiped clear.

As the roadway widened enough to permit two cars to pass the driver pulled in a half slide over to the side, braked to a stop, and killed the engine. *"Mikasa ryokan desu,"* he announced.

Through the heavily streaked windows on Marjorie's side Peter could see that someone had materialized outside carrying a large umbrella. As the door was opened he had a momentary partial view of an unpainted wooden structure that had apparently been built directly against the base of a quite steep hill.

Marjorie climbed out as the driver began to unload their baggage. When Peter attempted to follow he was motioned back, obviously to wait until the umbrella carrier could return. He did not mind; he was in no great hurry. He began to prepare himself mentally to enter into the life of a Japanese country inn where the odds dictated that no one would speak a word of English. After perhaps a minute the umbrella bearer reappeared and stood waiting for him to get out of the car.

It was only a few wet and slippery steps into a small flagged entryway; from there a single wide step in the form of an ancient flattened log gave access to the inn itself. He was about to step up when his escort literally thrust out an arm to stop him and then pointed to his shoes.

He should have known that: as he bent down he was surprised how stiff his back was. He pulled his wet shoes from his feet and then climbed the two steps up into the lobby.

Marjorie was there waiting for him, her face a dark and frozen mask. She looked at him with eyes that were dulled by shock. "They don't want to let me in," she said.

The simple words hit Peter like a blow. He turned, ready to do battle. He was an American paying guest, by God, and he would not tolerate his associate being refused! The possibility that his whole project might be jeopardized if she was not allowed to remain did not at that moment even occur to him. "Who the hell says so?" he demanded.

Marjorie raised her right arm halfway and indicated a Japanese man behind the tiny reception desk. Peter strode over and faced him squarely. "Do you understand English?" he asked, letting his displeasure show in his voice.

The man bowed and smiled. *"Irasshaimasu,"* he said, and offered a pen. Then he launched into what was evidently an explanation in Japanese and concluded by saying *"Irasshaimasu"* once more.

Peter understood the formal word of welcome, but all of the rest was gibberish to him. He did not care; he was in no mood to contend with the Japanese language while far more pressing matters were on his mind. He turned around for a moment and saw that their baggage had just been deposited in the center of the small, wood-floored lobby. That gave him a lever and he used it; with an unmistakable gesture he ordered that the luggage be taken inside to their rooms.

It did not succeed; the man behind the desk let out another flood of Japanese, this time higher pitched and even more intense. As he listened, understanding nothing, Peter thought of Archer Bancroft and wished to heaven that his department chairman hadn't gotten him into this.

He turned to Marjorie. "Can you talk to this man?" he asked.

She shook her head. "I tried to, but he . . ." She let the words trail off.

Everything was suddenly silent; the man behind the desk had had his complete say. No one moved. Without being told Peter sensed that the little car that had brought them was still waiting outside, prepared if necessary to take them back again.

Very carefully he began to corral his limited abilities in Japanese, trying to frame a suitable sentence out of the words that he knew. Unfortunately, he had learned only very polite phrases and he wanted none of them now. He was furiously angry and it was made worse by the fact that he could not express himself. He was about to try the futility of using English when by sounds outside he learned that someone else was arriving. He remembered then that he had ordered an interpreter; if this was his man, he could not have picked a better moment to appear.

The door slid open and a young Japanese came in. Although he was informally dressed for wet weather, Peter knew in a moment that he did not belong in the village — there was an urban look about him that any qualified sociologist could spot immediately.

The man behind the desk began urgently, *"Arone, Sensei . . . ,"* but Peter cut him off. "Excuse me," he said. "Are you my interpreter?"

The young man bowed slightly. "I would be honored to assist you," he replied.

"I am Peter Storm," Peter began, being careful with his pronunciation.

"Dr. Storm, I am most happy to meet you. Allow me, I am Akitoshi Kojima." He reached into an inner pocket, produced a small case, and offered his name card.

Peter had not thought of that and did not know that a supply of such cards was an absolute essential in every part of Japan. He searched his own wallet and by good luck found one that he had probably carried undisturbed for months. He handed it over and then turned to Marjorie. "May I present Mr. Kojima," he said, trying to pronounce the name exactly as he had heard it. "My associate, Miss Saunders."

The man behind the desk made another urgent effort to speak, but stopped abruptly when Kojima signaled him to remain quiet. The young Japanese spoke only a few words in his own language, but their effect was magical. Behind the counter the man bowed twice in immediate submission and then directed the porter who had carried the umbrella what to do with the bags that were still in the middle of floor.

"You must forgive us," Kojima said. "This is a small inn not used to having American visitors. You may be the first ever to come here. They do not understand English. I have only a very little myself."

"Your English is excellent," Peter said flatly, "and we are both much indebted to you. Is it possible that you could take dinner with us?"

Kojima bowed, not formally but with an easy blend of both East and West. "Thank you, it will be a great pleasure. I will come to your room."

Peter already felt much better. "Since my academic Japanese is completely inadequate, will you make the necessary arrangements for us?"

"Of course."

"Thank you. I don't know my room number yet."

Kojima smiled. "There are only two prepared at the moment, Dr. Storm; this *ryokan* is very small. I am in one and you and Miss Saunders are in the other."

Peter thought rapidly. "Is that what the clerk was objecting to?"

"No, not at all."

"We had not planned to share a room," Peter said, choosing his words like Eliza her ice cakes. "We are professional colleagues."

"I understand, doctor, but I am sure that the inn did expect that you would be living together. You can, if you wish, separate your *futons* by the width of the room."

Kojima thought for a moment, then he excused himself and held a short consultation with the man behind the desk. Peter could not follow what was being said, but he was acutely aware of the degree of respect that Kojima so clearly commanded. The porter was summoned and despite the inclement weather sent on an errand. The man donned a straw rain cape and went out the door.

"If you gentlemen will excuse me," Marjorie said. "I would like to go to the room and freshen up."

As she picked up her purse the man behind the desk understood her intention; he came out at once to lead the way. When they had been gone long enough to be out of earshot, Peter spoke to his new acquaintance once more. "Mr. Kojima, I've studied some Japanese, but I don't know your country and I've never been here before. Please answer me frankly; is the fact that Miss Saunders is black the reason for the trouble?"

"Yes, Dr. Storm, it is — you see, Negro people are almost unknown in this part of Japan. They did not know in advance that she is *kokujin* and the manager was upset."

Peter made a careful guess. "Is it possible that they also feared that her color would offend you?"

"I cannot deny that," Kojima said. "It was their misunderstanding."

"Of course. They obviously regard you very highly. You must be an important landholder here."

"No, I am nothing as important as that, Dr. Storm. I am only an artist, visiting here from Tokyo."

"Then I have reason to believe that you are a very good artist."

"A beginner, no more. Dr. Storm, on another topic. I understand your embarrassment concerning the room arrangements. In Japan a man traveling with a woman who is not a close relative is assumed to be sleeping with her."

"Not only in Japan," Peter added.

Kojima laughed. "How right you are. Unfortunately this inn is very small, and while I would be happy to share my room with you, there is another possible arrangement you might find better. We will know soon if it can be."

Peter left it at that. He had to be considerate of Marjorie's feelings and if they did share a room, no matter how circumspect their conduct, it would be sure to come out when they returned home. Many academic careers had been wrecked on such grounds; at least that had been the case a few years ago.

The desk clerk reappeared and sensed that he should do something. Kojima Sensei had laid down the law: Storm Sensei and his *kokujin* girl friend were to be shown every possible courtesy or he would leave himself. It would take the inn fifty years to recover from a disgrace like that; such a disaster had to be avoided whatever the cost. He could think of only one thing to do: motioning Peter to follow, he conducted him inside and proudly displayed for him the inn's one prize facility — its immaculately clean bath, which was very comfortably and well laid out to accommodate up to eight at a time.

With one of those changes of complexion of which nature is capable the steady downpour of the rain began to mitigate. A heavy nimbus cloud that had hung glowering over Mitamura throughout the day began to slide eastward toward the Pacific coastline. Although it was well along in the afternoon, the shadowless atmospheric light increased noticeably in intensity. Within a few more minutes a tiny bit of blue sky appeared at the zenith and the damp atmosphere gave way to a washed freshness that even contained a little warmth.

In a reflective mood, Peter Storm stood just outside the entry of the inn and listened to the voice of his surroundings. He watched the people who were still working so patiently in their paddies, taking advantage of the precious daylight that was essential to their livelihood. It was perhaps some kind of alchemy, but he began to feel that he could come to know them, to communicate with them, and even share some of their feelings and emotions. That mood still had possession of him when the porter who had been dispatched on an errand came into view, stamped the worst of the mud off his feet, and took off his shoes to go inside.

Shortly thereafter Kojima appeared. Peter turned, aware that the artist had a message to convey.

"Dr. Storm," Kojima said. "An arrangement for you has been

made. The inn much regrets that it has now only two rooms ready. They invite you to use their bath and other things as much as you would like. There is in this village a house where you will be welcome as a guest."

Peter was not sure what to say, so he took the safe path and remained silent.

"The house is owned by a lady — I cannot think of the word in English — her husband is not living."

"Widow," Peter supplied.

"Yes, of course, excuse me. She is widow who was left her house and also some small land. She can give you a sleeping room and also meals. The inn also offers food, but it is served always in the rooms — it is the way of *ryokans.*"

Peter realized immediately that in a village of that size finding someone to take him in had probably presented a problem. Also he was a foreigner, which unquestionably represented an added difficulty. Prudence told him to accept what had been arranged for him and to make the best of it; if it proved impossible he could make a change later. "How far is the house?" he asked.

"A walk of three minutes."

"Am I to go there now?"

"If you desire. The porter will carry your luggage."

Peter was about to say something about not needing the porter and then caught himself in time. Besides, the man would know the way. "You have been very kind to arrange this for me — and on such short notice."

"It was the inn that did it, I only made a small suggestion. I hope that you will be pleased."

"I'm sure of it," Peter responded. Privately he was disappointed. He would have much preferred to have stayed at the inn, where presumably he would have had some say concerning his meals and where he would have been able to confer with Marjorie much more easily as their work progressed, but the presence of the painter spoiled all that.

He quickly corrected himself; Kojima had saved their situation and he was doing him an injustice. He steadied himself and prepared to accept whatever was offered with good grace. When the porter reappeared with his two bags, he was ready.

The roadway was still very slippery, but the sturdy porter seemed to have no trouble despite his load. Peter followed him for a hundred yards, then he had to pick his steps more carefully as they started up a pathway on the slope of the hill. It was an easy climb, only the risk of slipping made it more difficult. The village seemed to consist of three rows of houses, all of which were close to identical in size, appearance, and design. All of them, too, were small, suggesting a maximum economy of space and a desire on the part of the individual builders to maintain the norm and no more. It was an interesting form of democracy and Peter noted it.

When he reached the upper row the porter turned left and led the way to the only house in the whole group which in any way stood by itself. It was a very limited separation and when he was closer Peter saw why: a harsh outcropping of rock had forced a break in the pattern of uniformity. It would have required a great amount of unnecessary labor to have cut the solid rock away. Before the door of the house the porter stood, called out, and then waited.

It occurred to Peter that he did not even know the name of the lady who had agreed to take him in, but he was expected and that would suffice for the moment. He only hoped that he would be able to eat and digest the food he would be offered.

The little house was straw-thatched and there were sliding panels in the side wall. One of them was drawn open and Peter found himself looking up at the lady who had consented to house him. Like the inn, the floor of the house was raised some eighteen inches above the ground, which changed his normal angle of vision.

She was much younger than he had expected. He had automatically assumed that she would be elderly, but the woman before him was not yet thirty, if he could judge at all. He knew very little about Japanese clothing, but he sensed that the attractive cotton *yukata* she wore had been put on especially to receive him. It was relatively commonplace, but even its simple lines and constrained blue and white pattern he found quite charming.

"Konban wa," Peter said. That was one of the first things he had learned.

His hostess-to-be bowed. It was not an elaborate gesture, but it was accomplished with such a grace of movement that he knew at once that this woman could not possibly have been raised as a field laborer.

She spoke very carefully. "I make you welcome." Then she smiled. It was very restrainted and proper, but the corners of her mouth seemed to quirk just a little as though some subtle secret was hidden behind them. Peter had heard a great deal from time to time about the supposed charm of oriental women, but he had not been prepared for this. She was being totally and absolutely proper, but as he looked at her smooth features and almost liquid eyes he found her compelling — there was no other word —and for just a bare moment he seemed to lose a small fraction of his normal self-possession.

Chapter Six

THE ROOM AT THE INN that had originally been assigned to Peter and Marjorie had to be at least a hundred years old, but it showed its age only with a rich patina; there were no signs of structural decay and it had obviously been maintained throughout the years with genuine loving care. As Marjorie walked around it in her stocking feet, she rested her fingers lightly on its inviting walls and loved every part of it. The shock of her refusal in the lobby had worn off enough so that she was genuinely and truly happy.

In a shallow lacquered tray she found two stiffly starched *yukata*, one in a small dark pattern and the other flowery light. Since they had clearly been left there for use, in a burst of romanticism she had put the obviously feminine one on and the garment too had charmed her. She wanted Peter to see her in it; anticipating that he would be back soon, she used the small mirror that had been provided to readjust and fix her hair. When a tap came on the panel she slid it carefully open and was confronted by Akitoshi Kojima. "May I come in?" he asked.

"Please," she answered, and stepped aside.

The artist dropped a cushion onto the tatami mat flooring and sat down with practiced ease. "I believe that Dr. Storm will be returning soon," he said. "If you wish, there is time for you to use the bath before dinner."

Marjorie took a cushion from the small pile in the corner and followed her guest's example. "I know that I should, but I just don't feel like it," she declared. "Will I be forgiven?"

"Certainly."

"When dinner comes, will I have to eat with chopsticks?"

Kojima smiled. "There is nothing else; it is the way in Japan."

"Then I will have to learn. And please tell me where to find the ladies' bath; I can't read Japanese."

"A ladies' bath they do not have. There is one bath and it is a very good one. It is for everybody."

"When?"

"In the afternoon and evening — whenever you wish to go."

"Men and women together — at the same time?"

"Of course. It is most convenient."

Marjorie looked up to see Peter Storm framed in the doorway, waiting to be invited inside. She noted an expression on his face she could not quite read — it suggested only that something was on his mind he did not wish to discuss.

She gestured him in. "Is the place all right?" she asked. As soon as she had spoken she realized how undiplomatic that had been in Kojima's presence and prayed that Peter would get her out of it.

He did. "It's a very nice house, quite close by. I didn't see much of it; I just left my things and came back."

"Did you like your hostess?" the artist asked.

"Yes, she was very nice."

"She is not a country girl; she comes from Kyoto."

"I see."

The brevity of that reply aroused Marjorie's curiosity, but before she could say anything a chunky little maid appeared in the doorway and asked a question in Japanese. Kojima obliged. "She would like to know if you are ready to have dinner, or if you wish to wait."

Peter looked at Marjorie and then answered for them both. "Anytime," he said.

Kojima spoke briefly and the girl disappeared.

Fifteen minutes later they were gathered around a low table that had been put in the middle of the floor. Despite the fact that he could not find any position that was even partly comfortable, Peter was enjoying himself. In Kojima he had an unexpected benefit: an English-speaking male companion who obviously had much to offer. And until the interpreter arrived, he would be a godsend.

The dinner that the inn had prepared was largely seafood, but Peter was fortunate in the fact that he could eat and enjoy almost anything that his system could be reasonably expected to digest. The chopsticks proved to be a minor problem for both Marjorie and himself, but with the artist's help they both managed moderately well.

"I want to thank you very much," Peter said, "for making the arrangements for me to stay in the house nearby. From the brief look I had it seemed to be very neat and nice."

"An untidy Japanese house is a hard thing to find," Kojima told him, "even when there are young people in the family. Mrs. Taminaka also has the reputation for being a very good cook."

Peter raised a point that was in his mind. "She is somewhat younger that I had expected; do you think that my presence in her home will bring about any unwarranted gossip in the village?"

"You can't possibly avoid it," Kojima replied. "But not to worry. It is known that I made the suggestion, so therefore both you and she are spared criticism for that."

"How about yourself?"

"Usually what I do is accepted; it is part of the way of Japan."

"Would it be better if I went there instead?" Marjorie asked.

Kojima answered her with the open candor that is a frequent part of Japanese conversation. "I think it would be better for you to stay now here at the inn. All of the arrangements have been made."

Marjorie swallowed and then looked at her dark hands. "Are all of the people of this village going to reject me?" she asked.

Akitoshi drank a little tea. "By this time, every person living in this *mura* knows that you are here and that you are *kokujin;* do you know that word?"

"Yes."

"It is something entirely new to them and they will not be sure what to do. In such cases they are very fearful of bad omens. But it is possible to overcome this."

"How much time?" Marjorie asked.

"I cannot answer that. It will depend on many things. If the crops were to fail . . . is that correct? . . . they might blame it on you. That is the worst. They will be very fearful and suspicious; every move that you make will be watched, even here in the inn. You will not see it, but you will be always under . . . I have lost the word."

"Surveillance?" Peter suggested.

"That is it. But understand that they are good people; they will do nothing but watch, wonder a little, and wait. It will then be up to you."

"What are my chances?"

"I hope for the very best. There is only one thing I wish to say to you: there is a path up the mountain behind us; it leads to a temple that is at the top. If you wish to go up there, do not do it alone. Ask me and I will go with you."

Marjorie did not understand. "Is it a dangerous path?" she asked.

The artist chose not to answer that; instead he reverted back to the previous subject. "You are not alone in your trouble. The lady who is accepting Dr. Storm for a guest, she also has problems which are not easy to lose."

Peter looked up at that. "Please tell us," he said.

"First, she was born in the year of the sheep, which is unlucky. Of course many share that misfortune with her. Then when her husband accepted her as his bride, he defied the ancient rules and looked in the wrong direction."

"A direction such as east or west?" Marjorie asked.

"Yes. Her home was to the northeast of his, which is very bad indeed. He should have found a girl who lived to the southeast or the northwest, but the southeast would be much better. Everyone knew that the marriage could not be successful and they expected him to return her. But he did not."

"They really believe that?" Peter enquired.

"Oh, absolutely. He was a good man and when he made that very great mistake, everyone was terribly upset. In four years there were no children, it was the first disaster. Then on a mountain road, in the rain, he was killed. That was the final proof. Now she possesses the house and a small bit of land because her unfortunate husband did not have a successor — either his own son or someone adopted for the purpose. She has land and is a good cook, but still no one wishes to marry her. It is most unfortunate."

"I'd like to meet her," Marjorie said.

"I am sure that you will. By the way, what is your plan for tomorrow?"

"I thought we would just walk around the village and get to know it," Peter replied. "If our interpreter comes, then perhaps we will be able to talk to some of the people."

"That will be difficult, Dr. Storm, because everyone will be working — this is the rice transplanting time. After the dark comes, they will all be very muddy and tired out. It is best to wait until the rice work is finished."

"How long will that take?"

"A week to ten days. But it must be done right now, it cannot be delayed. That is why they work even in the hard rain."

"I see. Then what can I do to be useful in the meantime?"

Kojima smiled. "There is one answer only, perhaps, in this village. Learn to plant rice."

During the short walk back to where he was to stay Peter thought about the things he had just learned. The astrological rules concerning direction he regarded as medieval, but despite his obviously fine education, Kojima seemed to half believe them himself. Or perhaps his own leg was being gently pulled. He considered that possibility as he climbed up the path toward the thatched house where his hostess awaited him. He did not for a moment believe that she was cursed with ill fortune, despite the fact that her history had not been a happy one.

He did not have to knock; as he approached the house the entry panel was opened from the inside. With a restrained bow that was full of both modesty and liquid grace his hostess welcomed him once more inside. For the fourth time that day Peter stooped over and removed his shoes, glad in a way that he would not be tracking mud into the immaculately clean house.

As he entered the small room that had been prepared for him he turned to say something appropriate and then stopped before he began. He sensed something and it was a moment or two before it focused for him; by her very restrained and submissive manner his hostess was showing that she considered herself to be inferior in status. She seemed almost to be apologizing for her presence in her own home. That was no way to get things started; Peter looked at her just for a moment and then deliberately smiled, thanking her in that way for her hospitality.

She looked at him in return as though she was uncertain, then she eased her very formal manner and smiled just a little in return. It was magical; once started it grew despite her until it was warm and friendly and made every part of her radiantly lovely.

The room he was to occupy was separated from the rest of the small house only by sliding screens held in shallow grooves set flush in the flooring. He guessed correctly that the panels could be easily removed if for any reason it was desired to open the whole house up into a single area. There was very little furniture, only a kind of wardrobe of modest size and a low table. Since the cabinet was already partway open he looked inside without thinking: there awaiting him were the clothes that had been packed in his luggage, hung with neat precision and in perfect order.

There were some drawers at one end which were slightly pulled out; he opened the top one the rest of the way and saw that his shirts were inside, carefully lapped so that he could see at a glance what he had available. Peter turned and broke the long silence. "Thank you," he said. "Thank you very much."

"You are welcome. Will you have tea?"

He turned to face her, not knowing what to answer. It had never occurred to him to drink tea at that hour, but he was sensitive to something in her voice. "Is it ready?" he asked.

"I have prepared it."

"Then I would enjoy some very much."

His hostess slipped out of the room, giving him a chance to gather his thoughts alone. He took note that there was electricity in the house; a single, low-powered naked bulb hung by its cord from the ceiling. What was obviously his bed was made up in the middle of the floor; it was somewhat larger than a sleeping bag and seemed to promise a fair amount of comfort. He would have preferred some sort of a mattress underneath, but the bare minimum was all that he could reasonably expect. Certainly he was being offered more than that. He looked again at the *futon* and convinced himself that it would provide a good night's rest.

He checked the other drawers in the wardrobe and found his socks, handkerchiefs, ties, and underwear. Something hung in his mind; he thought for a moment and then pulled the shirt drawer open once more. The soiled shirt that he had worn coming across the Pacific had been freshly laundered; as he picked it up he could smell the aroma of soap and warm water. It had been folded exactly like the others and placed into position with almost mathematical precision.

That was a helluva lot more than he had bargained for.

Before he could give birth to any more thoughts, his hostess reappeared carrying a simple tea service. On the tray she had put the essentials plus a single small flower in a little glass. Dropping to her knees, she set the tea things on the low table that had been put in the corner to make room for the *futon*. Holding the wide sleeve of her *yukata* out of the way, she poured a single cup of tea and set it in a fragile saucer. Then she looked up, awaiting his approval.

Peter got down next to the table as best he could. *"Anata no ocha wa doko desu ka?"* he asked carefully.

By the dim light he saw her raise her hand before her mouth as though she wanted to hide any expression that might be forming on her lips. "Please get another cup," he directed before she could speak.

She looked at him for a fleeting moment with searching eyes, then she rose to comply. When she returned she was carrying a small cup and saucer as though unsure that it was the right thing to do. Peter smiled at her and gestured that he wanted her company. In response she sank down at the opposite side of the small table and filled her cup carefully from the delicate china pot.

"Where did you learn English?" he asked.

"It was in school." As he lifted his cup she raised hers and looked at him almost across the rim. Her face was a study; it was totally Japanese, as well as intensely feminine and appealing. She was being very quiet in her manner, and very correct, but he felt that if she chose to let the bars down, she would be a very animated and perhaps even exciting person to know.

"I understand that you are from Kyoto," he said.

"Yes, Kyoto — most wonderful city in Japan." A touch of enthusiasm, and of nostalgia, crept into her voice.

"You speak English very well."

"No — only *sukoshi* — little bit."

He tried his tea once more. This time he tasted it and found it quite pleasant. Usually he took some sugar, but he knew better than to ask. If she didn't have it, which was probable, she would be embarrassed and he didn't want to risk that.

"Thank you for washing my shirt."

"It was nothing." She was pulling back into her shell.

"This is a very nice house."

"Thank you."

"I have heard about your husband — I'm sorry."

To that she bowed her head, but said nothing.

He let a few moments pass while he drank his tea in silence. He was very conscious of her across the table from him, but on this very first night in her home it was essential that he not give her the least reason to regret his presence. Finally he spoke once more. "I don't know your name."

"*Taminaka Midori desu.*"

"What would you like me to call you?" he asked. He knew that it was an unnecessary question; he could safely call her Mrs. Taminaka for the remainder of his visit and it would be entirely appropriate.

"In village here," she began in reply. "Most people have name Taminaka or Noda. Many Mrs. Taminaka, also many Mrs. Noda."

He realized that that answer gave him a small lever and he used it. "What is the custom in this village, then?"

"We other name use."

"And yours is . . ."

"Midori."

Remembering what he had already learned, from his seated position he leaned forward to suggest a bow. "How do you do, Midori. *Hajame meshita.* I like your name. What does it mean?"

"It is color — green. But also many times girl name."

"May I call you Midori?"

"Please, yes."

That was the point at which to stop and he knew it. He finished his tea and then stood up to indicate that he was ready to retire.

She quickly gathered the tea things before she rose. "What time *asagohan?*" she asked.

"How about eight-thirty?" He wanted to be considerate.

"*Gozen hachi ji san ju pun?* You not hungry before?"

"All right, then, eight o'clock."

She turned at the panel; as she held the tea things she looked exactly like a Japanese doll he had once seen somewhere in a case. It had had a wistful appeal that had captured his imagination despite the fact that he was not prone to fantasizing. The similarity of position, and the *yukata*, brought it all back with a rush as he saw the full-sized, living reality before him.

"Tomorrow, what you do?" she asked.

As he looked at her she was suddenly utterly captivating. He drew a deep breath and his hands unconsciously closed into fists.

"I'm going to learn to plant rice," he answered.

Chapter Seven

Wᴴᴇɴ Pᴇᴛᴇʀ ᴀᴡᴏᴋᴇ, the brightness in his room told him that the sun was already well up in the sky. A few times during the night he had stirred and had been dimly conscious of the fact that he was lying on the floor, but sleep had returned quickly as his weary body had demanded the rest that it needed. His first waking thought was that he had been much more comfortable than he had anticipated, the second was that the farmers would already be at work in their fields and paddies.

He stood up, stretched his muscles, and then slid open the panel that led to the outside. A blast of sunlight greeted him as he looked out and saw that his conjecture concerning the field workers had been correct. He had clearly overslept.

He never dressed until he had washed, shaved, and brushed his teeth, but there were no facilities whatever in his room and he was presumably alone in the house with his hostess. Judgment dictated that it would be best if he were to dress as quickly as possible. Closing the panel he went to the wardrobe, took out the work clothes that he had brought on the odd chance that he might need them, and put them on. He was just finishing when he heard a soft tap on the panel that gave access to the rest of the small house. "Come in," he called.

Midori entered carrying a tray. She too was dressed in very plain work clothing with her hair tied up in a cotton scarf to keep it out of the way. "Good morning," she said. Then she put the tray on the low table and bowed her respects.

"I'm afraid I overslept," Peter apologized.

She warmed him with a smile. "It is nothing." She gestured toward the waiting food.

He hesitated. "Midori, before I eat, I'd like to wash."

"Yes — you come, please."

She led him across another very small room formed by the same sort of sliding panels and then stepped down into the kitchen area. It was almost two feet lower than the rest of the house, its bare earth floor broken only by a narrow pathway of wooden planks laid directly onto the ground. The boards were cool under Peter's bare feet as he followed his hostess into what seemed the second section of the house; when he stepped up once more he discovered that he was in a kind of barn or workshed with a walkway on the south side. Midori stopped and indicated a narrow wooden door. Then she slipped past him and returned to the kitchen.

The small cubicle behind the door had one distinguishing feature: an open hole nearly twelve inches in diameter cut in the center of the flooring. A small pile of cut paper was neatly placed in the corner. It could hardly have been more primitive, but it would do.

When he returned to the kitchen area, he stopped to inspect it. The equipment was sparse: a kind of brick stove and oven, a few utensils carefully hung in their places, and a small work table. He saw no means of refrigeration, not even an icebox to keep things moderately cool in hot weather. If Midori had earned the reputation of being a good cook with nothing more to work with than this, she had to be resourceful indeed.

An idea hit him. "Midori, would it be all right if I ate here?"

"You would like?"

"It might be easier."

In response she disappeared and returned with the tray she had taken to his room. He was about to repeat his request to wash first when he realized that some of the food was hot and it would be unkind to delay any longer. By sitting on the edge of the raised flooring he could be quite comfortable. He moved the small table over and then took his position behind it so that his hostess would understand.

She did, and gave him an almost impish smile. "For *hakojin* maybe better," she said. Her eyes made gentle fun of him. "Big long legs," she added.

"Right," Peter agreed and surveyed what had been prepared for him. There was hot rice in a china bowl and three other dishes he could not identify by sight. Picking up the chopsticks he made a mental resolution — he would try to eat at least an acceptable amount of everything unless it was absolutely revolting. He put it into effect by testing the first unknown dish. It had a definite sea flavor, but it was tasty; a second small mouthful negotiated by his chopsticks confirmed that it was close to delicious.

"It is very good, Midori," he said.

"Arigato gozaimasu." She was beginning to credit him with understanding a little Japanese.

"What time is it?" He had left his watch in his room.

It took her a moment's thought to get her response into English. "Nine it is, also a little more."

He certainly had overslept!

He continued to eat until he had had more than enough for breakfast. His bed had been comfortable and he had certainly eaten well. He wanted to shave and comb his hair, and brush his teeth if he could arrange some way to do so.

Excusing himself, he went to his room and got his electric razor. He doubted if there was an outlet that would fit his plug, but there was power of a sort in the house and luck could be with him.

To his surprise there was an outlet in the kitchen; it was there to serve an electric fan which stood covered by a piece of plastic material. It was too much to hope that the plug would fit, and it did not. He was reconciling himself to the fact when his hostess surprised him once more; she rummaged in a box and came up with a small black object in her hand. It was an adapter and it worked.

He was just finishing his shave without the aid of a mirror when a knock came on the outside panel; a few seconds later Akitoshi Kojima was ushered into the kitchen.

"Good morning," he said. "Were you able to rest well?"

"Very well indeed," Peter answered. "I overslept shamefully."

"You were very tired last night, I could see it."

"Have you seen Marjorie this morning?"

Kojima laughed. "You were not the only one tired, and I believe that she is a little ill too. She was still sleeping when I left the inn."

"Have you had breakfast?" Peter asked.

"Yes, thank you. I hope you ate well."

"I did. I'll feel better after I've brushed my teeth."

Kojima spoke in Japanese; in response Midori filled a small pan with water from a pail and offered it to him. Peter excused himself long enough to get his toothbrush, paste, a tube of hair dressing, and a comb. He set out his simple equipment and in a matter of two or three minutes he was at last prepared to face the day.

"I have a message for you," Kojima said when Peter was ready. "A phone call was received from your interpreter. He met with a small accident in his way here and greatly regrets that he is no longer available. While they are finding someone else, will you allow me to offer my poor services?"

"I'm most grateful," Peter told him, "but it would be a great imposition on your time."

"On the contrary, it would give me the greatest pleasure."

"Then let's leave it this way: when you are free, it would be a great help."

Kojima changed the subject. "I see that you are wearing practical clothing."

"Yes," Peter answered. "I decided last night to take your advice. This is a rice-growing village, so I assume that most of the habits and customs revolve around the cycle of the rice crop."

"That is exactly correct."

"Then I should know something about the cultivation of rice. Since this is the transplanting time, I would like to learn how it's done."

"This is a very great liberty, Dr. Storm, but may I call you Peter?"

"Please do. How do your friends address you?"

"They call me Toshi."

"Toshi, I'm perfectly serious. I'd like to try transplanting rice for a little while if there is someone who'll show me how."

Kojima thought. "Perhaps Hideo Noda would be the right man. He is intelligent and will understand. Also he is very good-natured. Shall we ask him?"

"Yes. Is this clothing all right?"

"Perhaps at the inn I could get you a pair of Japanese work trousers — a pair large enough to fit you. Would you mind, if they have been well washed?"

"Of course not."

"Let us then try that."

In the bright light of day and without the shroudlike curtain of rain, the village appeared even smaller to Peter, but it was also much more picturesque. He began to feel a mounting interest in the work he had come to do, despite his still very limited knowledge of the country. For the moment the problems faced by his research partner were completely out of his mind.

At the inn the unusual request was received with apparent complete understanding, one more evidence of the high regard that

Akitoshi commanded. There was some scurrying in the rear of the establishment, two or three minutes of delay, and then one of the little maids appeared carrying a pair of blue shapeless trousers across her arm. She bowed in quick embarrassment and then handed them over.

Peter took them into Kojima's room and emerged shortly thereafter looking like a curious mixture of a Japanese farmer and a Western visitor whose conception of grooming was temporarily dormant. With characteristic Japanese courtesy the manager showed only a polite interest in knowing if the trousers were satisfactory. When Kojima advised him that they were, he seemed to be most pleased. Marjorie, it appeared, was still asleep.

From the inn Kojima led the way out into the area of the paddies. A narrow footpath ran between them on top of the dikes, a path just wide enough to allow free passage and to permit portable pumps and other essential equipment to be moved to where they were needed without disturbing the paddy floors two or three feet below. As Peter followed his guide he was acutely aware of the men and women who were standing deep in the thick ooze, setting out the seedlings. For a moment or two he was glad he was going to be one of their number — for a short while, at least. He rejected the idea of feeling superior to his fellow men, particularly when they were not only decent, but also hard working in the very literal sense. If he was going to know and study these people, the closer the kinship he could feel toward them, the better the job he would be able to do.

Kojima turned at right angles and started up another of the geometric walkways that bordered the paddies, no two of which seemed to be on the same level. In the lower one, to his left, three people were bent over planting the eight-to-ten-inch-high seedlings taken from the germination beds.

When Kojima stopped Peter looked at the workers more carefully and saw that there was a man, a woman who undoubtedly was his wife, and a girl who probably was their daughter. He did not catch any of the Japanese that Kojima exchanged with the man who had stopped his work to carry on the conversation, but he was most conscious that the two women had also stopped and were staring at him in complete bewilderment.

After some brief discussion, Kojima turned to him. "This is Mr. Noda, the owner of this field. He has consented to teach you the art of rice transplanting. I have assured him that your interest is genuine. He is a very fine farmer and he is happy to welcome you. Unfortunately, he cannot speak any English, but his daughter knows a little — she has been to school. She will assist."

"Please tell Mr. Noda how much I appreciate this," Peter said.

"I have already done that. One thing I must tell you before you enter the paddy: rice growing is a very precise and careful thing; only in this way can the farmers get the maximum yields from their fields. And they must do this, because the land is small and there are many people to feed. Each plant must be exactly right, not one inch out of the way."

"I'll try my best," Peter promised.

"Then I wish you the best of good fortune. If you are bitten by something in the paddy, tell Mr. Noda at once — it may happen."

That was a new element, but if the women could face it so could he. And they, poor souls, had no choice. Peter bent down and took off his shoes. He put them carefully aside and then rolled up the legs of his borrowed trousers as far as he could. When he stood up once more, he was ready to begin his lesson.

With a helping hand from Kojima he climbed down to the water level and thrust his left leg into the paddy; he did it carefully to avoid crushing any of the seedlings that had already been put into place. He felt with his bare foot for the bottom, but he encountered only semifluid mud, which finally compressed to the point where it would bear his weight. Then he brought his other leg down and saw that the bottoms of his borrowed trousers were already wet. The paddy ooze came up between his toes, reminding him of a brackish pond he had waded in as a boy. He had felt the same sensation then and it had forced him to retreat as rapidly as he could for fear of slimy things that might be hidden in the water.

He brushed that juvenile conditioning out of his mind and reminded himself that he was standing in the paddy for the purpose of learning something about rice cultivation. With careful movements forced on him by the thick mud around his feet, he made his way to where Noda was patiently waiting. As soon as he was close enough the Japanese farmer bowed energetically two or three times and then spoke to him just as though he could understand.

"He is welcoming you," Kojima explained from where he stood on the dike.

"Thank you," Peter acknowledged. "I'll try to do all right for him."

"You will. I'm going to leave you now; Miss Saunders may need some help."

"Good. Thanks a lot." With that Peter was ready to begin his work. He nodded to Noda, then picked up one of the rice seedlings to examine it. As he did so, the young woman who was at work in the paddy made her way to where he stood. She was somewhat foreshortened like her father and in her very round features he found little that could be described as beauty, but he instinctively liked her nonetheless. She was moon-faced, there was no doubt about it, but she was also most agreeable.

When Peter spoke to her, trying his Japanese, she bowed. "My fatha . . . ," she began with considerable effort. "He make show."

Peter nodded that he understood. "*Arigato,*" he said.

The girl bowed again. "Hideko," Noda said. "Hideko."

Fortunately he recognized the "ko" on the end and knew that

it was the girl's name. He was being introduced. He pointed to himself. "Pete," he declared. He had already learned that the Japanese had serious trouble with *r*'s.

"Peta," the girl acknowledged. "Noda Hideko."

Peter bowed as best he could. The formalities over, Noda took three of the seedlings in his left hand and picked up a notched stick with his right. Holding the stick horizontally, he positioned it along the row of tiny clumps that he had just set out. Peter saw that each cluster corresponded exactly to a notch on the measuring stick. That seemed an almost unnecessary refinement, but Noda clearly thought differently and presumably he had been growing rice most of his life.

Bending over, Noda thrust his left hand down into the mud and set the three seedlings together so that they were precisely opposite the next notch on the stick. That done he moved up a step, took three more of the seedlings and handed them to Peter.

Shifting his position so he could reach, Peter judged the distance, plunged his hand into the water, and felt for the soil underneath. It was quite easy to put the thin roots into the almost liquid mud; when he measured with the stick he was barely an inch off the mark.

Noda nodded his head in quick approval, then he reached down and corrected Peter's planting until it was exactly right.

Peter tried again; using the stick this time he managed to do a little better job. Noda seemed to take great satisfaction from his simple success; once more the farmer adjusted the roots and then, by gesture, told Peter to continue the row. A string stretched across the top of the water would help him to keep it straight.

Three quarters of an hour later Peter began to feel that he was getting the hang of it. He was exceedingly slow in comparison with the Nodas, but he had still set out a respectable number of the supple little plants and his eye told him that his row was straight and true.

Noda was working by himself now, but he was coming over every few minutes to see how his pupil was doing. He did not hesitate to make adjustments and to check the root placements under the water, but on the whole he seemed pleased. He offered multiple smiles of encouragement, each tinged slightly by embarrassment. A guest in his paddy was a totally new experience for him and it defied all rational explanation. Particularly he could not comprehend why the very rich and high-level foreigner would ever condescend to perform manual labor; it was totally against every rule of conduct that he had ever learned. But the *sensei* had approved the arrangement, so it was up to him to cooperate without question.

Peter realized that he was free to stop whenever he chose, but the Nodas had taken time from their work to teach him and he owed them something in return. Also he didn't want to be seen giving up too soon, especially since two women were working in the paddy too and they had to keep at it even when it poured of rain. He determined to hang on for a while, despite the fact that his back already ached like sin.

As Marjorie Saunders came out of the inn, her camera in her hand, she was careful to give no outward signs that would show how tightly she was holding herself in check. She did not know how much longer she would be able to endure all of the reactions she was causing simply because she happened to be dark-skinned, But she kept the raging within herself and only someone who knew her very well would have been able to detect its presence.

She had sensed the fear of the maid who had come to fold up her *futon* and store it away in the cupboard; she had handled it almost as if it had been unclean. A different girl had brought her breakfast tray with obvious hesitation; her required bow and *"Ohayo gozaimasu"* had been delivered as though she had been addressing the devil. Most particularly Marjorie had been aware of the surveillance — the constant watching of her movements. It might have passed unnoticed, but she had been conditioned much of her life and therefore was more sensitive to what was taking place.

She had eaten her breakfast at her own pace, determined not to give the slightest indication that she knew. Mercifully she was only the object of intense curiosity; there were no signs of raw hostility. She did not expect to be accepted until they knew her better, but there were ways of counterattacking, most of them built on the simple formula of being a reasonable and pleasant person until prejudice would be shamed into silence, if not oblivion.

Taking her time, she walked slowly down the roadway of Mitamura and drank in all that she saw. The bright, beautiful day had its own magic and began to evaporate the poison in her system. As she looked about her she realized fully that she was at last in Japan — the real Japan that was mercifully far from the economic and industrial chaos of Tokyo. And Japan was beautiful.

She gathered her thoughts and then spoke aloud, softly and gently as the circumstances demanded. *"Ohayo gozaimasu, Mitamura San. Ohayo gozaimasu Nippon. Watakushi wa anato o dai sukidesu!"*

Japan, she hoped, would understand her and return the affection she was offering. She looked about her once more at the colorful village and hoped almost desperately that it would be willing to be her friend too.

And Japan responded when Marjorie heard her name spoken and turned to find that Akitoshi Kojima was coming toward her and there was indeed a welcoming smile on his face. She waited for him and was rewarded when he said, "Miss Saunders, I am happy to see you."

With her camera held in her two hands in front of her Marjorie bowed and said her good morning once more — in Japanese.

Kojima did not fear being seen with her; he came and stood

directly before her so that they could talk easily. "To start the day right, am I allowed to call you Marjorie?"

"Please!"

"Then call me Toshi. May I show you around the village a little?"

"I would love it. Have you seen Peter?"

"Yes, he is in one of the rice paddies, working with a farm family. He asked me to arrange it."

"Am I expected . . . ?"

"Of course not. The women here are used to such work, but it would be very hard for you. Especially just after your long trip. Let Peter break the ice; he is, I think, very good at that."

She understood perfectly what he was telling her. "Would it be all right if I took some pictures?" she asked.

"Of course! If people are concerned, I will be your interpreter."

Together they walked up the road past the closely packed houses. Kojima talked pleasantly about the seasons in Japan, but Marjorie was not listening as she should — there was something else on her mind. When he paused and she had an opportunity, she brought it into the open. "I have observed something," she said. "Everyone here holds you in high regard; whatever you ask for is done immediately. I'm a foreigner and I'm *kokujin* — I know the word. By being with me I think you are damaging your own image."

She was not sure that he understood despite his excellent English. "I mean, it will hurt your reputation."

Almost visibly Kojima's pleasant good humor retreated and he became more serious. "Marjorie, there are many things in Japan that outsiders do not know — we keep them hidden. One is our concern for the color of our skins. Some Japanese are very dark; this suggests to us that we are not pure Japanese after all, but a mixture, far back in our history, of other races. We are very sensitive about this."

"I have been told."

"Then you will understand. Also in this particular village there is something in addition. I do not wish to speak of it now, but please do not go outside the village, especially up the hill, unless someone is with you — Peter or myself."

"Because of my skin?"

"Yes — but it may pass. Perhaps I may be able to help a little. Just because I am a poor artist, the people here look up to me."

He turned off the main road and indicated a footpath that would take them to the higher part of the village. "If it is true that being seen with you will harm me, it is not to worry — I can afford it. If the people see that we are friends, perhaps it may help them to feel better in their minds."

"Will I be able to conduct interviews?"

"Yes — but they will not tell you very much."

She stopped and turned to face him. "Then how can I do the job I've been assigned? I should not have come." She swallowed very hard.

"Do you like Japan?" he asked.

"I've wanted to come here for a long time."

"Then be glad that you have. By status and education you are *tokken kaikyu* — a privileged person whose superiority is understood. Against this is your blackness of skin. It is possible that the two may balance." He paused. "Here is what I want to show to you."

He indicated a house which, to Marjorie's eyes, was similar to all of the others: it was a simple thatched square with its apparent twin beside it. "I will explain," he said. "In this prefecture the style of houses is different from what it is up north. But it is always necessary to have the *nagaya*. It is not what you call in English the barn, it is the workplace where is also located the bath and the toilet room. Sometimes also live animals, such as a cow for milk. In this house is a special workshop, you will see. It is now time for you to meet the *yuryokusha,* the important man who is the chosen head of this village."

Marjorie held the strap of her camera in a suddenly tightened grip; at that particular moment she did not feel ready to meet anyone. Ordinarily she would very much want to see the head man, and in Akitoshi's company, but her treatment at the inn had started her off very badly and not even the warm blessing of the sunshine had been enough entirely to break that mood. The discussion she had just been having with a man she trusted and liked had not helped either. He had been too honest with her and she was badly on edge as a result.

She had no opportunity to express herself; with a nod Kojima left her and walked rapidly toward the barn-workroom.

She waited for almost five minutes, which gave her time to think. Perhaps she was too sensitive. She had been shielded, she knew that, as much as had been possible, but not even her father's wealth and position had been able to insulate her completely. When she had encountered serious problems she had sometimes solved them by communicating, on other occasions she had rationalized that she did not really care — and had almost succeeded. Now she was in a different situation because she could not communicate as she wanted to; the barrier of an enormously difficult language stopped her from the kind of human contacts in Mitamura she so desperately wished to achieve.

When she saw Kojima coming back to get her, she swept those troublesome thoughts out of her mind. She knew quite a bit about Japanese customs; from that knowledge she guessed that hasty preparations were being made to receive her. Tea had to be served; it was obligatory. She made a conscious effort to relax and from her slender knowledge of Japanese tried to frame a proper expression of greeting.

Then Akitoshi stood before her and she saw in his face what he was about to tell her.

"I am very sorry; the *yuryokusha* is very superstitious. He fears that a black person is a symbol of great ill fortune and he will not allow you to enter his house."

Chapter Eight

Peter Storm could not remember any time in his life when he had been so stiff and sore. His back stabbed with pain and each step he took was an effort of will.

Once more he cursed himself for having had the idiotic notion that he should get down into a rice paddy and try his hand as a day laborer, but despite his acute discomfort his more rational judgment told him that now, at least, he had some conception of what these people he had come to study went through in trying to earn a living. And not a very good living at that.

He had held out until he had finished a full two rows, setting that goal for himself and achieving it. He believed that life had to be a succession of goals, otherwise it would just drift along until, on some grim and deadly day, all hopes for a brighter future would have to be abandoned on the altar of reality.

It had been a short walk from the inn to the paddy; the route back was interminably longer. While he had been planting his body had seemed to find a well of resource that kept it going; as soon as he stopped the well was suddenly dry and every painful muscle demanded immediate rest. It could not be, the village was still several fields away and there was no possible way to get there except to walk. So Peter walked.

As he plodded up the dike path he remembered that the inn had a hot bath that he had been invited to use as much as he wished. He headed that way, the idea of soaking in a hot tub drawing him like a magnet.

When at last he crossed the narrow roadway and entered the shelter that protected the doorway, he was barely equal to bending down to take off his shoes. He managed it somehow and then climbed up into the lobby, where the manager bowed quickly before him. Peter had no time to waste in trivia; with his hands and arms he pantomimed his need for a bath.

He had no idea that he was creating a minor crisis; the bath was not due to be ready for hours and there was no hot water. Also there was only enough fuel to heat it once a day; by requiring a tub while the sun was still close to the zenith, he was throwing things completely out of gear.

In the village of Mitamura almost nothing went unseen and Peter's progress back from the rice paddy had been followed with interest. Kojima Sensei had given orders that the foreigners, even the *kokujin*, were to be shown every possible consideration. The manager had had one good look at Peter as he was plodding his weary way out of the paddy area and with penetrating insight had read the handwriting on the wall. When Peter turned toward the inn rather than Midori's house, he had fearlessly given the order to begin heating the bath at once. The job had therefore been well started before Peter had fumbled his way out of his first shoe.

Since Peter's progress had entertained three quarters of the adult population of the village (the children were in school), Akitoshi Kojima knew of it too. In an effort to restore Marjorie's equilibrium he had taken her to a vantage point where she could get some panoramic photographs of the whole surrounding area. As they were coming down again he clearly saw the slow progress of Peter's walk to the inn and knew that it might be well for him to be on hand when he arrived. But when he suggested to Marjorie that they return to the inn, she did not want to accompany him. "You go ahead," she told him. "I want to be alone for a while. I can find my own way back."

"You do not mind?"

"No, of course not. Go help Peter, please."

So Akitoshi went and walked into the lobby while Peter was still sitting and waiting, wondering why it was taking so long.

Without formality the Japanese artist sat down beside him. "It is very hard work, transplanting rice."

Peter looked at him like the ghost of Christmas yet to come. "It was invented in hell," he declared. "I did about all that I could; when I left, Mr. Noda and the women were still at it. Now I need a bath," Peter continued. "They're getting it ready, but it seems to be taking quite a while."

"It must, because a Japanese bath is not like yours. But if you wish to soak your body in hot water, that you can do."

"That's exactly what I want — I never wanted it so much before."

"It will be ready in a few minutes. Do you understand the Japanese bath?"

"No. But a bath is a bath is a bath."

"Ah yes, you have read Stein Gertrude. What you said is correct, but there are a few minor points. In Japan you wash yourself thoroughly first, *then* you enter the bath. Many people use the same bath water and it is cleaner that way. Just as in America many people use the same swimming pool."

Viewed in that light, it was understandable. "Then I'm not to empty out the water after I'm through."

"Not unless it is your wish to institute a small riot. By the way, here the bath is not for one person alone, so if it is your wish, I will join you. Then after your bath I suggest you have a massage; one of the maids here is skilled in that art."

A quick added spasm of back pain made Peter wince and then think only of the joys of relaxing hot water. That one thought so dominated the forefront of his mind nothing else could penetrate. "Sure — why not," he said.

As she came down the hill, alone for the first time since she had been refused entry to the house of the *yuryokusha*, Marjorie formed a decision in her mind. She knew then that no matter what she did, or how she conducted herself, her presence in the *mura* would only handicap Peter Storm and impede his work. In this beautiful country it was like the America of fifty years ago and the island of Kyushu was the unfortunate equivalent of the Deep South. The only sensible thing for her to do was to clear out, as quickly and as quietly as she was able. The college had paid her fare over, but she had her return ticket and her father would reimburse the expenses she had incurred.

Her mind made up, she came carefully down the path, anxious now not to fall and possibly come up with an awkwardly sprained ankle that would delay her departure. If Peter Storm needed a new partner, he could get one easily in a matter of a few days. The assignment was a choice one and the replacement would be a very lucky girl — if she wasn't black.

She stopped for a moment, looking at a small cluster of tiny fields that hardly covered an acre of ground. Three of them were fallow, the other two had been planted as kitchen gardens with rows as precise as those in the paddies themselves. She raised her camera to record the scene on film, a last souvenir of the country she had wanted to visit for so long. As she focused she saw that there was a single worker down on his hands and knees digging in the soil.

She took her picture and then hoped that she had not once more given offense; some people resented having their picture taken when they were at hard labor. She could have retreated, but she refused to be ashamed of herself or her own innocent actions. She continued on down at the edge of the tiny fields, steeled against any further hurt.

She was only a few feet away from the field worker when she saw, with a slight shock, that it was a woman. She was doing a man's work with her hands dug deep into the soil, but she had about her a certain aura which suggested an educated, possibly even a sophisticated person. When the woman in the field looked up, she did not flinch from the sight of dark skin. Then to Marjorie's considerable surprise she said, "Good afternoon."

Then Marjorie knew who she was. Once more she put her hands together and bowed, as she had practiced so many times before she had come to Japan. "Good afternoon," she repeated. *"Konnichi wa."*

The woman in the field stood up and returned the bow with a grace that is bred in the bone in the Far East. As she did so Marjorie detected something else: despite the unflattering work clothes, the dirt on her hands, and the cloth tied around her hair, she was lovely. Her eyes were magnificent and the bones of her face were classic in the Japanese pattern. With sure feminine instinct Marjorie knew that if she were given an hour or so in which to bathe and dress herself for an occasion, this woman would be devastating.

"Anata wa Nihongo ga hanase masu ne!"

For the first time Marjorie understood Japanese without being aware of it. "No," she protested, "I don't speak Japanese at all. Just a very little. I learned from records."

"I cannot . . . Englishu. Only . . . little . . . bit."

Despite all of the pressures that had been building within her since morning, Marjorie found the courage to smile. "I am Marjorie Saunders."

"Taminaka Midori desu."

"How do you do."

There was an awkward pause then as neither of the women knew what to say or how to put it into a language that the other could understand. Then Midori put down the gardening tool in her hand. "Please, you will have tea?"

For a moment Marjorie hesitated; she had unconsciously sworn never to enter any of the houses in the village. But this was the widow of whom she had heard; the fellow human cursed with misfortune. "That would be nice," she said, "if I can help."

A few minutes later, sitting in the kitchen of the little farmhouse, Marjorie Saunders raised a teacup to her lips and drank the somewhat bitter green tea she had been given and found it ambrosia; for in the cup was the soul of the Japan she wanted so very much to know and as the hot liquid passed her lips it took no notice of her complexion.

She spent the better part of an hour with Midori Taminaka and it never occurred to her that she was keeping the hospitable widow from her work. She did not know either how strained her hostess' circumstances were or how much of a godsend a paying guest represented, even though the gossip that he would provoke would degrade her standing in the community even further.

At the invitation of Akitoshi Kojima, Peter remained at the inn, sprawled out on a *futon* in the artist's room, until dinnertime. When the meal was brought in, Marjorie joined them in a very quiet and reflective mood. Shortly afterward she announced her decision to go home. "I want to get out of here the first minute that I can," she declared. "I can't possibly make any useful contribution. The Japan that I had hoped to find doesn't exist — at least not for me. At home things are a lot better now and I'm sure that I'll be able to find a project where I can be useful."

Peter put down his soup bowl. "I want you to stay here and work with me. If you don't, the effect of your leaving could be the worst thing that could happen."

"I agree," Akitoshi added. "You are here now. Remember that these people know only this simple village — they have never before seen anyone like you. They are like little children in being fearful. But they are good people and they will learn."

"*But how soon?*" Marjorie asked.

"Much sooner if you stay than if you go. Now they have seen you, they must get to know you. When they do that, they will not fear any more. Tomorrow, perhaps, I will explain something else to you about this particular village — why everyone is so careful."

"Tell me now," Marjorie urged.

"Tomorrow would be better, I think." The artist hesitated. "Anyhow, I agree that Marjorie must stay with us. I know it is hard, but did not your country put all Japanese-Americans into concentration camps, like the Nazis, in World War II?"

"Yes, we did," Peter admitted.

"It was hard for them, but they had the character. It is, I think, that Marjorie has the character too."

The meal continued after that in a quiet so thick it was almost unnatural, but each of the three persons gathered around the low table in the middle of the floor was reluctant to break it.

When the meal was almost over, Akitoshi remembered that he was the host. "It is an intrusion," he said. "but would you care to see some of my poor work?"

"Yes," Marjorie answered suddenly, "I would like to very much."

Kojima stood up and crossed to the side of the room where he had some objects hidden under a covering cloth. "First I make sketches," he explained, "then I make them again in color with water paints." He took a piece of artist's board from a small pile and turned it over.

The moment that Peter saw it he knew that it was magnificent. It showed the workers in the rice paddies just as he had seen them in the rain, but it was more than a painting — it breathed with life and reality. It was hardly two feet square, but its effect was so magical it seemed almost to fill the room.

Marjorie looked a long time before she spoke, then without taking her eyes from the painting she said, "Oh, Peter!"

"Yes, I know."

"It is not a very good thing," Akitoshi commented, "but it is what I like to do." He put the painting down and from the waiting pile produced another. It was of a farmhouse in what appeared to be close to the last light of day, the sun shining goldenly on its thatched roof with its final bit of glory before setting. Within the borders of the picture the whole atmosphere of the village of Mitamura had been almost magically captured in the simple scene.

When he had looked his fill, Peter asked urgently for more.

In response Akitoshi produced another work. It was a portrait of a young woman; elusively beautiful, but overlaid with an aura that defied definition. It transformed her from just a certain type into a vivid human being, a person fully alive and finding her way in the world. It was so subtle it had to be experienced rather than felt.

The picture captured Peter completely; he looked into the face of Midori and knew that Akitoshi had discovered more about her than he, a trained sociologist, would learn living in her home. It was a Japanese face, but deep within himself he felt that it was a universal face — she could have been born in any country at any time, and she would have been the same person. And if she had been born, say, in England in medieval days, many a knight would have aspired to have carried her token into battle.

The maid came in to remove the food trays and leave a fresh pot of hot tea. Neither Peter nor Marjorie took especial notice of her presence; they were too completely absorbed in the dozen or so pictures that Akitoshi was showing them.

When the last of them had been seen, Peter sat very still — looking into himself and seeing something that had eluded him up until that moment. He had come to Japan to do a study, and because of it he had been holding himself a little aloof. He had been playing the role of an agreeable scholar from a more sophisticated environment. He had not intended to do that, but he was guilty of it and he knew it. He had worked in the rice paddy, but it had been a condescension. Not once had he truly let himself go — he had been on stage, at least in his own mind, all of the time.

He resolved to stop it at that moment, to be himself and to tear away the academic cocoon he had let build up around him. Akitoshi's pictures had told him that Japan was not a smaller country to be unconsciously patronized, it was a nation that could produce superbly talented people. He was ashamed of himself.

"Akitoshi," he said, "I've never seen anything finer in my life. They're superb, that's the only way I can put it."

Marjorie spoke very thoughtfully. "I don't know all of the customs in Japan, and above all I don't want to be rude, but are any of your pictures for sale? If they are, I want to have some for our home." She changed her tone and became more urgent. "Toshi, what I'm trying to say is: I don't think I can ever be truly happy until I have something of yours. Will you sell at least one of them to me?"

"No," Kojima answered, "but I will give you one — if you will stay here and help us both with our work."

"I can't accept that!"

"Then perhaps you will allow me to make a picture for you. Whatever you would most like to have. It will be my very great pleasure."

Marjorie pressed her lips together; for a few moments she could not, or would not, speak. Akitoshi turned and addressed himself to Peter. "It has occurred to me that you will write a very learned paper that will be quickly published in a famous journal. But this has also been done many times by others about Japan. Not of your brilliance, but they have studied our cities, our villages, and our people, sometimes for years. Is it possible that you might write also something about this village, not for the scholars, but for all of the people of your country that might be interested? I am sure that you and Marjorie can do that. If perhaps it would be of any small added benefit, I would be honored to illustrate it. It will be a lessening of the whole, but it might help people to understand a little of our appearance."

Peter was still fighting with himself, wondering if any Japanese had ever presumed to go to the United States to dissect a typical Midwestern rural community. Why in hell hadn't he seen that before!

He caught hold of himself "Your idea is wonderful, Toshi, but I have one objection: your work is great art — I mean that —you can't be classified as an illustrator. What you do is far too good to go with any words we might put together. I don't think we could write anything that would even approach the level of your work."

Akitoshi laughed. "Peter, you say that you know so little of the Orient, yet you speak with the modesty we so highly esteem and in a manner we perfectly understand. I do not wish to intrude myself into your project; I offered only a passing suggestion."

Marjorie had been thinking her own thoughts. "Listen: Toshi is right: there's a considerable literature about Japan, and more is being added all the time. But instead of analyzing this village, I want to *understand* it. Instead of statistics, suppose we offered real people — their thoughts and ideas, how they live, what their ambitions are and what they're trying to achieve. Instead of how many rice plants will grow in one acre, how about all the work that it takes, the skill, and the care."

Peter felt a vibration run the length of his spine, he was beginning to find himself. "And how they raise their families. How they worship, and perhaps why. We could do it that way if we wanted to. Nothing in the grant says that we have to come up with a dry dissertation that only recites facts and figures." He stopped to think. "In fact, I know that Arch Bancroft would prefer something different. That's his gift: a warm relationship with all kinds of people. He's always open to new ideas and fresh approaches to learning."

"I want it to be an art book," Marjorie declared. "I mean a larger format so that Toshi's pictures will have more room — let them be the main attraction. We can add the text. It could be printed in Tokyo; they do wonderful color work there, I've seen some of it. And they do do books in English." Her face was full of sincerity, her mistreatment for the moment thrust out of her mind.

"I could possibly arrange that," Kojima responded. "In some places I have a small reputation."

Peter made a decision. "All right, it's a deal. Our obligation is to produce something that will satisfy a foundation, but its basic purpose is international understanding."

Akitoshi turned to Marjorie. "Will you stay?" he asked.

"If you want me to."

"Yes, please. It is best, I think, that our village be seen both through the eyes of a man and a woman. That was the plan when you came."

"Then I will," Marjorie promised. "I will — if they will let me."

While Peter was having his breakfast in Midori's kitchen the following morning, a young man presented himself and bowed most respectfully. "Dr. Storm, good morning, sir. My name is Hiroshi Kitamatsu. I have been sent to be your interpreter."

Peter stood up and shook hands, an action that told the new arrival that this distinguished foreigner knew nothing whatever about proper manners in Japan. "I'm glad to meet you," Peter said. "How did you find me here?"

"I was instructed from the *ryokan* — the inn."

"Tell me about yourself," Peter invited.

Kitamatsu remained standing. "I am a student, sir, in my last year at the university. I shall graduate with a major in the English language. I have studied it for eight years."

"You do very well."

"I thank you, sir, but I strive to do much better. I hope that my poor abilities will be of help to you. I regret also the lateness of my arrival."

"Are you the man who met with an accident?"

"No, sir, I am not he."

"What happened?"

"His lady friend is also desired by a larger and more powerful person. This person found them together in the embrace of love. The accident then occurred."

Peter looked at his hostess, then back at his new employee. "Why don't you sit down and have a cup of tea," he invited.

"You honor me, sir."

"How much do you know about our project?" Peter asked.

"I understand you are to study this village, talking with the people and obtaining the details of their lives. You have a lady to assist you."

"Have you met her yet?"

"No, sir, I have not done so, but I am aware of her misfortune."

Peter took a little more food with his chopsticks. "Is it a misfortune to be Japanese?" he asked.

Kitamatsu did not know how to answer that, but he had been trained to speak with total candor to a teacher. "For you, perhaps, sir, it would be undesirable — I do not find it so."

"By the same token, I do not think that Miss Saunders considers it a misfortune that she is Negro. She is a very intelligent young woman and I believe that you will find her attractive."

"Attractive, sir — then she is at least part Japanese?"

When Peter did not answer him the young man almost literally turned pale. "Honored sir, Dr. Storm, I entreat your pardon; I did realize that she is your . . ."

"She isn't," Peter snapped.

The young man turned four shades of purple and two of green. "Sir, my blunder . . . can you possibly forgive? If you wish my resignation, I offer it to you at once!"

Peter waved his free hand. "Forget it. Just remember that Miss Saunders is a very capable young American scientist and a very nice one. You will like her."

Kitamatsu would have shaken the laces out of his shoes if he had had them on. "Sir, you are most generous. I promise you . . ."

With excellent timing Midori set a cup down before her new guest and poured in the tea. At last confronted with something that he fully understood, the interpreter went through all of the proper gestures of appreciation, turning the cup in his hands to admire its design despite the fact that it had no pretensions in that direction.

"Do you have a place to stay?" Peter asked.

"Yes, thank you, sir. I possess a car and it is here with me. I shall drive the short way into the city where I have a place arranged. I will be here as early as you require me each morning, typhoons permitting."

"Fine. By the way, this is Mr. Kitamatsu, Midori. My hostess, Mrs. Taminaka."

The young man jumped to his feet and bowed energetically three times when once would have sufficed. Inside his skull his brain was still on fire with embarrassment; only by displaying great tact and perfect manners could he hope to redeem himself. Therefore if Storm Sensei chose to introduce a farm woman cursed with misfortune to him, he would at once accept her as his equal, irrational as that might be.

While his new interpreter drank the tea he had been given, Peter calmly finished his breakfast; it had been too well prepared for him to hurry eating it. He was beginning to acquire a taste for Japanese food, at least the sort that he was being served in Mitamura. There was a notable absence of meat, but he attributed that to a lack of refrigeration. Apparently the inn did not have any way of keeping food cold either, because he had seen no ice and he had not been offered any type of cold beverage — even water.

By exercising great care Kitamatsu managed to nurse his small cup of tea so that he finished it exactly when Peter put down his chopsticks and was ready to begin the business of the day.

"Please go down to the inn," Peter instructed him. "Introduce yourself to Miss Saunders and advise her that I will be with her shortly."

Kitamatsu bowed his instant obedience and left at once, glad to have a few moments to himself. When he had departed, Peter turned to his hostess. "Midori San," he said. "I have not yet paid you anything for my room and meals."

"It is all right."

"It is not all right." Peter took out his wallet and laid a ¥5000 note on the table. "That is not very much; it is only a small advance to buy food." He smiled at her. She looked so appealing he did not trust himself to remain any longer; he got into his shoes and set out to do his day's work.

After he had gone Midori waited until she was sure that he was not going to return, then she picked up the note and examined it. Five thousand yen was a considerable amount of money to her; it was, in fact, a godsend. Her cash resources were very slender and she could not have gone another two days without having to borrow on the strength of having a temporary paying guest. Now she could buy food and pay cash, something that would help to restore her face.

Because of her guest, she was preparing far more elaborate meals than she would have allowed herself and the added expense was considerable. By His blessed will the Lord Buddha had granted her help at the very moment that it was needed most. Very reverently she took the note and placed it carefully before the miniature shrine she maintained faithfully in a corner of her home that Peter had never seen.

That done she placed her hands together and bowed her head in grateful prayer. She gave thanks for many things, asked a blessing on both Peter and Marjorie, and then, with particular supplication, asked that the secret of Mitamura would be kept and that Marjorie San would never be forced to face the danger that awaited her on the hill.

Chapter Nine

Wʜᴇɴ Pᴇᴛᴇʀ ʀᴇᴀᴄʜᴇᴅ the inn, Marjorie had made all of the preparations for a day of fieldwork. She had clipboards well stocked with paper, some model interview forms she had drawn up, and her camera with a full supply of film. Peter presented their new interpreter to her and noted with satisfaction how the Japanese student outdid himself in trying to be polite to her. He was young and he would learn.

As he started out to begin the formal work on his project, Peter felt a rich, full satisfaction that he was back doing something that he understood and for which he was fitted. The first thing would be to gather basic facts: the number of houses in the village, the population, the approximate number of domestic animals excluding pets, the amount of land owned and cultivated by the villagers, and the makeup of the households. All of this would take two or three days, but it was the point from which any sort of sociological research would have to take departure.

In response to Peter's direction, Marjorie began the preparation of a detailed map of the village showing all of the individual houses. From the narrow roadway that was as close to a main street as anything that Mitamura had, he tallied the houses and paced off the distances between them while his partner diagramed them in place. This activity was intensely observed by young Mr. Kitamatsu, who was taking careful note of how everything was being done.

It was close to eleven when they reached the small schoolhouse, where the one telephone in the village was installed. The windows were open and the children inside could be heard as they recited *en masse*. Peter paused for a few moments to listen, as he did so Kitamatsu asked, "Is it your wish to visit here?"

Peter had not planned any stops during the morning's work, but he was intrigued because the sounds he heard coming out of the schoolhouse faintly suggested English. "Is it customary?" he asked.

"They would all be most honored. It is known, of course, who you are."

"We don't want to interrupt the lesson," Marjorie said.

"I would not fear that problem, Miss Saunders. The children will be anxious to see you."

As soon as those words were spoken Marjorie became quite still. In her enthusiasm for the work they were now doing she had temporarily forgotten the blow she had received at the home of the *yuryokusha*. If she were to step into the classroom, and some sort of a panic would result because the children had never seen a black person before . . .

"I think you should go in," she said to Peter. "It will give me more time to work on the map and there are some things I want to check."

He was still unaware of the incident of the day before, but he knew enough of her situation to grasp her concern and her wish to go slowly. "All right," he said.

Miss Emiko Noda, who was the teacher, knew, as the entire village knew, that the foreigner and the *kokujin* woman were making an examination of the village. She also knew that her schoolhouse was almost directly in the path of their progress and therefore the poor children might be coming out just when they were going past. They would have to see these strange, round-eyed people sooner or later, and probably some of them already had, but while they were in her care it was up to her to protect them as best she could.

Miss Noda was a very conscientious girl and she took her job seriously, this despite the fact that she had been married twice and had been returned both times. Since approximately half of the girls who are married by arrangement in rural Japan are returned within a year for one reason or another, her position in that regard was neither very unusual nor particularly to her discredit — it was only unfortunate. Of course no experienced *nakado* would risk his reputation as a matchmaker with her any more unless someone were to ask for her specifically. Since she was not very beautiful in either face or body, and since she had been to school in the city and educated well above her normal station, she had been an obvious choice for schoolteacher and there she was likely to remain as long as she could foresee. Occasionally she wished that it might have been otherwise, but when she sometimes looked out at the workers in the paddies, she was grateful that she had at least been spared that.

The authorities, far removed from the village, and therefore only lightly regarded, had ordered that English instruction be given. That was hard on the children as the foreign language was fiendishly difficult with countless strange sounds and irregularities that made it all but impossible to learn. In Japanese there were two irregular verbs, to be sure, but everyone knew what they were and consequently no trouble resulted. But the *yuryokusha* had personally instructed her to follow the orders and teach English. That authority was immediate and final, therefore while she knew almost no English whatever herself, she obediently put it into the curriculum.

The children were reciting their English when a knock came on the door and a man she did not know informed her that the *gaijin* was directly outside and wanted to come in. Miss Noda thought very quickly. She knew that the foreigner could not understand Japanese, since no one but a true Japanese could, so she did not hesitate to ask in her own language, "Is the witch woman with him?"

"No," Kitamatsu told her, "she has gone away."

"We will receive him then." It was not her decision, it was Kojima Sensei who had dictated that response. Everyone knew that the great artist had befriended the foreigner and the black woman, therefore any insult to them would be an affront to the *sensei* himself — which was unthinkable. Only the *yuryokusha* had dared to take such a position and despite his status, she considered that to have been most unwise.

She turned to her students. "Children, you all know that the language you are now learning is spoken by strange people on the far side of the world. One of them is here in our village, but he is reported to have a good heart and there is no need to fear him. You will have a chance to see him, because he is coming in here now. If anything happens, I will tell you what to do."

She had just finished when Peter came through the doorway. Miss Noda, who knew her manners, bowed low before him at once and spoke words of welcome.

Kitamatsu translated. "This is Miss Noda, the poor teacher of this humble school. She and the children are greatly honored by your distinguished visit."

"Please tell Miss Noda that I greatly appreciate her hospitality. I am honored to be here. Everyone tells me that she is a very fine teacher." That last part was pure invention, but Peter was beginning to get the knack.

When that was translated, little Miss Noda bowed again furiously, partly to acknowledge the compliment and partly to expiate her serious mistake in assuming that foreigners had no knowledge of proper deportment. "I present to you the children of this village," she said.

Peter looked at the blackboard and saw the few words in English that had been painstakingly block lettered by an inexperienced hand. "In America I am a teacher," he said.

"In a public school?" Kitamatsu asked, slightly shocked, before he made his translation.

"No, at a college. I'm an assistant professor."

That was another matter entirely and the interpreter was properly impressed, something which he conveyed fully in his rendition into Japanese. Miss Noda was deeply affected and the children regarded him almost as they might have a member of the imperial household.

Miss Noda rose to the occasion. Making her utmost effort, she succeeded in saying, "We make Engilishu."

At once she gained great face in the eyes of her students by her ability to speak to the *gaijin* directly in his own tongue, and they were all properly awed. To know English was one thing, but to be able actually to speak it was a far more lofty achievement.

Peter looked at the eager faces of the children and had an idea. A glance at Miss Noda reassured him that anything he might choose to do would be well received, so he picked up her pointer and indicated the first word. "House," he said clearly.

An enthusiastic chorus responded. "Ha-o-su."

"House," Peter repeated very carefully.

"Ha-su."

With that improvement he went on to the next word. For fifteen minutes he taught the children and never in the long history of the schoolroom had there ever been more rapt attention. As for Peter, he enjoyed it immensely, feeling that he was adding his tiny bit to the bridge of communication. His young pupils were alert and intelligent with a clear eagerness to learn. He began to understand how Japan had been able to make such huge strides in industrial development since World War II.

When he felt that he had intruded long enough, he put the pointer down and smiled his thanks. Miss Noda clapped her hands and commanded, *"Rei!"* At once the youngsters bounded to their feet, formed ranks for a moment, and then bowed their appreciation in unison.

Peter knew that he was expected to bow in return, and he did. That set off a chain reaction: the children bowed once more, Miss Noda bowed, and Kitamatsu, apparently inspired, bowed also. To extricate himself Peter smiled at the children and lifted his arm in a farewell greeting. By the time he went out the door, he was an overwhelming success; long before nightfall every person in the village would know that the great *sensei* from America had consented to teach English at the local schoolhouse. The children who carried the exciting news could hardly wait for his next appearance.

Little Setsuko Taminaka was only eight years old, but she had already made one of the most important discoveries of her lifetime. She was still entirely innocent of sex beyond the bare facts that there were boys and girls and that she was one of the latter, but she had somehow come into possession of the knowledge that she had a magnificent gift from the Lord Buddha — a mind of her very own that she could operate herself and which would produce for her all sorts of wonderful thoughts and ideas. She listened carefully to all that she was taught at home and in the schoolroom as an obedient Japanese girl should, but afterwards she liked to think about it all and wonder if perhaps there was not something more beyond — something she had not yet been given the opportunity to learn. Had some of the learned professors at the great universities in Tokyo been given the opportunity to test the power of her intellect, they might well have been astonished at the result.

Because she grasped things so quickly, some of her playmates thought she was a bit queer and some of them were convinced that she was dumb. None of them suspected the truth.

Setsuko herself understood that she had to follow certain rigidly prescribed rules of conduct and she did so unfailingly — but at times she wondered why. She had heard, of course, about the witch woman who had been turned all black as punishment for her evil deeds, but Setsuko lacked one vital bit of information — what it was that the foreign grown-up person had done to deserve such treatment. When she asked no one gave her a satisfactory answer, and that disturbed her. The only avenue left open to her was direct and elementary — to find out for herself.

If the witch woman cast any bad spells over her, she would simply pray to the Lord Buddha to have them removed. She was quite unafraid.

While Peter was in the schoolhouse, Marjorie continued her mapping of the village. She wanted very much to visit the school too, but she had to accept the situation she had faced so many times before when she had been a little girl: a present prohibition, but also a genuine hope that it might be lifted in the not too distant future.

She was well down the roadway when the children were dismissed for lunch and was not aware that the morning session was over, until some as yet unexplained sense told her that she was under observation. She was quite sensitive to that, but she continued her work for a few more seconds until she had completed the line she was working on. Then she looked around casually as though she had no intimation that she was not alone.

To her considerable relief she saw only a little girl who was thoughtfully observing her with unblinking eyes. Children could be very cruel, she knew, but they seldom had the ingrained hostilities of their elders. And she liked children very much. So she smiled at the little girl, who stared gravely back.

Even though there had been no response to her gesture, Marjorie ventured one step further. *"Konnichi wa,"* she said.

"Konnichi wa." The little girl spoke in a clear voice unstrained by fear. No one had told her that the devil woman could speak Japanese, which was a tremendous point in her favor. She had said "good afternoon" most politely, and evil spirits did not do that.

Marjorie dropped down onto one knee and looked again at the first citizen of Mitamura, other than Midori Taminaka, who had willingly shown her the least consideration. *"Watakusha wa Marjorie desu,"* she said. For the first time she regretted that there were two R's in her name, but she could not help that either.

The little girl advanced half a step *"Hajime mashite. Taminaka Setsuko desu."*

Despite the fact that her own Japanese was very limited, Marjorie recognized that the child had spoken almost like an adult. One of the things her language records had covered was introductions; she had practiced them patiently long before she had foreseen any immediate opportunity to visit Japan and use her knowledge. The child before her had addressed her as an equal.

Then it began to fall apart; the little girl poured out a long sentence in Japanese and all that Marjorie understood was the "ka" at the very end, which meant that she was being asked a question. Regretfully she shook her head and gestured with her hands to show that she did not understand.

It was remarkable how well the child grasped that and abandoned further attempts at involved conversation. Instead she drew fresh breath and pronounced "Ma-jō-ri" very carefully. Her *r* sounded like an *l,* otherwise she had caught and remembered the name very well. She came one step closer and gravely bowed.

At that potent moment Marjorie herself knew precisely what she was expected to do. She got to her feet, placed her hands on her knees, and performed her return bow with equal gravity. "Setsuko," she acknowledged.

Thus it was that two young ladies, separated almost by a generation, by ethnic origins, by totally different languages, and by the cultures of two different hemispheres, met and communicated. To Marjorie it was a wonderful experience that proved it was possible for her to be accepted as a fellow human being in this utterly fascinating Japanese village. It was a sunray of hope coming out of what had been oppressively leaden skies.

To eight-year-old Setsuko Taminaka it was proof that the person called the witch woman wasn't that at all because no witch could ever be so properly polite, even though she only knew a tiny bit about the correct way to speak. Strengthened by her new knowledge, she ran almost all of the way home to report the news. Since her father was the *yuryokusha* and had authority over the whole village, obviously he should be told first of all.

Chapter Ten

By the end of his third day of work, Peter Storm had completed his preliminary survey of the village of Mitamura and was well satisfied with the results. It gave him a solid foundation from which to go forward and with it he found a freshened enthusiasm for the job he had undertaken. He had also acquired a new respect for Marjorie Saunders as a research associate; she very obviously knew what to do and she came up with some ideas that were of real value. As their professional relationship continued to develop, Peter became less and less conscious of her color and increasingly aware of her femininity. And that, he learned, she possessed by the carload.

After each day's work he had been making use of the hot bath at the inn with a growing appreciation of its merits too. Soaking in the steaming hot water relieved the stresses in both his mind and his body, and uplifted his spirit. The local rules permitted him to share it with Marjorie, a prospect that he found highly attractive, but he was not about to make the suggestion. That would have to come from her, and he sincerely hoped that it would.

He was enjoying the last few moments in the relaxing water when the panel slid open and Akitoshi appeared. "How about eating here?" he proposed.

"I'd like to, Toshi, but Midori is expecting me."

"Then will you take a cup of tea before you go?"

"You're on."

When Peter tapped at the artist's door five minutes later Marjorie let him in. She was wearing the blue and white *yukata* that the inn provided in its own distinctive pattern. He had seen her dressed in Japanese style before, but the effect was still quite startling. He watched her for a few seconds, studying her movements as she walked back into the room, and his blood pressure rose a few points.

"The tea is ready," she informed him.

Peter came in and sat on the floor. It was still uncomfortable for him, but there were compensations. As soon as he was settled Marjorie poured three cups and passed them around. The role of hostess fitted her well and for a few seconds Peter wished that he was staying at the inn too, then he remembered Midori and the thought, agreeable as it was, evaporated.

Akitoshi began. "Peter, I am very interested in your project, especially now when I may have a small part in it."

"A big part," Peter corrected.

"Thank you. May I now be very un-Japanese and come right to the point. I have not your knowledge of social research, but I do know the customs of Japan. To help you to understand this village, it would be good for you to have some of them explained. Otherwise . . . I now use an expression taught me by an American officer . . . you will spin your wheels."

Peter responded immediately. "Toshi, we want all the help you can give us. Please tell us whatever we need to know."

Kojima picked up his cup of tea and drank. "Then allow me to say this: you have made a fine map of this village and of its fields. I understand why. You said that you next wish to find out the names of the owners of each of the fields and paddies. You can't do this, because they don't belong to people — they belong to families. This is also true of the houses and other property. It is like nature: the individual means little, but the species, or the family, is all important."

"But isn't there a *danasama*, a head in each family?" Marjorie asked.

"Yes, that is true, but he is just that — the head of the family. When he speaks, it is for all. When he retires, he passes the farm and all of its possessions on to his first son; the others get nothing. If he does not have a son, then he will adopt one from another family."

Kojima paused and drank more tea. As Peter watched him he saw almost two men — one the modern-day artist of fine education and sensitivity, the other a samurai of the old school so much a part of Japan he could never be completely separated from his homeland. The way that he sat, the way that he held his back as he ceremoniously used his teacup, those were the clues. Peter was not entirely sure which was the real man: the modern sophisticate or the strict traditionalist who had managed a fine veneer overlay of Western culture and language as a necessary means to an end. He did not doubt the man in any way, but when he spoke of Japanese traditions some invisible new element seemed to come into his being and he was like a part of the court of the Shogun.

The Japanese artist had now revealed a depth of dimension that frankly surprised Peter and told him how little as yet he really knew about Japan. But he knew that it was, indeed, a remarkable country.

"Peter, do I bore you?"

"Of course not!"

"Then let me say this: the most important concern of each family head is to have someone to inherit. That is one of the problems Midori faces; her husband died before there was a proper heir. Under the law passed in 1947 she can legally inherit, but it is against tradition. A woman cannot head a family, even if it is only one person."

"Suppose she remarries?" Marjorie asked. It was precisely the same question Peter had in his own mind.

"Then her new husband will be considered the son of her first husband and that way he will inherit the property. Does that sound strange to you?"

"Yes," Peter said.

"Then let me tell you a little story. In this village there was a man who did not wish to be a farmer. Since property is almost never sold, he adopted his younger brother as his son and then retired. At once his younger brother inherited, because we do not wait here for someone to die first. Now the elder brother was free to do whatever he wished. He went to the city and became a salesman."

Peter had nothing to say to that. It was a strange system at the best, but obviously it worked — and had worked for a good many generations.

As Marjorie refilled the teacups, Kojima changed the subject. "Peter, you remember Miss Noda, the young lady who worked in the rice paddy with you? She is to be married in a few days. It is usual to do this in September after the rice crop is in, but this time it will be sooner. Mr. Noda has asked me to say that you are both invited to the wedding."

"Me too?" Marjorie asked.

"Yes."

"The Nodas treated me like one of the family," Peter said. "I'd like to send a gift if that would be appropriate."

"Most appropriate — and also necessary. It will be much appreciated because it comes from you."

Peter enjoyed a few more minutes of luxurious leisure, then he excuse himself and set out on the short walk to the house where his evening meal awaited him. He was quite hungry after his day's work and he was looking forward to a good dinner.

When Midori slid open the panel to admit him he looked at her and thoughts of food were for the moment sidetracked. She was completely circumspect in her manner, but when she smiled just the proper amount to welcome him in, Peter could not help wondering how in the hell a girl like that had ever consented to make her life in a little farm village. The man she had married must have been some remarkable guy to sell her a bill of goods like that.

He looked forward to having dinner with her. At first she had insisted on serving him while he ate alone, but he had not cared for that arrangement; it smacked too much of her being a servant in her own home. When he had first asked her to join him she had complied somewhat reluctantly; he had solved that by asking her to instruct him in Japanese. She had looked at him sidewise out of her almond eyes and asked, "You sure?"

"Very," Peter had told her.

Within ten minutes after that she was laughing and happy, pressing her lips together to suppress her mirth when he came up with some particularly atrocious attempt to pronounce a Japanese word. The one that gave him the most trouble was "ryokan," the word for a Japanese inn. It sounded more like "lyokan," and that he could not manage no matter how hard he tried.

The food that she had prepared for him tonight was delicious. As he had learned to expect, it was served in small bowls with no one of them designated as the main course. There was some fish, two interestingly seasoned vegetables, and for a small wonder a tiny quantity of meat that had been cut up into little cubes and mixed with barley.

"Midori, how long have you been alone?" he asked her.

"It is two years, Peta, since my husband die."

"After that why didn't you go back to the city — to Kyoto?"

"I live here now. I care my husband's farm."

He had expected something like that, despite the fact that she certainly didn't fit the role of a farmer's wife — particularly a farmer whose landholdings were the smallest in the village. It must have been very hard for the young couple — the farmer with almost hopelessly inadequate little fields, the city-raised wife who was not used to the hard work required to wring the last bit of yield from the available soil.

Good Lord, how had they managed at all!

Peter remembered at that moment that no firm arrangement had been made concerning his payments. He had been told that Mrs. Taminaka would accept him as a paying guest, but no terms had been mentioned. He decided to discuss the matter with Kojima as soon as convenient and indicate at that time that he would like to be as generous as possible. It would only be a temporary help to her, but it would be something.

"Midori," he said, "This food — it is very good."

She leaned forward in a half bow. "Thank you, Peta."

He finished his small cup of tea and she refilled it for him. Once more he noted the innate grace she put into everything that she did; it was either a remarkable gift or else the product of rigorous training. No one could duplicate her flow of movement without one or the other — or perhaps both. It was that way also when she bowed; Pavlova would have had trouble trying to duplicate it. Simple as the action was, she could invest it with a grace that was liquid in its purity. And this was the woman who had come to an isolated village with her new husband to eke out a living on a farm hardly an acre in extent.

It made him think again about the times when he had felt that he was hard pressed; he had not known what real difficulty was. He had had his ups and downs, but in a situation such as Midori and her husband had been in, there could not have been any ups at all. He asked himself why some people had to work so hard for so little return while others became millionaires before they were thirty-five. It was not the economic system, because under any known system yet invented there always were the haves and the have-nots.

Perhaps it would always be so, but he still wanted to do something about it. Present before him was a good place to start.

When he had finished, he laid down his chopsticks and took a final drink of tea. Then, since it was still fully light and he was not likely to be misunderstood, he asked, "Midori, may I see the rest of your house?"

For a scant moment he saw her hesitate and he drew breath to withdraw his request, but before he could do so she gave her consent. "I show you," she said simply.

She took him first to the *nagaya*, the workshed that adjoined the house proper and closely resembled it from the outside. He was already familiar with the bathroom that contained a cubically-shaped tub of clean unfinished wood; to sit in it he would have had to have folded himself up until his knees would have been close under his chin, but it did have the virtue of not requiring too much hot water.

Next to it was the toilet compartment, the door of which was always kept carefully closed. The thought was in his mind that it might be better to keep it ajar for the sake of ventilation when Midori spoke on that exact subject. "Always door fasten shut. Not fasten, can baby fall down open place in floor. Many times happen."

The visual impression of that gave him quite a jolt. "What a way to get hurt!"

"Not many times hurt, Peta. Wash baby carefully and then usually all right. But better keep door fasten."

She showed him the rest of the shed which, like the kitchen, had a packed earth floor. In the principal work area the tools that had probably belonged to her late husband were carefully hung up and, Peter noted, were free of dirt or rust. The area for a milk cow was empty and had been for some time. The storeroom contained an almost painfully small stock; after the crops had been harvested it could have been comfortably full, since it could not hold a great deal under the best of circumstances.

With Midori leading the way, he returned to the kitchen area and stepped up into the house proper. His room, on the south corner of the house, occupied about a quarter of the total available area. Midori slid open a panel that gave access to the north half of the little house and motioned for him to go through. He did, and realized that he was in her room.

Her *futon* had been carefully put away, but this was where she slept. It was only a few feet from where she put out his own *futon*, but because it was at the opposite corner of the structure it was effectively separated by at least one full room, small as it was. For Japan that was considerable privacy.

He noted her low, simple dressing table that he'd a few bottles of the usual feminine sort. None of the products had been elaborately packaged, therefore they were probably quite inexpensive. On the wall she had pinned up a small mirror. There was also a wooden chest set in a corner; on it there was a simple lamp and a tiny potted plant.

When he had seen enough, she opened a panel that gave access to the northwest corner. As Peter stepped through he thought at first that the small room he had entered was unfurnished, then he turned and saw that against the *fusuma* wall through which he had just entered there was a plain table and on it a miniature shrine. Before it there was a small supply of food: a bowl of cooked rice, three or four unopened cans of vegetables, and a modest quantity of fresh produce.

Peter did not know if the altar was Shinto or Buddhist, but he did know that by allowing him to see this very private part of her house Midori had gone far beyond the requirements of hospitality. She had offered him something more, but precisely what he could not define.

He wanted to say something — to express his appreciation of the privilege she had given him — but he was not sure that he could put his exact thoughts into words she could understand. A better idea came to him: with careful restraint he reached and took her hand. She allowed him to do that and for a few moments they stood together.

"Thank you very much," he said.

"You are welcome."

The physical contact that he had with her was minimal, but it was almost electric. She worked very hard, he knew that, but her hand was still soft and delicate, warm with the life of her. He felt the vein in the middle of the back of her hand, so very like his own, and marveled that they were so much alike as two human beings.

Because she had trusted him in admitting him to this place, he was compelled to ignore the slowly growing desire within him to take hold of this woman and bring her to him, to press her body against his own, and look much more closely into her pure, classic, exotic features. He forced the thought out of his mind because he knew that he had to, let go of her hand, and walked back through her bedroom into the kitchen area. When he had done that he turned and read gratitude in her eyes. He reminded himself that she had been married, that she had undoubtedly loved her husband very much, and that she had had to sustain the shock of his sudden violent death.

Married meant that she had slept by his side every night and to a considerable extent she was still his.

He did not want to think about it any further. For the time being he would be content to leave things as they were. He had a job to do and he would have to concentrate on that. If any change in that plan was called for, he would know it when the time came.

When Hiroshi Kitamatsu reported for work the following morning, Peter had a proposition for him. "Hiroshi," he said. "Miss Saunders and I would like to take the day off and go into town.

Since you have a car here, would you care to drive us? Of course we will meet the expenses."

Kitamatsu was immediately willing. "It will give me great pleasure," he replied in his carefully academic English. "If you wish, I will also serve as your guide."

The drive did not take as long as Peter had anticipated. Kitamatsu's car proved to be almost absurdly tiny, but there was room for the three of them as long as they did not breathe too deeply.

It did have the unquestioned advantage of being able to negotiate the very narrow Japanese roads without difficulty. A half hour brought them to the outskirts and the beginning of pavement; after that the ride was far more comfortable. A few minutes later Kitamatsu pulled into a parking facility close to the heart of the central shopping area.

They were soon in a maze of stores, most of them tiny and all of them apparently employing three times as many clerks as seemed necessary. The area was crowded, but it was nothing like Tokyo and there were none of the signs in English for the benefit of foreigners. It was a new Japanese experience for Peter and he drew added enjoyment from the way that Marjorie so eagerly took it all in. Kitamatsu kept up a running commentary which he managed to make quite interesting; he had his heart set on becoming a guide and he was wasting no part of this precious opportunity to get in some practice.

Now that he was a little more attuned to the Japanese character, Peter noticed how much attention Marjorie was attracting. It was like a strong undercurrent that surrounded them both whatever way they happened to go. Once a small boy with a curious, unblinking face stood still and just looked at the two of them. Peter winked, but the child did not know how to regard that and he maintained his stoic immobility.

"I am sure that everyone believes Miss Saunders to be your wife," Hiroshi told Peter.

"Then let them," Peter answered.

For almost two hours he toured the shopping area with Marjorie, going in and out of many of the small shops, watching the people, and whetting his interest in everything that he saw. He was thoroughly impressed by the vast variety of merchandise available; as far as he could see there was no shortage of anything that might be wanted or needed by the people of the surrounding area.

With Hiroshi's help he bought an attractive box of bean cakes for Midori, after which the question of a wedding gift for Miss Noda came up.

"Let's eat first," Marjorie proposed. "Then I'm sure we'll be able to find something nice in the department store."

That suited Peter, so with an assist from Hiroshi he picked out a restaurant. Like all of the eating establishments, in the front window there was a display of wax models of the various things on the menu. Even beverages were shown with a card beside each item identifying it and giving the price.

When they had made their selections they went inside to discover that the restaurant was crowded to the walls with every inch of available space being utilized to the utmost. Within a minute or two they were able to take possession of a small table just adequate to meet their needs. A tiny waitress somehow managed to wedge herself between the other tables and took their order from Hiroshi. She nodded her head quickly as each item was named and wrote on her pad. She was frantically busy and Peter could not see any way in which she could get everything right. Nevertheless she did; their food came quickly and each dish was properly put before the correct person.

After lunch they went to the department store. It too was crowded, but the displays were attractive and dozens of girls were on hand to give immediate service.

"Where shall we look?" Peter asked. Like most men, he felt somewhat awkward when he had to shop in the sections principally dedicated to women and he was glad to pass the responsibility over to Marjorie.

"I've been thinking," Marjorie said. "Miss Noda is a farm girl and after she's married, she will probably go right on working in the fields with her husband."

"Yes, but that doesn't make her any less a young woman."

"Bravo, Peter, but it might be a mistake to give her a filmy nightgown; she might prefer something more practical."

To Peter that made excellent sense. He turned to Hiroshi and asked, "After she's married, is it likely that she'll have electricity in her new home?"

"A very good chance, yes, sir. Almost every house has that now, sir."

"Then perhaps we could get her a small appliance of some kind. Something to make her work a little easier."

In the rear of the store they found a profusion of electric fans and many other pieces of equipment. Marjorie selected a toaster and examined it carefully. "Hiroshi," she asked, "is toast popular in Japan — in places like Mitamura?"

"I am afraid not, Miss Saunders. We do not eat much bread in rural parts of our country."

"Then a toaster would not be a good idea."

"I do not believe so."

Peter was exploring on his own, investigating the various items on display and evaluating them with a man's eye. "Look at this, will you?" he asked.

He was standing in front of a small electric oven; it was splendid with shining chrome, a clear glass door, and a sufficient number of control knobs to suggest its versatility. Marjorie looked at it and leafed through the accompanying booklet, but since it was in Japanese, it did not tell her a great deal. "It's very nice," she said, "and probably very handy, but isn't it a little elaborate?"

"Perhaps," Peter agreed. "On the other hand, the Nodas were uncommonly nice to me. The girl is getting married only once and this could give her some real help in her kitchen."

Marjorie hesitated. "Well, if they have electricity, there's no doubt this could be a wonderful help to her. Do you think she would like it, Hiroshi?"

The interpreter was in silent agony. He had sworn before his ancestors that he would never again risk disaster by volunteering anything. This was his first assignment working for foreigners and if he blew it, his face would look like pea gravel at the bottom of a reed pond. He resorted to answering the question literally. "I am sure it would be very wonderful for her."

He justified himself by rationalizing that it was all but impossible that his American clients would actually purchase the fabulous piece of equipment. They were vastly rich, of course, but there were limits to everything.

"Let's take it," Peter said.

"All right," Marjorie agreed. "That's fifty-five dollars apiece."

"No it isn't. In the first place, you haven't even met the Nodas yet. Secondly, gifts of this kind are legitimate expenses and the funds are more than ample. If the foundation doesn't see it that way, I'll gladly pay for it myself."

Hiroshi could not believe what he was hearing. The lightning had struck and he was still in shock. Half of his being cried out that he had to tell them what they were doing; the other half demanded that he keep his mouth shut and not risk another disaster that would ruin his career before it had fairly begun. His lips formed words and he spoke mechanically, fighting for time in which to recover himself. "Shall it be wrapped as a gift?" he asked. Since gift giving in Japan is approximately ten times what it is in the United States, practically all stores are prepared to gift wrap anything from a paper fan to a sizable piece of furniture.

"Yes," Peter said.

Hiroshi shut his eyes as his lips moved in prayer.

They did not start back toward Mitamura until they had made some other purchases. Peter acquired some after-shave lotion, a bottle of shoe polish, and two or three other small items. When Marjorie rejoined him she had some packages of her own in a plastic shopping bag. By that time the oven was ready and Peter carried it himself despite the protestations by Hiroshi that that was his duty. With some small effort it was stowed in the car on the remaining vacant seat.

With hands that were wet with nervous perspiration, Hiroshi climbed in behind the wheel. Before he turned the ignition key he considered one more time whether or not he should speak. But he knew that he had waited too long; any retreat now would involve drastic loss of face for his clients as well as himself. He only hoped to almighty Buddha that if he kept his mouth shut, everyone would understand.

On the way back he tried to tell himself that it was not his duty to question his employers' actions. It was a weak defense and he knew it. He tore the curtain of rationalization aside and at last admitted to himself that he had horribly failed in his duty. His clients were people of good heart, but there was nothing he could do about it now.

Chapter Eleven

Pᴇᴛᴇʀ ᴅɪᴅ ɴᴏᴛ ꜱʟᴇᴇᴘ well during the night.

As he lay on his *futon,* he was disturbed by a wild and furious dream that churned through his mind and would not allow him to rest. It was incoherent and preposterous, but he could not shake it off. He was married to Miss Noda and her father had adopted him as his son. He was working in the rice paddy under the hot sun, striving to please his new family, but he could not understand a word they were saying to him. They were trying to tell him something urgently important, but even though they shouted to him in their desperation, he could not comprehend.

Meanwhile the strong sun was turning his skin black until they called him a *kokujin* and he became a symbol of evil. He came out of the paddy to reach the shelter of Midori's house, but each time he tried to take a step, some mighty force held him back until he could barely move with great and painful effort.

At last he reached sanctuary, but now the maddened villagers were massing outside, pulling and tugging in a frantic effort to tear the house down. He heard the sound of their fury and the creaking of the structure as it swayed under their attack.

Although his eyes were tight shut, he still saw an ominous black shadow crossing the panel of his room. They were after him and they were after Midori because she had been born in the year of the sheep and that made her a woman of ill fortune. He struggled to find reality and he was still struggling when a noise he could not identify jerked him awake.

For a moment he could not sense anything, then he heard the wind. A moment later he was aware that someone was directly outside the panel of his room. Fully conscious, he got to his feet. reached the panel, and pulled it open.

Midori was there, clad in a robe of some sort, but almost hidden behind a large wooden panel she was sliding into position.

Although he was only in his pajamas and barefooted, Peter did not hesitate; he motioned her aside and took over the handling of the panel. As he did so, he felt the force of the wind. It was not too great, but it was much stronger than it should have been. The panel was heavy and solidly built, but as he pushed it along in its groove, it was not too difficult to manage. He slid it home and then assayed the situation.

At each end of the house there was a kind of tall box that housed the storm doors. At the one on the west side Midori was moving the next panel out of the container. "I'll do it," he said, and waved her aside.

"Big wind," she told him, "Come many times each year."

"I understand. Now go inside, I'll take care of this." The panels were old and weather-beaten, but their very age testified to their ability to withstand whatever blows might come through. Ten minutes' work in the whistling wind gave him the satisfaction of seeing the south side of the house closed off and protected from the possible storm. Then he walked around past the kitchen to the north side and found Midori at work bringing out the panels there. She had the job half finished before he took over and completed it. The wind was still blowing hard as he finished, but he could not detect that it had gained any additional strength during the short time that he had been outside.

He went back in through the kitchen to find Midori waiting for him there. "Thank you," she said. *"Arigato gozaimasu."* For a moment he sat on the edge of the flooring and gave his attention to the sole of his left foot; he had stepped on something while he had been walking around the house and the hurt persisted.

"I will make tea," Midori said.

He did not want tea — if anything he wanted a very long, very cold glass of water. As he rested for a moment he gestured that he did not require any tea.

Midori came to look at his foot. As she bent over to inspect it he felt the closeness of her; he looked down, inadvertently, inside her nightgown, and saw the tops of her breasts. He did not want to take advantage of her that way, so he looked aside and then down at his foot which she was probing with her fingers.

"Would you like water?" she asked.

"Yes, please — mizu, kudasai." There were moments when she seemed able to read his mind.

She brought him a small cupful that he tossed down his throat in a single motion. She refilled it for him twice until he was partially satisfied, then he got up to return to his room.

"Thank you," she repeated, "for making help the *amado.*"

"Glad to," he answered. He turned to say good night to her once more and she was close enough for him to have taken hold of her if he had reached out. He almost did, but stubbornly he refused to exploit the minor emergency that had brought them together at that hour.

He hesitated, hoping that she would give some slight gesture, some sign that he could reach out and take her, but she stood as she was, lovely even with her hair uncombed, looking her trust at him. He could read nothing else.

"Good night," he said, and went back to his room.

Taminaka San, the *yuryokusha*, sat with the dignity that befitted his station on the tatami floor of his house and contemplated the tea service that had been set before him. The panels that normally divided the house into rooms had been removed so that the center pole with its hanging *shimenowa* was the only interruption. Sitting respectfully on the mats before him were most of the family heads of the village.

They had been summoned and they had come, still in their blue work clothes, but with almost the same sense of awe and respect they would have shown in the temple. The *yuryokusha* was far more than their elected head, he was by a wide margin the wealthiest man in the community. His sixty-four years entitled him to the high respect due to an elder. But more than anything else, his position as a great doll maker, the sixth generation of his family to live in the village and carry on that important work, raised him far above the assembled farmers, who earned their slender livings by almost continuous hard physical labor. Most of the men gathered in his presence felt themselves highly honored just to have been allowed to enter his home.

The *yuryokusha* drank his tea calmly, his stern features remaining set in the true Japanese tradition. The members of the village knew that he would speak when he was ready and they had no wish to hurry him. When he was at his workbench he took vast pains in the creation of each individual doll, which was why the wealthy collectors in Tokyo and Osaka not only paid high prices for his signed creations, but also waited patiently for months for the chance to acquire them.

At the *yuryokusha*'s right sat his eldest son, a living symbol of the stability of his home and household. The son, fully aware of his role and the dignity he represented, remained as still as his father. From the day that he had been adopted on his twentieth birthday, he had unceasingly done his best to live up to the great tradition he had been chosen to carry on. His dolls were now of such superior quality they bore the seal of the shop and were second only to those signed by his father himself.

The *yuryokusha* put down his teacup and placed his hands in his lap. Sitting formally like that in his *uchi kake* with his black *hakama* over it for receiving visitors, he personified traditional Japan and the heritage of the samurai. Had Dr. Archer Bancroft been privileged to see him and the others who were waiting for him to speak, the question that he had asked in his office some weeks before would have been answered. Old Japan still lived, and it was not destined to die an early death.

The *yuryokusha* raised his head and looked at his assembled audience. "It is time for us to consider together the several outsiders who have recently come into our village," he declared. His words were encrusted with authority. "First, we are honored by the presence of Kojima Sensei. It was at my invitation that he came here, and I have already expressed my wish that everything possible be done to make his visit a most happy one. His work is a great credit to Japan."

The last statement was the most potent. The edicts handed down by the national Diet in Tokyo and the prefectural government deserved a certain respect and sometimes obedience, but the *yuryokusha* was the immediate local authority, which meant that he had to be obeyed without question.

"We also have here in the village Sutoramu San from America. I am informed that he is a man of great learning and a distinguished teacher who is here seeking to improve his knowledge of our true culture. He has humbled himself to work in a rice paddy in order to learn. This is not our way, but it is possible to understand that this is the American system."

He paused and made a small ceremony of drinking more tea. As he finished his wife removed the teapot almost like an invisible shadow and replaced it with a fresh one that was steaming hot.

"I only cannot understand the fact that he is a full-grown man of vigor, more than twenty-five years of age, and he is not married. This is most unnatural, unless he is an unfortunate, and I do not believe this to be the case."

A farmer seated in the front bowed very low and then spoke. "Kojima Sensei has honored me with conversation on this point. He informed me that the American *sensei* is not an unfortunate. I believe that his wife has died."

The *yuryokusha* nodded. "If that is the case, then it is proper that he is observing a period of respect for the family of his late wife, and it is to his credit. Presumably he will remarry shortly."

Mr. Noda also bowed. "It was in my paddy that he worked," he said. "He has not great physical endurance, but I observed that when he set the plants out, he did so with careful attention. After he left us I went back over the work he had done and fewer than half of the seedlings had to be replanted. I wish to speak of him favorably. He was also most polite to both my wife and my daughter."

Another farmer bowed with firm vigor. "He is living in the house of a woman to whom he is not married."

The *yuryokusha* poured himself some fresh tea. "That arrangement was made by Kojima Sensei. In his wisdom he persuaded the *ryokan* to state that it had only two rooms when, as we all know, there are nine. In this way he was able to send Sutoramu Sensei to the house of Taminaka Midori where he is paying her for his food and *futon*. If she is prudent, it is possible that the money will last her for some time. By then someone will be found to marry her. Meanwhile she is doing the correct thing in refusing all offers for her land."

"She has honored the memory of her husband, my cousin." The voice came from the back of the room.

"In her conduct I find her blameless," the *yuryokusha* declared. "The women will talk, but what they say is of no importance

whatever. It is now necessary that we speak of the black woman."
He stopped, as was his prerogative, and enjoyed his fresh tea. "I
have not met this person, but I am aware that she was polite to my
daughter. She knows a few words, incorrectly, of our language."

The manager of the inn bowed his wish to be heard. "We were
very much concerned when we were forced to accept her as a guest.
We protect everyone from using the bath water after her. I have
heard many reports and there is much gossip. But in fairness I must
say that for a woman who has not been properly raised in Japan,
she has acceptable manners and if she were a *hakojin*, we would
find her a good person."

"Have you observed any evidences of ill fortune about your
ryokan since her arrival?"

"No, honored sir, and her habits are very clean. Only one accident occurred, and it was a very strange thing. Our maid Miyoko
fell and cut her knee open, but the black woman was not there.
When she returned and saw the girl's injury, she asked for our
medical supplies. Then she told the girl to come to her. Miyoko
was terrified, but she was forced to obey. The black woman applied
medicine to the knee and then wrapped it very skillfully in a
bandage. She said than in America her father is a doctor — is this
possible?"

At the side of the room little Setsuko had been listening. She had
been keeping herself properly out of sight, but her remarkable mind
had missed nothing. Now, in a great breach of etiquette, she dared
to come in and bow extremely low before her father. "I ask your
gracious permission to speak," she said.

No child, least of all a female, had any right to intrude in so
formal a discussion, but the *yuryokusha* had a very deep affection
for his little daughter and he was well aware that her mental
abilities were quite exceptional for her age.

Since she had addressed him properly, and with excellent manners, it pleased him to grant her request. He lifted his fan in consent.

Again Setsuko bowed to show her profound respect. "Most honored father," she said. "I have spoken with Kojima Sensei and he told me that it is true, Majōri's father is a very great doctor. Most important people, equal almost to yourself, travel to his hospital to be cured."

"This is interesting information," her father acknowledged.

"I have also spoken with Majōri myself, and I do not believe that she has been turned black by devils. I believe she is good. What I think means nothing, but with your great wisdom you can tell us after you have talked with her yourself. Please to do this so that we may all know what we should do."

She bowed once more, almost completely to the floor, and then backed away from her father's presence in a show of complete obedience. Because the Japanese love children almost more than any other nation does, her performance was visibly approved by the farmers who sat behind her on the mats.

It was not until she had left the room that her father realized how, quite unintentionally, of course, she had put him on the spot. Now it was unavoidably necessary that he speak with the black woman himself, face to face, or he would suffer a loss of dignity, because of his failure to provide guidance to the rest of the village.

He strengthened himself with the realization that his personal conduct was so correct he was undoubtedly well beyond the reach of any demons that might be associated with the black woman. There was no ego in that: the rules he had meticulously followed all of his life had been part of Japan almost since the first emperor had been given to the land by Amaterasu, the Sun Goddess. Therefore they were immaculate and, if properly observed, complete insurance against evil.

He lifted his head once more. "In order that you may all be guided properly," he announced, "I will do this."

He immediately gained face, for everyone present knew that Kojima Sensei had no fear whatever of the black woman and the *yuryokusha*, by proving himself equally as brave, once more cemented the authority of his office. He felt the approval of his fellow citizens so strongly he silently forgave Setsuko for what she had, unwittingly, done to him.

Akitoshi Kojima, clad in a sports shirt and a pair of custom-tailored double knit slacks, tapped on the panel of Marjorie's room and listened for a reply. A few seconds later it was slid open and he was invited inside. He accepted with an easy air since the *futon* had already been removed and the breakfast dishes were on the low table in the middle of the room. "Are you still eating?" he asked.

"Yes, I overslept a little. All of this quiet and peacefulness must be getting to me. How about a cup of tea?"

"Thank you." Akitoshi sat down easily on his heels before the low table. "I made a deal with Peter last night," he said. "I bought you."

"That's interesting," Marjorie replied. "How much did I bring?"

"The final details haven't been worked out yet. But anyhow, you are mine for today."

Marjorie poured tea. "What am I to do — sing and dance? Or do you have other plans."

Akitoshi laughed. "Plans of that sort should be . . ." He paused. "It begins with an *m* . . ."

"Mutual?"

"Yes, that is it. It should be mutual, only then is it truly wonderful."

"I'll drink to that," Marjorie said, and raised her teacup.

"Today you will work very hard holding still. I am going to make a picture with you."

Marjorie's eyes opened wider. "Toshi — why?"

Kojima shrugged his shoulders. "Because I have an idea. You

gave it to me, but you do not know that. It will be something different. So you will spend all day holding still and I will do my best."

A thought crossed Marjorie's mind. "Toshi, you don't mean in the nude, do you?"

Kojima had never considered that idea, but he put a very serious expression on his face and spoke with dignity. "Why, yes. You don't have any objections, do you?"

She did not know what to say. He could be joking, but she was not sure, and above all she didn't want to give him any offense. She thought very quickly. "My fanny's too big," she declared.

"Fanny?"

In answer Marjorie reached partway behind her and patted her hip.

"Oh, *oshiri.*" Very gravely Kojima walked around and surveyed her from the rear. "It looks all right to me," he announced. "Besides, I was going to paint you from the front anyway."

Marjorie was still uncertain whether he was in earnest or not. "Here?" she asked.

"No, out of doors — by one of the rice paddies."

She knew then that she had been had and she broke out in laughter. "Toshi, you amaze me. But then, I opened my big mouth."

"But I mean it. I ask you now to put on the clothes I chose. You will do this?"

"If you want me to."

He went quickly through the limited wardrobe she had brought with her and made his selections. When she met him in the small lobby ten minutes later he had his painting materials with him, a good-sized easel, and a young man from the inn to help him carry it all.

"I can take some of it," Marjorie offered.

"No. You're the model — your work begins later."

She discovered that he had been serious about taking her into the area of the rice paddies when they headed in that direction; moments later he was leading the way down the narrow dike that separated the first two fields. There were still a good many workers in the flooded terraces, but at least three quarters of the huge transplanting job had been completed as paddy after paddy displayed a perfect pattern of growing green seedlings.

It was a seven- or eight-minute walk to the spot that Akitoshi had chosen; a little island of dry raised land barely ten feet square in almost the exact center of the paddy area. "At this place," the artist said, "the farmers can leave equipment overnight. It is sometimes necessary to use pumps to keep the water in the paddies just at the right level. They are hard to carry, so this is a place to leave them."

He dismissed the young man from the inn and then began to set up his equipment. It took him several minutes to do that and as he worked, Marjorie watched. His physical build was not as heavy as that of some men that she knew, but there was no evidence of weakness about him. His forearms were smooth and not too thick, but when he picked something up, the muscles were there and they obeyed without complaint. His fingers were firm and strong — he was a man who could do things with his hands.

When he was ready he turned to her. "I will ask you to stand up," he said. "It would not be the same thing if you sat down."

"Whatever you'd like," she answered.

At one corner of the working area there was a small pile of rice straw; when Akitoshi picked up a quantity of it and began to arrange it to his satisfaction, Marjorie knew that it had been put there for a purpose. He made up a long sheaf and then adjusted it several times, twice adding a little more straw and once taking some away. When he was satisfied he motioned to Marjorie to come where he was. He turned her to face his standing easel and put the sheaf of straw into her arms.

For several minutes he made adjustments in her pose. He was all professional now; the easy manner that she had come to know was gone as he studied her exact position, the light, and then scanned the sky for possible clouds that would alter the pattern he was establishing. When he adjusted her shoulders she was aware that he had touched her for the first time, but it was quite impersonal — he was completely absorbed in what he was doing.

He went back to his easel and studied her until she felt that he was counting the pores in her skin, but he could have been on another planet as far as any emotional communication was concerned. He came quickly back to where she was standing and made several more very small adjustments, so slight she could not see that they made any difference at all, but he was intent and she did her silent best to oblige him as best she could. She only feared that after he had everything just the way that he wanted it, she would not be able to hold the pose for more than five minutes. She was not tired as yet, but how long could she stand absolutely still in the hot sun?

Finally he was ready. "Please give me ten minutes if you can," he said. "Then we will rest. After that, it will be easier."

"I'll try," she promised. "Shall I smile?"

"It doesn't matter; we will come to that later."

She studied him as he began work; it gave her mind something to do and blocked out the discomfort of not being able to move. Her nose developed a slight itch, but she had no choice but to endure it — the straw in her arms made it impossible even to rub a fingertip across the irritated spot.

As he stood behind his easel, Akitoshi seemed to be making almost sweeping movements with his right hand. She did not understand how he could produce the exquisitely sensitive things that he did that way, but she had seen enough of his work to be completely convinced of his ability. She drew in a sharp breath through her nose, but the itching refused to go away.

She shut her eyes and began to relive in her mind all of the good things about her first trip to Japan. The interview with Dr. Archer Bancroft when she had first heard of the project. The electric moment when she had answered the phone and had been told that she had been chosen to be the female research associate. The meeting with Peter Storm when they had gone over together what he planned to do. The morning at the airport when they had boarded the trans-Pacific jet for the Far East — that moment of a dream come true.

It was harder after that to think of only good things, but she remembered the comfort of the Imperial Hotel in Tokyo and the moment when she had first seen the rice paddies of Mitamura in the rain and it had been a glowing wood block print from the past. She remembered the little girl called Setsuko who had done her childish best to talk with her and who had succeeded unexpectedly well.

"You can rest now," Akitoshi said.

"You mean I can move?"

"Yes."

At that exact moment her nose stopped itching. "May I see what you have done?"

Kojima shook his head. "No, please, I don't want you to. Not until it is finished. Will you be patient with me?"

"Of course." She took a step or two each way to ease the muscles in her legs and then rotated her shoulders to loosen them up. That done she did her best to resume the pose she had been holding. "Anytime," she said.

It went on like that through the rest of the morning; she did not get any real relaxation until they broke for lunch at the inn. Before he left his easel Akitoshi threw a dropcloth over it; as soon as he had done that he became again the relaxed, amiable man she had come to like so very much. "You've been very patient," he told her. "One of my best models. Perhaps I should paint you in the nude after all."

"Let's see how this one comes out first. I don't doubt you —I doubt myself."

"Why?"

"I don't know," she answered. "I should have more sense. But right now I feel terribly inadequate."

"You shouldn't, not at all." Then for a moment he hesitated as though some alien thought had just come into his mind. When he continued, the timbre of his voice was slightly altered. "You may not like my picture," he warned, "but it is what I want to do. At least one thing, Marjorie, it will be a little different, I think."

When Hiroshi reported for work, he had information. "Dr. Storm, sir, I have learned that the Nodas have completed the work of transplanting their rice. Today they will be at home during the morning. Since morning is the time when all important gift giving should be done, perhaps you would wish to present your wedding gift." He stopped very suddenly and it was not until several seconds had passed that Peter realized that the speech had been rehearsed. He saw no reason for it: the interpreter spoke English well enough to say whatever he wished without having to practice first. But he was sure that his deduction was correct. As indeed it was.

"When is Hideko going to be married?" he asked.

"I am unaware of the date, sir, but soon, I think. She is going to live in a village northwest of here. It is very fortunate, for that is a lucky direction. She has already met the man she is going to marry and the signs are all good. They like each other."

"I take it that it is an arranged marriage," Peter said.

"Yes, sir, it is the usual way. The older people have much better judgment and they choose very carefully to be sure they do not make a mistake. Of course sometimes they do, then the girl is often returned. Like a store where the merchandise is not as represented. But this is all right, because the marriage is not registered until a child is expected."

Peter was interested. "About how many girls are returned?" he asked. "In percentage."

Hiroshi thought. "I am not certain, sir, but it is close to one half, I think. It is hard to say exactly, because nobody counts. Some girls are returned two or three times, but it is not always their fault. If they marry in the wrong direction, or if something else is bad, then it comes apart, I think you say."

"I see. I hope everything works out well for Hideko."

"I think it will, sir. She is not beautiful, but the man knows that and he does not seem to mind. He is not beautiful himself, so it is possible they will be very happy together."

"Let's take the gift over," Peter suggested.

This time the interpreter insisted on carrying the package and Peter let him. It was only a short distance and the package, while bulky, was not too heavy for one man.

When Peter tapped on the panel it was opened very quickly by Noda himself who immediately bowed his welcome. *"Irasshai mase,"* he greeted. *"Irasshai mase."* He gestured for his visitors to come inside.

Peter took off his shoes and stepped up into the farmhouse determined to make his call a very brief one. He had had his breakfast and he wanted to avoid being served more tea, if that was possible. The Japanese drank tea as the Navy drank coffee; there seemed to be no limit to their capacity. But it probably kept their systems in good condition.

Mrs. Noda appeared and bowed, repeatedly in fact, as though

she could not recover from the impact of having the American *sensei* in her own home. During the performance Kitamatsu came inside bearing the oven. He set it down on one of the mats and then stepped aside and delivered a short speech, bowing himself once or twice during the discourse. Whenever he did, the Nodas bowed back: apparently all of the right things were being said. When it was all over and an abrupt silence fell, Peter pointed to the large package. "For Hideko," he said. "Hideko San." As soon as he had finished he realized that he could have managed that in Japanese, but there was no need; Mr. Noda understood at once.

"Hideko, hai, wakari masu." With his words Mr. Noda bowed two or three times until Peter wondered how he could do it so easily after several long days planting in the paddy.

At that point Hideko herself appeared and a fresh cycle of formalities began. Peter sensed, quite correctly, that the Noda family was doing its best to show full appreciation of his gift. That made him glad that he had decided on something substantial; they were fine people and he genuinely appreciated them. Hopefully Hideko would be married only once, so it was her one chance to gather a little loot.

Relaxed and happy, he produced enough Japanese to decline tea and to thank them for their hospitality. Then, with the feeling that the day had started out very well indeed, he took his departure. He bowed as many times as seemed necessary after he had his shoes back on and then started back down to the inn with Hiroshi bringing up the rear.

As soon as he was safely out of sight, the three Nodas sat down and looked at one another, each aware of what was in the minds of the other two. When Peter had returned from the city bearing a huge package that was clearly gift wrapped, the entire village, the Nodas included, knew that some family was probably going to be put into an almost desperate position and they greatly feared that it might be themselves. Now the uncertainty was over; the incredible gift stood in the middle of their small room and it would not go away.

"Perhaps we ought to look at it," Mr. Noda said. It was a very simple speech, which was all he felt capable of at that moment.

"It must be done," his wife answered. Her hands were cracked with hard labor, but she still had the courage to face great misfortune.

Hideko was crying; as she sat on the matting her stocky little body shook with sobs. Understanding, her father reached out and comforted her.

She buried her head on his shoulder and found solace in his great strength of both body and spirit. "I have brought this upon you," she said with a choked voice. "Please, please forgive me!"

"You could not help it," her father answered. To the outside world he might have appeared only a simple Japanese farmer, but not visible on the surface was his deep and abiding love for his small family. He had looked forward to his only child's marriage as one of the most joyful events of his life, because it would mean her happiness and also provide him with the son he had never had. All this was shattered now, but somehow he would manage.

When the great typhoon had come eight years before and had totally destroyed the rice crop, wiping away hundreds of hours of back-breaking toil, they had endured it and had managed to survive. As *danasama* in his little household he put his sturdy arms across the shoulders of his wife and daughter and gave them his protection.

Then they unwrapped the gift. When the finely designed electric oven stood fully revealed, Hideko stared at it with a mixture of shock and disbelief. It was magnificent — no other bride in any village within miles would have another equal to it. In it she would be able to cook wonderful things for her husband for many years to come, for she would care for it with every bit of skill she possessed.

But even that should-have-been-happy thought stabbed her with searing agony. She would never be able to use it without remembering the terrible thing it had done to her parents. Because every gift received at the time of a wedding had to be returned through another gift to the donor which, by inviolate custom, had to be almost precisely half the value of the original.

The fabulous oven had cost a staggering amount of money. They had almost no possessions left that they could sell in order to raise enough money to buy a return gift worth half the value of the gleaming, beautiful, wonderful present that they were far, far too poor even to dream of receiving.

Chapter Twelve

Wʜᴇɴ Pᴇᴛᴇʀ Sᴛᴏʀᴍ ᴀʀʀɪᴠᴇᴅ back at the inn at the end of the working day, he was more than satisfied with what he had accomplished. He had conducted several very good interviews and through them he had gained a considerable additional insight into the life of Mitamura and its people. There was still a long way to go, but he was learning rapidly. He was also increasingly grateful to Archer Bancroft for having given him this assignment. Japan was beginning to get into his bloodstream.

He was still amazed that it took 870 man-hours of labor per acre to raise rice in Japan while in his own country, thanks to vastly more available land and mechanization, only 26 hours were required. There was no comparison in the yield; forced to work with their hands in tiny fields that an American farmer would not bother to plow, the Japanese achieved astonishing results. Under the pressure of vast overpopulation, they had to.

At the inn he was warmly welcomed and advised that the bath was ready. By a somewhat devious process the inn had managed to reveal without serious loss of face that it had a number of additional rooms and one of these had been placed at his disposal. Because of his growing understanding of the Japanese character, Peter had never raised the issue as to why no room had been ready when he had arrived with a bona fide reservation; he was happy with the way

that things had worked out and there was no point in rocking the
boat.

He had put down his notes and was starting a brief progress
report to his superior when Akitoshi knocked and came in. The
artist's face was a little more serious than usual and Peter read it
out at once. "Is Marjorie all right?" he asked.

"Oh, certainly. She is a little tired, but that is to be expected."

"Something seems to be on your mind."

"Yes." Akitoshi hesitated. "Peter, it is all over the village that
you and Marjorie gave Hideko Noda a very lavish wedding present."

Peter put down his pen. "It wasn't really that much. The Nodas
were very good to me and I like them a great deal. So I got her
a little electric oven I thought she might like."

"Forgive me, but how much did it cost?"

"A little over a hundred dollars, but don't worry — the foundation will probably pay a good part of that."

Akitoshi was visibly troubled. "Peter, in your country you have
certain customs, like allowing a woman to go first through a doorway. We also have ours. One is that each wedding gift must be
exchanged by one worth half as much, so now the Nodas will have
to give you a gift worth fifty American dollars."

"I don't want them to do that!"

"Unfortunately they must — your interpreter should have told
you that. So we have a little problem."

"In their circumstances . . ." Peter stopped. "Look, Toshi, help
me out. Please, for me, call on them and explain that American
custom does not allow me to accept a return gift. Explain that I
value their friendship far more than anything they could give me."

"I am sorry, but now they must offer it to you, otherwise they
will lose terrible face in the whole village. We cannot get out of
it that easily."

Peter got up and paced the straw-matted floor in his stocking feet. "What in hell can I do?" he asked.

"First, do nothing. Pretend that you do not know of this. But if the Nodas do offer you a gift, you must accept it. If you refuse, it would mean that you consider them unworthy to offer anything to you. So you must not do that."

"All right," Peter promised, "I won't. But I'll have Hiroshi's neck for not telling me this."

Akitoshi raised a warning hand. "Go easy," he advised; "sometimes in this country students who fail an assigned task with too much disgrace kill themselves. I will think about this and see if anything can be done."

Marjorie was having her breakfast in her room when Akitoshi knocked and came in. "Something has occurred I must take care of today," he said. "Could you work with Peter today and me tomorrow?"

"Yes, of course. Is anything wrong?"

"No, I do not believe so. But there is something that must be done. I will explain later."

In his own room he picked up his drawing materials, two pieces of board, and a small easel. Two minutes later he had his shoes on and was out of the inn. He walked briskly, because he did not want to encounter anyone if he could help it; within five minutes he was before the door of the Noda home.

Because of the forthcoming wedding, the family was still at home. As soon as Mr. Noda saw who his caller was he began immediate frantic bows while he poured out his profound respects. He was overwhelmed that Kojima Sensei had come to his humble home; he called to his wife to prepare tea at once. In her own tiny room poor little Hideko did her utmost in a few seconds to make herself presentable.

In a manner that Peter Storm would not have recognized, Kojima seated himself formally on the backs of his heels and made small talk with his host until the tea was ready. Noda himself was almost too overcome to say even one word to his astronomically distinguished visitor. On her knees Mrs. Noda poured for her guest and her husband, then drew back to indicate her unworthiness to participate in whatever important discussion the men were about to have.

At the proper moment Kojima began. "I have been asked by a magazine in Tokyo to do some sketches for them while I am here. It has occurred to me that Hideko might be a suitable subject for one of them. May I borrow her for a little while?"

Mr. Noda was so honored he he could not express himself. In the presence of the great artist words simply would not come until he had recovered himself. Then he at once summoned his daughter and informed her of the overwhelming honor that had befallen her.

Mrs. Noda, in one of the climactic moments of her life, overcame the training of a lifetime and dared to speak. Would Kojima Sensei like her to wear her kimono? They could have her in it and ready in an hour.

No, that elaborate a preparation would not be necessary. Just as she was would be fine. The idea was to depict the people of Miyazaki as they were from day to day.

The joy in the Noda household was so great it was forgotten that not one member of the family had slept a single wink during the night. The ruination that they faced was for the moment thrust aside. Hideko was produced and as she bowed on the mat before her father, she was sternly instructed. She was to do at once whatever Kojima Sensei wanted, no matter how difficult. She was to do exactly as directed — nothing else.

She bowed vigorously several times, her forehead to the mat, to show that she understood and would do her utmost to oblige. The thought of remaining home to receive any additional wedding presents could not have wedged in sideways. The excitement of having been selected by the great and immortal artist was so overwhelming, everything else was totally blocked out. She looked at her hands and almost wept that she had been planting rice for the past two weeks and as a result they were cracked and swollen. Hideko Noda knew that she was not beautiful, but despite her limitations in that respect, she was still thoroughly female and therefore wanted to make the very best of what she had.

Terribly fearful that in some unexpected way she would prove to be unworthy of her incredible good fortune, she left her home with the man who was her exalted social superior and followed him obediently as he led her up into the hills behind the village.

Although she was a virgin, she had already decided that if the great *sensei* wished to honor her with his intimate attentions, she would acquiesce immediately. Perhaps that was what he wanted: he had been in the village for some time, far removed from the ravishing beauties of Tokyo who must be panting for his return. She recalled her father's instructions and awoke to the fact that he had had the same idea — but of course he would have had no choice in the matter. However, it was still quite early in the morning for that.

They were high above the village, and far removed from everyone else, when Kojima stopped at a level spot and set up his easel. He placed his model on a convenient rock, told her in direct language to hold still, and opened his case of drawing materials.

In a little more than an hour he had what he wanted, a sketch of Hideko that almost spoke from the paper. He had made a few subtle changes: he gave her a face that was a little less round, a slightly improved eye separation, and a mouth almost invisibly better than the original.

When he had finished he let her rest for a few minutes while he talked with her about her forthcoming marriage. Inevitably the subject of Peter Storm came up and his rice planting exploit was once again discussed. There was a little stream nearby from which they drank cool water and refreshed themselves. Hideko was ready then for her fateful moment, but it did not arise. Kojima took her back to her rock, produced his second drawing board, turned his subject in the opposite direction, and went to work once more.

It was noon by the time he had finished; once again he had created a portrait that almost possessed a life of its own. Satisfied, he sprayed both drawings with fixative and then packed up his materials. "It is past time for your lunch," he said. "I will take you home so that you can eat."

"It does not matter, sir," Hideko answered. "I am only anxious to please you."

"That you have done, and very well. I am sure that the magazine will be delighted." He stopped and set out the two drawings that he had made. It was the first time that Hideko had seen them, as she had not dared to ask for that privilege, and she was spellbound. She had never dreamed that she could ever be so near to beautiful, yet the sketches were unquestionably of her — they could not possibly be anyone else.

"They are marvelous," Hideko said. "I cannot believe that you have done this wonderful work from my poor face."

"It isn't that poor," he told her. "I rather like it. I am sure that your husband will be most pleased."

The conversation concluded because he wished it that way, then he led the way back down the hill to the upper edge of the village.

While the tea was being poured once more in the Noda home, Hideko recounted her wonderful adventure. Her mother and father listened with deep appreciation, profoundly grateful that their daughter had been found worthy and had conducted herself so well. They were also greatly relieved. "I could not have asked for a better subject," Kojima told them. "She has such a pure Japanese face, and, of course, nothing in the world can be compared to that."

Hideko was ecstatic.

As he rose to go, after taking his refreshment, Kojima paused. "I made two pictures," he explained, "so that I might choose the one I wanted. I have now made my selection. I have no need of the other, so I will leave it here with you. Perhaps you will have a use for it some day. I have signed it, so in almost any gallery it will be worth more than fifteen thousand yen."

That said he bowed his way out, put his shoes back on, and turned back toward the inn.

Ten minutes later the Noda family — husband, wife, and daughter — knelt in utter respect before the little shrine in their home and thanked both the Lord Buddha and their own ancestors with all their humble hearts for the restoring miracle they had been granted.

For more than twenty-four hours they had been racked by the knowledge of the great obligation they owed. The only possible way to discharge it would be to sell Hideko's kimono, and that they had to have if she was to be married, Mrs. Noda had parted with hers to keep the family alive after the great typhoon of eight years before. Beyond that they had nothing more than their little farm, and without it they faced only slow starvation.

Hideko had been to school. She had been able to figure out, and tell her parents, that ¥15,000 was a little more than fifty American dollars.

It was a day off for the village of Mitamura. The long rice transplanting job had at last been completed and a brief period of rest was in order before the particularly arduous and exhausting task of harvesting the mat rush that had been growing during the winter and spring months had to be started. It would call for the hardest kind of work in a bent over, twisted position that was agony in itself. Before that annual purgatory had to be endured, the farmers of the community declared a holiday.

Since everyone else was knocking off work, Peter Storm wisely decided to do so also. A group of the younger men set out some flat filled sacks and enthusiastically prepared to play basebaru. When Peter arrived at the playing area the serious business of choosing up sides had just begun. The team captain who first saw Peter coming sensed a golden opportunity and at once chose him, because of his height, to play first base.

No English was spoken and none was needed; Peter was ushered to his assigned position and someone threw him the ball to see if he could catch it. When he did so easily with one hand, the tryouts were over and the game began in earnest five minutes later.

Marjorie had chosen to remain at the inn. When she was with Peter she was politely tolerated, but she knew that because of her color she did not want to go out alone. She had been declared *persona non grata* at the most important house in the village and she did not want to risk a similar rebuff from anyone else.

When Hiroshi tapped on her door she recognized his knock. As soon as she admitted him, he had a small piece of news. "You have a visitor outside, Miss Saunders. She wishes to see you."

"Who is it?"

"A little girl of eight or nine years. She wishes me to say that her name is Setsuko and that she knows you."

"Please invite her in."

A few moments later Setsuko entered gravely and bowed her respectful greetings. Then she produced a surprise. "Gudo moriningu," she said with careful definition of each syllable. "Gudo moriningu, Majōri."

Marjorie wanted to gather her up into her arms, but knew that

that would be the totally wrong thing to do. Instead she bowed in return and replied, "Good morning. *Ohayo gozaimasu.*"

The formalities concluded, Setsuko stood properly erect with her hands at her sides and declared herself in Japanese. She was perfectly aware of the fact that Marjorie could not understand her, but she also knew who Hiroshi was and what his function was supposed to be. So she did things as a young lady should and used proper language.

Hiroshi performed his duty. "Miss Setsuko wishes to inform you that her father is a doll maker. He is presently at home in his workshop and has sent his daughter to ask if you would like to see some of the poor things he has prepared."

Marjorie was suddenly delighted. "I would love to! I heard that there was a doll maker here and I would like to meet him." She did not add that should would have been happy to meet anyone; anyone, that was, who would be willing to regard her as a human being, as she regarded all the citizens of the village.

There was a further swirl of Japanese around the room and some formal bowing in which Marjorie did not participate for the very good reason that she did not know what was going on. Then Hiroshi spoke again in English. "Miss Setsuko will be your guide. She is very happy that you have accepted her father's invitation. She knows that he will like you very much."

It was too much to hope.

Marjorie put on a pair of sunglasses and tied a scarf over the top of her head. It was partly to keep her hair in position, but most of the Japanese women did the same and it might help her to be a little less conspicuously different. As she walked out of the inn into the bright sunlight, she almost reached her hand down to her little guide, but once again she remembered. She made sure that Hiroshi was coming, then set off down the road, a new adventure singing in her heart.

When Setusko turned up the hill Marjorie followed, but with the hope that she would not have to walk past the house where she was unwelcome. She had been carefully avoiding that area as much as possible.

Unfortunately they were headed in that direction. However, if the people who had refused her saw her walking past, perhaps it would tell them that there were others in the village who were not as bigoted.

Setsuko did not go past the forbidden house, instead she turned right up toward it. As she did so, Marjorie stopped dead in her tracks. It was the house of the *yuryokusha*, she knew that, and she would not go one step further.

Hiroshi came up beside her. "It is here that you have been invited," he said.

Marjorie did not believe it. Firmly she shook her head and turned away.

Setsuko came running toward her, demanding attention. When she spoke Marjorie could not understand her, but she could grasp very clearly the emphasis in her words. When she had finished, Hiroshi functioned. "Miss Setsuko wishes you to understand that she was sent by her father to invite you here. He now awaits you. Since he is the head of this village, I ask permission to advise you that it would be best to accept. Please to go in."

Marjorie swallowed, looked for a quiet moment at Setsuko, and then braced herself. If it came down to that, she was better equipped to endure a reprimand than her little friend and for her sake she was willing to risk it. She turned and allowed Setsuko to lead her directly up to the door of the workshed. She remembered then that the invitation had been to visit the workshop — not the house.

A young man appeared, bowed and said in Japanese, "My father awaits you." Although Marjorie understood that, Hiroshi translated and then, remembering his recent training, he did the irrational thing of stepping aside so that a female could go first. Setsuko led the way in; with unsteady knees, Marjorie followed.

The shed was elaborately fitted out; there were shaded electric lights above the workbenches. Racks of carefully-filed baskets contained materials and supplies; against the wall, on shadow boards, there was an impressive display of small shining tools. A wooden floor had been provided and a large fan was running almost silently in the corner.

All of these things Marjorie saw, but her main attention was claimed by the man who stood waiting, turned away from his bench and facing her. She had often imagined what a Japanese samurai might look like in his home; now she felt that she was confronting the reality.

Since she was the guest, she bowed. She could not do it as the Japanese did — it would take years to acquire that skill, but at least she could display good manners — and the man before her had once failed that test. For she had no doubt whatever that this was the person who had forbidden her entry into his house.

"*Konichi wa,*" he said. It was the minimum welcoming courtesy. Then he returned the bow in the traditional and correct manner.

"*Konichi wa,*" Marjorie replied. "*Watakusha wa Marjorie Saunders desu.*" She sensed that she should bow once more, and did.

Very gravely, and very carefully, the *yuryokusha* surveyed her. Her black skin was not quite as dark as he had expected. He had known that there were people in the world born like that; not everyone could be Japanese. He recalled a man who had been terribly burned and who, after much intense suffering, had recovered. His skin had been left in a frightful condition so that many people turned away from him, but despite that awful affliction, he had remained a Japanese gentlemen.

He first returned the bow, then he gestured toward the bench.

"Would you care to examine some of our poor work?" he invited.

As soon as Hiroshi translated Marjorie stepped closer to the bench, where a single doll stood in the center of the cleared area. Having been granted permission, she bent over to look at it more closely.

After a few seconds she became so interested she forget momentarily where she was; putting her hands on the bench she bent over still farther to study the doll as closely as she could without picking it up.

It utterly fascinated her. It was far more than just a doll, it was a miniature sculpture done in clay, fabrics, and other materials with a realism that was startling. The finely detailed model of a human being of another era that stood there on the bench seemed to possess everything but the breath of life itself.

In her admiration of the superb piece of work Marjorie blocked all other thoughts out of her mind. She continued to study the doll and the costume that it wore, unmindful of the others who were present, until at last she remembered and straightened up once more. "I have never seen anything to equal this," she said. "Nothing that even came close."

When Hiroshi had translated that, the *yuryokusha* bowed once more. "It is the work of my son," he said. "I find a slight satisfaction in his achievements."

"It must give you great pride," Marjorie answered, "to have a son of such wonderful talent. Also you must be a very great teacher."

She had no intention of saying anything other than what was truly on her mind, and her words were quite sincere. She was entirely unaware that by a very fortunate chance she had said precisely the correct and proper thing from the standpoint of the finest Japanese etiquette.

"It is really very poor," the son said. "It cannot be compared to the work of my father. Your praise is far too much."

At that moment Hiroshi Kitamatsu realized something with a smashing impact. He could put aside the things he had been taught about rude foreigners who talked at the top of their voices and who sometimes wore their shoes indoors, even in their own homes. He was translating in the big league now. He gave his renditions with great care, striving to preserve the flavor of correct speech. Belatedly he realized that he had had no appreciation of the true quality of the black woman: she had been educated!

Marjorie turned to look at the doll once more. "Is it of the Kamakura Period?" she asked. She knew only a little about Japanese history, but the miniature warrior could be consistent with that time. Or she thought so.

Taminaka San, the living treasure of Japan, had never faced a more difficult moment. He knew very well that there were demons and other forces of evil that rose to plague the Japanese islands; he had guarded against them all of his life. But demons were rude — and so were the people possessed by them.

The strange foreign female before him could not speak Japanese, but she was both thoughtful and courteous.

By the unquestionable statement of Kojima Sensei, her father, who presumably was black in color also, was a physician who healed the sick and therefore frequently had to drive out evil spirits.

And, incredibly, she also knew something of Japanese history. He had not believed that there was a *gaijin* anywhere, except perhaps on the faculty of some great university, who could identify correctly the costume of a Kamakura Period samurai.

As he collected his thoughts he looked down at his little daughter. She was standing obediently still and looking back at him with complete innocence and respect, but in his inner mind he knew that she was thinking, "I told you so!"

As indeed she was.

For just a brief moment he entertained the idea of presenting the black woman with the doll — it would serve to correct one of the few blunders he had ever made. But it would be far too much and the whole village would know it within the hour. No one in Mitamura, even his oldest friends, had ever dreamed of receiving such a lavish gift from his hands.

However, there was something else. Locked into Japanese tradition through the long centuries of the past was the absolute dictum of courtesy. Even those who had been directed to perform anguishing ritual suicide had always expressed their thanks and gratitude to their superiors for having been granted the honor of thereby clearing their names.

It was now time, according to the all but sacred tradition, to observe the requirements of courtesy. Because this woman understood them despite her origins, and if he displayed a flaw now, she would detect it.

He bowed moderately, as was correct, and then spoke in an even voice.

"Would you care for some tea?" he asked.

Chapter Thirteen

During the next several weeks the farmers of Mitamura and their families blessed the fact that the weather held good. The rain came at reasonable intervals to water the dry field crops and to augment the precious supplies upon which the vital irrigation system depended. The rice grew taller and by the great benevolence of the Enlightened One, the rice blast was kept well under control. If the insect hordes did not descend upon them, and if the typhoons remained small ones, then all of the signs were in for a bumper crop.

The harvest time was still a long distance away, but those who had predicted continuing disaster, because of the presence of the witch woman with the black skin, were forced to concede that they were having the best year for a very long time. The final verdict was not yet in, but if the crop did prove to be as good as was hoped, and if the prices for the grain were at least adequate, then there would no longer be any reason to believe that she was a bad person.

Meanwhile the village had acquired, at least temporarily, a new son. Peter Storm had entered into his assigned research project with a properly objective attitude, but as he talked to people, and gathered his facts and figures, he discovered that Mitamura was no longer a small community he was putting under the sociological microscope, but a place that was becoming so familiar he felt himself to some degree to be part of it too. The little twists and turns in the pathways, the ruts in the road that ran through the village, the layout of the paddies and the dry fields, all began to mix a little into his bloodstream.

He very much missed Akitoshi, who had left before all of the mat rush had been cut, and no one seemed to know when he could be expected to return. The inn had been told that he was coming back and his room was held for him without his asking. He had left behind a number of his things, so there was no doubt that he would return when he was able. A thin flow of travelers came and stayed at the inn, but the big front room that had been given to the artist was left strictly alone except for the maids who went in to dust.

Peter could have moved to the inn at any time, but he was enjoying himself far too much where he was. Midori he found fascinating; now that he knew her better he discovered a certain impish charm about her. She had a trick of looking at him sidewise out of the corners of her eyes that would have laid any man low, but he never had the feeling that she was flirting with him. The meals she prepared for him were one of the highlights of his day and her companionship was delightful, but despite his natural inclinations he was still careful not to assert himself.

He held himself in check for several reasons. There was the presumed trust that Akitoshi had put in him when he had made the housing arrangement. He certainly had a need to maintain a proper posture in the village to carry on his work. But most of all, he was unwilling to take unfair advantage of a very attractive woman who had taken him in because she almost desperately needed the money.

There was another thing: despite their warming relationship, he had never received the least direct encouragement from Midori to go beyond where they were, and a certain language restriction between them tended to keep things that way. Peter was content to leave it at that, but if she ever indicated to him that he was welcome to put his *futon* in the same room with hers, then he knew he would not waste any valuable time in moralizing.

In his work he had reached the point where he was ready to study the irrigation system in detail, since its maintenance and operation was absolutely essential to the continuing life of the village. Well up on the hill there was a small lake or reservoir from which the water came. The same source supplied a number of other communities; consequently there were frequent meetings at which the distribution of the available supply was discussed in minute detail. This summer there would be enough water, but only if it was judiciously allotted until it was time to let the paddies go dry during the last phase before the harvest.

At nine in the morning of Hiroshi's day off, when data gathering in the village itself would have been impractical, he collected Marjorie at the inn and proposed that they inspect the water system firsthand. It was a beautiful day and despite the fact that it was quite warm, it was close to ideal for climbing up the hill.

"I'd like to go up to the lake very much," Marjorie told him. "I've been wanting to, but Akitoshi insisted I had to have an escort."

"You've got one now. Perhaps the inn could put up a lunch for us; I understand it's very nice up there."

With his limited Japanese Peter managed to make himself understood; a lunch would be prepared, he was assured, and would be ready in fifteen minutes. The manager, however, did not seem to be happy. He drew breath as if to say something, but then held back when he realized that Peter's Japanese was inadequate for what he had in mind. Akitoshi was not on hand to translate and the interpreter had the day off, so he was powerless.

While the lunch was being packed Marjorie changed into a pair of slacks and a white blouse that emphasized her dark skin. The people of the village knew her now, she was no longer a novelty. She chose a good pair of shoes designed for possible rough going and declared herself ready.

"Bring your camera," Peter advised. "If you'll take it and a clipboard, I'll carry the lunch."

"We'll take turns, but you save face while you're still in the village. Do you know the way?"

"I haven't been up there, but there's only one trail. I don't see any chance to get lost."

As soon as the lunch was produced, Peter took it and after getting back into his shoes, led the way to the path that went up the hill.

Ten minutes after they had left the inn they were well above the village and in the shade of substantial trees. The path was narrow and in places very steep, but with reasonable care they climbed without difficulty, pausing occasionally for a few moments' rest. When they found a stream of clear cool water they drank gratefully; it was the best and coldest water Peter had had since he had first arrived in southern Japan.

"At this point in time," Peter said, "despite the exercise of climbing, I feel completely relaxed."

"So do I," Marjorie agreed.

"Are you happier now?"

She knew exactly what he meant. "Yes."

He wanted to add something, but he could not find the right words. He profoundly admired her spirit, but to say so at that moment might be exactly the wrong thing. Instead he treated her like the companion and associate that she was and pushed everything else aside. "Shall we go on?" he asked.

"One more drink and I'll be with you."

It was further than they had expected up to the lake, but when they arrived the scene was beautiful. The lake itself was quite small, but it was set like a jewel on the side of the mountain. It was evident immediately that a great deal of careful and ingenious engineering had been done at some time in the past. In all probability the lake was artificial; there were obviously ancient retaining walls of carefully piled stones and a system of sluices that merited respectful attention. Everywhere it was clear that a massive amount of labor had gone into the construction and that more was being expended constantly in maintenance.

It took the rest of the morning to walk around the lake, study it, and make a reasonably accurate estimate of its size and volume. As Peter caught up his notes, Marjorie spread a mat and set out the lunch that the inn had provided. Her brief experience in Japan had already taught her much; she was careful to arrange everything to have maximum eye appeal and even precisely judged the place where she should put down the chopsticks.

When Peter joined her, she put her hands together and bowed.

She was utterly captivating when she did that, and Peter was not immune. He knew her so much better now, and found so much to admire in her, including her determination to stick on the job when with full justification she could have fled home to the sanctuary of her family's mansion. He sat down beside her. "You're a helluva girl," he said. "I shouldn't say that to my research associate, but you are."

"As for you," she responded, "there's only one thing wrong: you don't know how much of a man you are."

"You're giving me ideas," he told her.

"I know; I'm a doctor's daughter. A damn good doctor, by the way. But it would be inappropriate for the great Sutoramu Sensei from America to be discovered *in flagrante delicto* in a semipublic place, don't you think?"

"*Touché,*" he admitted.

"Eat your lunch."

When they had finished Peter went about his measurements while Marjorie put everything away and carefully gathered up the bits of litter that remained until the site was as clean as it had been when they had arrived. Then she unslung her camera. "I'm going up a little way," she called to Peter, "I want to get a picture of the lake."

Confident that she had been heard, she returned to the path that led upward through the dense trees toward the temple high above. She hoped to pay it a visit eventually, but it would have to be after the principal work on the project had been completed.

With a sense of freedom she had not felt for weeks she started up the path, climbing easily and enjoying the exercise it gave her. The higher she went, the better the panoramic view that spread out below her wherever there was a break in the trees. She did not want to take too long away from Peter, but the day was intoxicating and she wanted to make the very most of it.

Presently she found the spot she was looking for; the trees were thick around her, but an outcropping of rock provided a ledge where she could stand and see the whole plain with its intricate pattern of glittering rice paddies and small clusters of houses that were the individual villages. She poised herself carefully, aware that ten feet in front of her there was a direct drop of almost a hundred and fifty feet and below that the broken gravel of a sixty degree slope; if she went over the edge that would be the end of everything.

She studied the scene and adjusted her Nikon to the prevailing light. As she did so she wished that Peter had been there with her; she would have asked him to take her picture against the rich background of rural Japan with all of its varied pattern of paddies and dikes that now meant so much to her. She focused carefully and took her first picture, then turned to move back a few steps. At that instant every muscle in her body locked tight and her eyes went wide with horror.

There was something there. With the instincts of a trapped animal she knew that it was hostile and that behind her there was no possible escape. Her mind was so shocked she could not grasp what it was for the first second, then she saw that it was a man, but not like any man she had ever seen before. It was more like an erect animal, wild, ferocious, and totally savage. She looked into the creature's eyes and saw the sure signs of insanity.

When Marjorie Saunders had been four years old she had discovered that she was "different" and that she would have additional battles to fight as a result. She had learned to tell, almost instantly, when she faced a serious challenge.

She faced one now and she knew it completely. She was much too far up the trail to call to Peter for help; he would not possibly hear her. To the best of her ability, she would have to fight. Her camera was an expensive instrument, but without turning her head she tossed it into a bush; it would be no good as a weapon.

The thing she faced shrieked and plunged toward her. To counter Marjorie snapped her knees forward and let her body collapse. She had had a few lessons in aikido when she had been in high school; desperately she hoped that she could remember *something* of her limited training now.

To escape the attack she rolled forward, away from the deadly edge and then, throwing herself on her back, she bent her knees once more and held her feet ready to kick in any way that she could. There was no science to that; it was raw instinct and nothing more.

She saw the madman close above her, but not close enough for her to land a blow. His black hair fell to his shoulders, partially covering his eyes. He seemed to wear nothing but a tattered robe wound around himself and tied. His eyes were awful and his mouth was open with his lips drawn back from his teeth. He was reaching for her.

Somehow she managed to push backward and regain her feet — she did not know herself how she had done it. Then the inhuman thing she faced charged her again and this time the simple trick of dropping out of the way would not work. Concentrating on one of the few specific things she had learned, she fixed her eyes on the left hand that, like its partner, was reaching out for her throat. As the lunatic rushed her once more Marjorie seized his left hand, spun herself to the left to get out of his way, and then folded the hand back in *kotogayashi* position, twisting it at the same time toward the outside of the wrist. As she did so, she whirled herself to the right to increase the leverage.

The feet of the man came out from under him and he crashed down onto his back. It was a good throw, but it was almost the only one she knew. The madman rebounded to his feet and then rushed toward her, arms outstretched.

She had no defense against that and the cry in his throat almost paralyzed her. In desperation she curled her fingers to scratch and then, from nowhere, Peter plunged onto the man's back.

Both of them went down, the wild man a total animal in his ferocity. Marjorie sprang forward herself, determined to do anything that she could.

Like two fighting cats in a thicket the men thrashed on the ground; the lunatic astonishingly strong, Peter giving his all with fierce intensity. Then Peter was on his back and violent hands were at his throat. Setting herself, Marjorie kicked quickly at the attacker's groin. She succeeded in causing a yell of pain, but the hands were still locked tightly around Peter's throat. Peter had hold of the wrists, trying to tear them away.

Knowing that a desperate, frantic effort would probably fail, Marjorie forced herself to move into position, to gauge her distance, and then to focus her strength so that she could kick once more with maximum effectiveness. When she was ready, she drew her foot back and then drove it forward with the full power of her body.

It was difficult to deliver a groin kick from the back, but she caught her target squarely and with authoritative power. It had taken her four extra seconds to do it right, but it was the thing that saved Peter and herself. With a scream that came from a shattered mind, the demented creature plunged into the trees, still crying in agony.

"Let him go!" Marjorie gasped.

Peter got to his feet, a little slowly and massaging his throat; the skin was red and almost raw and his hands were shaking.

"I remembered just in time," he panted out. "Akitoshi told me not to let you be alone, up here."

Marjorie sat down and began to cry. It was a pure nervous response and Peter knew it; he left her alone, standing guard while she got it out of her system. He saw her camera and recovered it.

When she was in control of herself once more, he spoke to her as calmly as he could. "Let's go back down to the lake. There are a few more things to do there, and I don't think that we'll be disturbed." When she did not respond immediately, he took her by the hand, helped her to her feet, and then led her back down the trail.

When they were at last back at the inn, Marjorie disappeared into her room without a word. Peter was more than ready for his evening bath; it had become a well-seated habit and a dangerous one, because there was no really good way that he could continue it once he was home again. He had a bathtub available, to be sure, but it was a minimum thing in which it was quite impossible to stretch out and let the hot water do its relaxing job.

In his room he undressed, put on the *yukata* that was always laid out for him there, and went directly to the bath. With a strong sense of gratitude he poured hot water over his body, soaped himself, and then rinsed off. That done, he climbed into the hot tub and slid down into the water until just his head and neck were above the surface.

He had been there two or three minutes when there was a tap on the door. Before he could gather the energy to respond, it slid open and Marjorie was there in her *yukata*, her hair streaming down her back. "I ache in every muscle of my body," she said, "and, after what happened, I don't want to be alone. Do you mind if I join you?"

"Of course not."

Besides, it was the Japanese way.

She turned her back, hung up her *yukata*, and then sat down to wash herself. Peter noted that her dark skin seemed more evident, but on the other hand, what real difference did it make? She finished her washing process, used some shampoo on her hair, and then rinsed thoroughly, dumping a half dozen small buckets of hot water over her head and shoulders so that it flowed down her whole body.

Then she stood up, an ebony sculpture, and came over to the big tub. Since she was now used to the Japanese bath, she got in easily despite the high temperature and let her body stretch out to its full length. Peter admired her for that, because she didn't try to be coy or pretend unnecessary modesty; she was a woman like every other woman and that fact did not embarrass her.

"Thank you," she said, "for what you did for me — up there."

"Anytime," Peter responded.

"I think that you bailed me out of a pretty dangerous situation. The poor thing seemed to be completely insane."

Peter nodded. "There isn't very much doubt about it. More like an animal than a man. Apparently he's been on the loose up there for some time; a literal case of the village idiot."

Marjorie deliberately changed the subject. "Dad shipped me over my typewriter, just in case I might need it. Guess where it was made."

"Japan."

"Correct, of course. Since it's here, I'm going to start writing up things in narrative style, there's so much feeling I want to put down. Things beyond my shorthand notes. Like that little genius, Setsuko Taminaka, and Hideko Noda's wedding, and that blow we had when you helped Midori to put up the storm doors."

All at once Peter was thoroughly relaxed. He knew that the Japanese bath was frequently something of a social event, now he understood why. In the almost steaming hot water mental strains tended to disappear along with the physical ones. As any normal man would, he had visualized Marjorie nude now and then when they had been together, but the reality was much superior to his conjectures. He wondered what idiot it had been who had first said that it was good to leave something to the imagination. Imagination always exaggerated, and therefore distorted. Marjorie just as she was was quite something, and complexion had very little to do with it.

There was another tap on the door.

Peter resented it although he knew that he had no right to; he was just beginning truly to enjoy himself with Marjorie and he did not want to be interrupted. Also the fact that she had accepted him as a bath companion did not mean that she was ready to welcome anyone who chose to walk in the door.

He looked quickly at her and discovered that he had been at least partly mistaken, because she called out, "Come in," without turning a hair.

The door slid open and Akitoshi was there. "May a road-weary traveler join the party?" he asked.

"Toshi!" Marjorie greeted. "This is wonderful. Come in by all means."

Five minutes later he joined them in the tub. A maid came in and deposited a small stack of towels for them to use when they were through. From somewhere the aroma of food being prepared penetrated into the bath and gave promise of things to come.

"How have you been doing while I was gone?" Akitoshi asked.

"Up until this afternoon, fine," Peter answered. "Almost everyone has been really helpful, we've even been told a lot of things we didn't think to ask."

"You were so right about the family unit," Marjorie continued. "It's even stronger than we had realized. Everything is designed for the preservation of the family; it's the whole key to the social structure."

"And whatever you do," Peter added, "don't ever cross up the family head."

"I congratulate you," Akitoshi declared. "You are really getting an insight into our culture now. There is a Japanese proverb you should learn: 'The things one has most to fear are *jishin, kaminari, kaji,* and *oyaji.*' Do you understand that?"

"No," Marjorie admitted.

"Earthquake, thunder, fire, and father."

He ran his fingers through his thick, wet, black hair and then made an announcement. "I've been in Tokyo taking care of some business. While I was there I had lunch with a friend of mine, a publisher. If your foundation is willing, he would very much like to put out a book on your studies here. It would be as we discussed — an account by you of this village — and I will do some pictures to illustrate it. If you wish to publish your work also in an American magazine of science, he would not mind if it is not the same words."

"I'm all for it," Peter said. "Now I think we had better tell you something." Quietly, and making good use of understatement, he told of the madman on the mountain. When he began his account, saying that they had gone up to visit the lake, he could see that Akitoshi had anticipated him and was uncomfortable. When he had finished, Peter concluded by saying, "We didn't ignore your warning, Toshi; I was with her. It was my fault that I left her alone as I did."

The artist was grave. "It is also very much my fault that I did not tell you all: I must do that now. It is because I like Marjorie so much and I did not wish to give her any hurt. I waited until I thought that it might be the right time. I waited too long."

He shifted his position in the water and rested on his elbows against the edge. "It is a thing that Mitamura knows, but does not tell to outsiders. The man you found: he was once a fine person, good and hard-working. He lived here. He had a wife who had given him no children, but he loved her very deeply just the same. With his wife he left this village and went to the city, where he had work. There were also near to his home a place where there were American soldiers. Most of them were very welcome, but there was one who was very bad. The people feared him greatly, but they also feared to complain of him."

Marjorie saw it coming. "Was this soldier a Negro?" she asked.

Akitoshi nodded. "Yes, he was. A very big and strong man with a very bad temper. One day, when the Japanese man was away, the American followed his wife home from the market and forced his way into her house."

"*Oh, my God!*" Marjorie said.

"There he forced her to make love with him. It was very brutal and she was covered with blood, even though she was a married woman. When her husband came back, he almost went crazy then. But he did not; he took his wife and came back to Mitamura, where his brother lived. Here, at least he had a home. For a month the husband did nothing but take care of his wife, he loved her so. Then it was discovered by her that she was going to have a child and she knew it was not her husband's. So with a dagger she stabbed herself in the throat, which is the woman's way of asking forgiveness for her sins. It was her husband who found her. He ran up the mountain, screaming. It was thought that he was going to the temple to ask for the help of God, but his mind could not endure the terrible thing he had seen."

Marjorie turned up a tear-stained face. "And I kicked him like a mad animal," she said.

Akitoshi looked at her. It is a good thing that you did," he told her, "because he is very dangerous. The monks at the temple put out food for him, because they show charity to all. Usually he is not seen, but people have been hurt."

"Can't they put him in an asylum?" Peter asked.

"It would be difficult. He is used now to living on the mountain. He has a place to hide, although no one knows where it is. He never comes down. If he were locked up, he could not survive."

"But you said that people have been hurt!"

"Yes, that is true, but not recently. It is believed that he will not live too much longer, and it is the decision of the village to leave him alone." He looked at Marjorie and she sensed that he was communicating with her in a person-to-person empathy she had never discovered in him before. "Perhaps you will understand now why this village, of all the places in Japan, has been perhaps the most difficult for you."

"Yes," she answered very quietly. "I understand."

Peter waited until he sensed that it would be all right for him to speak. "You said that he had a brother here. Perhaps he can help. If it is a question of money, then I would be willing . . ."

Akitoshi shook his head. "His brother is dead," he said. "He was Midori's husband."

Chapter Fourteen

IN THE MORNING Marjorie left for the city with Hiroshi in his tiny car to get some camera film and a number of other items. Peter declined to go along; he had a considerable amount of thinking to do and he wanted to reorganize his notes. As he ate his breakfast he turned over in his mind the idea of dual publication; it appealed to him because it could open a new avenue of interest in sociological studies. If the book that the three of them did for the Tokyo publisher proved to be a success, then the door would be wide open for others to follow the same format.

Midori sensed his mood and kept silently in the background. When Peter looked at her suddenly, she was almost startled. He read that and smiled at her. "*Gomen nasai,*" he apologized; "I was just thinking."

"So hard you think! Too hard, maybe." She returned his smile and his mood softened in response; he could not help himself.

"You may be right," he agreed. He picked up a small brown bowl and drank the last of the thin, delicate soup that was part of the breakfast menu. Then he turned back to the boiled rice. "May I have some water?" he asked.

"*Mizu? Hai,* I will get some."

Peter rose. "No, let me." Before she could protest he took the bucket and went outside. The well was behind the house and up at the northwest corner of the yard, about as inconvenient a location as could be found. He drew the water and took it back into the house. "Whoever put in that well didn't plan very well," he remarked. "It's three times farther away than it needs to be."

"No, Peta, it must be there — right direction."

"Now look," Peter began, "out in front of the house there is plenty of room for a well. You could just step outside the door and get your water. You wouldn't have to carry it more than a few feet."

Midori sat down beside him, making him happy. "Peta, house is looking south, yes?"

"That's right, the house faces south — they all do. I found that out."

"South is warm side, you believe?"

"*Hai, so desu.*"

"Then if well on south side, too hot. Well dry up. So never put there."

For a moment he was baffled. He looked at her carefully again, but her lovely face was perfectly serious; she obviously meant what she was saying. "Has anybody ever tried it?" he asked.

"No, Peta, everybody know better." She sat quite still for a few moments, then she rose to her feet and held out her hand to him. "Come," she said.

He took her warm fingers and allowed himself to be led outside into the small yard of the farmhouse.

"My Englishu bad, Peta, but I make try." She took up a position almost in the center of the yard and then pointed southwest toward the corner. "Best direction. Good fortune this way. I think maybe you come from this way. Man want wife, he look in this direction and he find."

With her left arm she pointed northwest. "Also very good. When farm have stronghouse, always put this direction. Good fortune come from southeast, travel to northwest. So put stronghouse there to collect good fortune. Understand?"

"Keep on," Peter invited.

Midori pointed northeast. "Very very bad, Peta. Not marry this way, not travel if can help. If move, never in this direction."

She turned once again and faced southwest. "Also very bad. Farmer not want field this direction from his house. Rice not grow good, wrong direction. Bad comes from northeast, go to southwest, so we fix."

She took his hand once more and led him down to the extreme southwestern corner of the yard. There she pointed to an opening in the low stone wall that he had not noticed before. "Is not accident, Peta, hole made here to let go out bad luck. So when it comes from northeast, it go out here. Look other houses, same thing. No one want bad luck collect his house, so everybody have hole for bad luck go out. Very important, Peta; you not know this America?"

"I'm afraid that we don't," he replied. "Where do these rules come from?"

"Very long time, Peta, and everybody know is true. I come from wrong direction; my husband die. I cry, but cannot help. Everybody know I wrong direction girl."

There was no doubt whatever that she was completely sincere, and despite the fact that he did not believe at all in the rules she had recited, Peter thought no less of her because she did. It was what she had been taught, and God knew how many falsehoods had been circulated in his own country just in sociology. She was trying to share with him something that she knew, and it was up to him to take it in that light. And perhaps, who knew, she could be right after all.

It occurred to him that the girl who had broken their engagement had lived almost exactly northeast of his own bachelor apartment. So it had worked out in that case. On the other hand, Marjorie Saunders had flown in from the northwest when he had first met her.

"You learn this, Peta, important I think. Name is called *hōgako.*
Everybody in Japan know and respect."

As she looked up at him, eyes wide open and asking to be
believed, he had a consuming desire to kiss her. He didn't only
because they were in public view and he had learned that in Japan
kissing was considered practically a sexual act not too far removed
from intercourse. One hasty moment of gratification would ruin
her; after that no one in the village would believe that they were
sleeping in separate rooms.

To calm himself he turned and looked over the cluster of houses
just below him and the paddy fields beyond. The rice seedlings,
now grown taller and sturdier, stood in fascinating geometric pat-
terns in the water, drawing strength from the soil and from the
fertilizer that had been so carefully measured out and added. The
sharp blue of the sky, dazzlingly high overhead, added a brilliance
to everything; for a long moment Peter wished that he had Akitoshi's talent so that he could commit what he saw to canvas.

The small village of which he now felt himself to be a part was
made up of human beings whose lives were irretrievably controlled
by the cycle of rice cultivation. Whatever their hopes, ideas, pas-
sions, and aspirations were, they were all regulated by the inexorable need to raise rice. It was part of their lives and souls: a calendar
drawn not by men, but by the rotation of the seasons and the
experience gained through generation after generation of raising
the same crop in the same paddies; a constant combat in which
thousands of hours of patient toil were matched against the constantly growing need for more and more food throughout the
length and breadth of Asia.

Mitamura was rice: the white cereal was its cause for existence
as well as its means of support. The planting began almost on May
first with the plowing and irrigation of the fields. After a soaking
period of three or four days came the long hours of working the

entire soil by hand into a smooth, clodless consistency while the seed was soaked in salt water for two days to cull out the infertile grains. Then the seed was distributed into the thick puree of liquid mud, two quarts per acre, after which the whole thing was covered by a thin layer of charred rice hulls and reflooded.

For a few weeks the seedlings were left alone to sprout and grow, then between June twenty-second and July first the ultracareful transplanting began. After that back-breaking job was concluded, there came patient hours of more hard work culling out weeds, thinning out the poor plants to increase the yield of the good ones, and always the constant watch over the water level in the paddies. At last, in mid-October, came the harvest; not only the precious grain, but also the straw that during the winter months would be woven into bags and put to a hundred other uses. Practically nothing that the earth was willing to yield up was put to waste; a use was found for everything.

All this Peter knew now; he would have to write the story of the village against the background of the growing of rice, and very little else. A good wife was one who could make a man comfortable at home and help him in his rice fields — but only if she came from the right direction.

Even the houses of Mitamura reflected their closeness to the soil from which they too seemed to have sprung. None of them were painted or ever had been painted; they were made of charred board, which cost less and lasted a lot longer — another bit of learning handed down through the years. It was simply another way of extending the generosity of nature close to its utmost limit.

As Peter stood, surveying the quiet peace of the village as it lay cupped against the base of the mountain, a picture postcard of rural Japan, in the schoolhouse the telephone rang. Miss Noda answered it, but she was interrupted before she had finished the flow of formal salutations with which she customarily acknowledged a call.

She listened, had time to ask just one question, and then was cut off.

She instructed her pupils to continue studying, then she hurried as fast as she was able, her face pale, toward the house of the *yuryokusha*. Her breath did not come as easily as usual and her eyes were wide with fear.

Shortly before eleven the tiny car that Hiroshi drove pulled up in front of the Mikasa Ryokan and Marjorie got out with her purchases. The she turned to the interpreter. "Hiroshi," she said. "Thanks much for the ride. Why don't you take it easy and come back after lunch."

"Thank you, Miss Saunders." He was still being carefully correct to her. "I will be available when you require me." He drove away to park his vehicle.

Marjorie went inside to find Akitoshi standing in the door of his room. "Have you had lunch?" he asked.

"No, not yet."

"Then I have a suggestion. It is today my turn to have a picnic with you, and I know a pleasant place. The *ryokan* will pack a lunch."

Because of her recent experience, Marjorie hesitated. "Peter might need me."

"I do not think so, at least not for a little while. He is this day, I think, enjoying the company of Takinama Midori."

"I don't blame him," Marjorie retorted. "I like her very much myself."

"Shall we go, then?"

"All right. Give me time to change."

They left the inn a half hour later, Akitoshi with a sketch pad, and accompanied by the young man employed by the inn who was carrying the lunch basket. Marjorie could have handled the lunch quite easily and certainly Akitoshi could, but it would have represented a loss of face and deprived the young man of a further excuse for his being kept on the payroll. So the three of them walked together a scant mile to a small grove at the base of the mountain. There Akitoshi located a spot where the sunlight painted the ground with little splashes of color and warmth. He dismissed the lunch bearer and then stretched out on his back, fully relaxed, to enjoy a respite from every other form of human contact.

Sensing his mood with a sure instinct, Marjorie sat down with her back against a tree and quietly studied him. His features were sensitive, yet strong and firmly masculine in a way that she found magnetic. He did not suggest the rugged durability of the farmers in the village, but he did not have their stockiness either. In action, she decided, he would be able to give a good account of himself.

"What are you thinking?" Akitoshi asked.

"I was thinking that you are a handsome man."

He turned on an elbow and looked at her. "Why?" he asked.

"Because it's so."

"Nonsense." He rolled back to where he had been, but she could see that he was pleased. And not for reasons of vanity. "You must remember that I am Japanese," he added as he looked up toward the sky.

"I don't see what that has to do with it," she answered him. "Besides, we're in Japan. You must remember that I'm an American."

"I prefer simply to think of you as a woman."

That was more than she had dared to hope for and she felt a surge of emotion that ran the length of her spine. He had always been very considerate to her, but she had attributed that to his good manners and his unwillingness to show any awareness of physical handicaps — or blackness.

"What kind of a woman?" she asked.

"A kind that's nice to be with. And a very female kind."

"Thank you. You see, in America we still have some puritans hanging around. And some bigots."

"My English is very small, but is that not the same thing?"

"They do have a great deal in common."

He folded his hands behind his head. "Let us then wish them both *sayonara*. In Japan we do not require their services."

For the second time in two days Marjorie set out a picnic lunch. This time the inn had outdone itself so that Kojima Sensei would be pleased. A vacuum bottle held hot bean curd soup. Each dish, as she unwrapped it, revealed careful design in its packaging. She arranged things as well as the inn would have done. When she had finished she sat on her heels and announced lunch as a proper hostess should.

He came to the mat she had spread out with the formal manner of an invited guest. As the mottled sunlight patterned him, Marjorie found herself responding to her inbred instincts that told her it was very good to be alone in the company of an attractive man.

Akitoshi caught her mood and understood it. He accepted his soup from her outstretched hands and then sipped it from the bowl. As he did so he thought of his unfinished painting of her and hoped that she would like it when it was ready. He wasn't sure, but it was a risk he was prepared to take.

"I'm very happy," Marjorie said.

"So am I," Akitoshi responded. He looked at her again. "You are a very attractive woman; will you pose for me in the nude?"

"Yes," she answered and quirked a smile at him. "After all, you got a good look at me in the bath, didn't you?"

"I certainly did — and I liked it."

"Thank you." She drank her soup and loved its taste.

"Also," he added, "your *oshiri*, you called it — fanny?"

She nodded.

"It is, I think, exactly the right size. I made special notice." She decided to risk everything. "You did not object to its color?" He shook his head. "I was considering other things at the time." She drew her breath in quickly and covered herself by reaching for one of the bowls and picking up her chopsticks. When she had split them apart and adjusted them in her fingers, she felt that she was in control of herself once more.

Akitoshi was looking over her shoulder. She turned to see that the young man from the inn was hurrying toward them. Her heart caught up as the thought raced through her mind that something had happened to Peter.

She got to her feet, but the messenger ignored her. That was understandable since he had no English, but as she watched he talked quite urgently to Akitoshi for several seconds. Then Akitoshi got up as well.

"I think we had better return to the village," he said. "A warning has been received. The weather service has advised that a very large typhoon is coming this way. When it arrives, it is possible that it could be very dangerous for everyone."

Marjorie began to breathe again; at least Peter was all right. She turned to take care of the picnic things, but the man from the inn was already hurriedly packing up what she had so carefully put out and stuffing it into the basket as fast as he could.

The news that had been received by telephone spread very quickly throughout the village; in literally a matter of minutes everyone knew. From the shimmering rice paddies the men and women climbed out to hurry home and leave their tools. Then as the women began to prepare for what lay ahead, the men headed toward the schoolhouse to organize for the pressing work that now would have to be done.

Peter was having his lunch in Midori's kitchen when Hiroshi

arrived with the news. Peter immediately put his chopsticks down and asked, "How soon is the storm expected?"

"I believe, sir, that we will have one day before it comes."

"And it's reported to be an unusually bad one?"

"That is correct, sir."

A quick concern came into Peter's mind. "Is this house likely to be in any danger?"

"I cannot be certain, Dr. Storm, but it has been here for a long time, and there have been many typhoons. It should be all right, but it will be necessary to prepare some things."

Peter finished his tea quickly and then rose to his feet. "I'll help with whatever has to be done here. What are the rest of the people going to do?"

"They are holding a meeting now, sir, or they will be very soon, to organize the work that will be necessary. Above all they will have to protect the irrigation system, for without it Mitamura cannot survive."

"I'd like to go to the meeting," Peter said. "I think it's very important that I be there."

"Then we should leave at once, sir."

On the way down to the center of the village Peter had another question. "Who is going to run the meeting? The head man here is a doll maker; will he know enough about farming?"

"He will be present, but the agriculture chief, he will be the leader. There is usually in each village a head man, as you say, and also a chief of agriculture. In Mitamura it is Mr. Noda. You know him; it was in his rice paddy that you worked."

"Good," Peter said. He remained silent after that until they reached the schoolhouse, from which the children had long since been dismissed. It was already full, but he managed to find room at one side with Hiroshi next to him. Tension was very strong in the air, proof that the typhoon warning was being taken very seriously. There was no evidence of panic, but the sturdy men jammed into the schoolroom were in a grim and hardened mood.

Almost as soon as Peter had found his place, Noda San began to talk. He was clearly in charge and beside him Taminaka San, the *yuryokusha*, lent him the authority of his own office.

"What is he saying?" Peter asked softly.

"He is repeating the news of the storm, sir. Now he is beginning to make plans for the work to be done."

"Keep on translating," Peter directed.

"Yes, sir. He is now talking about the irrigation system. He is sending ten men up to the lake to make protection there."

"How?" Peter asked.

"Sandbags; they will fill them and put them where they are needed. Perhaps several hundred."

As Noda continued his organizing, Peter was impressed with his ability; he might be lacking in formal education, but when it came to the business of rice farming and all of its aspects, he could speak with a voice of authority. Furthermore, the rest of the community was unquestionably accepting him as the man best qualified to deal with the emergency.

Hiroshi continued to translate. "He is saying now, sir, that there will be very little sleep for anyone tonight. It will take many hundred of filled bags to protect the dikes and they must all be prepared and placed during the next several hours."

From his position in the front of the room Noda began to point to certain individuals. "He is choosing the men who will do the important work at the lake. They will be the best and most experienced. All the rest will work here, filling bags and putting them into place. He will supervise that himself."

The door opened once more and Akitoshi came in. He had put aside his usual trim attire and was dressed in substantial work clothes.

"He is saying now, sir, that the women will prepare food and it will be ready at the inn all through the night."

"What about you, Hiroshi?"

The interpreter almost paled. "Sir, if you require me I will try to come here, but it may be impossible. Also my mother . . ."

"Stay home until it's over," Peter directed. "Kojima Sensei will help me if I need it."

"Thank you very much, sir, thank you! My father is away in Osaka . . ."

Peter gestured him into silence; he was much more interested in what was going on in the room. Noda was again pointing to certain people and giving them instructions. "What is this about?" Peter asked.

"He is naming the men who will pile the bags against the dikes. Some will fill, some will bring them out with . . . machine with one wheel in front."

"Wheelbarrow."

"Thank you, sir. Some will use wheelbarrow, some will pile bags."

Peter put up his hand. Noda saw it quickly and asked a question. Hiroshi translated. "Noda San asks what you would like to know."

"Tell him I will help to pile the bags."

"That is very hard work, sir!"

"Tell him!" Peter snapped.

Hiroshi obeyed. As soon as he had done so, Peter could sense the reaction in the crowded schoolroom. One of the farmers put a question which Noda quickly answered.

"Mr. Taminaka, over there, thought it would not be suitable for you, but Mr. Noda said that you are very strong and a good worker."

Peter was grateful to Noda for that endorsement; he knew perfectly well that that he was not as physically hardened as the

Japanese farmers who surrounded him, but he was still an able-bodied man capable of doing a day's work. In the face of a major emergency he did not intend to be found wanting. For some transient reason at that moment he thought of Midori, then he forced the image out of his mind.

Soon after that the meeting broke up. As Peter made his way out through the doorway one of the farmers gave him a wide smile. All of the men of the village had been unfailingly polite to him even when he had interrupted their work, but he had felt many times that they had been standing on different shores. Now, in the atmosphere of men who faced a staggering amount of unexpected, all out heavy labor, he thought that he detected a subtle change.

"How soon will the work begin?" he asked Hiroshi.

"Almost at once, sir."

"Then I'd better get into some suitable clothes. Why don't you go home now; come back after the storm has gone through."

"You are sure, sir . . ."

"Yes, I'm sure. You look after your mother."

Alone once more and somewhat glad of it, Peter climbed back up to Midori's house. He went directly to his room, shut the panel, and changed into his work clothes — already pacing himself for what might turn out to be a marathon effort. The sunlight was still bright against the shoji panels and it was a little hard for him to accept the idea that a possible disaster lurked somewhere only a few hours away. Apart from the high winds on the night that he had helped Midori to put the storm doors in place, he had had no experience whatever with typhoons. Or hurricanes either, for that matter. He knew that they could be highly dangerous and that they frequently caused serious property damage, but they remained something he had read about in newspapers. Then he remembered the seriousness of the meeting he had just attended, and his good sense told him that the farmers of Mitamura knew a lot more about storms in Japan than he did. He was satisfied to take his cues from them.

There was a tap on the panel and when he opened it, Akitoshi was there. Without a word he handed over a pair of Japanese work pants similar to the ones he had worn before. "Thanks," Peter said, and put them on.

When he had finished Akitoshi bent down to tie the legs. "Last time you rolled them up, but that is not the right way," he explained. "You should tie them tightly around your legs. Then if there are any creatures in the paddies that wish to climb up inside, they cannot do so."

"So that's why," Peter said.

"Yes, but they did not wish to tell you so, because it would not have been polite."

"Toshi, is the village itself in any real danger?"

"Peter, just because the sun shines now, do not be deceived. When the storm comes unless the right things are all done, lives could be lost. It happens all the time."

"I want to take care of Midori."

"When it is time, I will help you to do that. Now we must go to the inn; it will be headquarters. Also one thing more, Peter — I know the great size of your heart, but remember that the men of Mitamura are very tough from much constant work. Do not try too much: do not overdo yourself. I do not wish you to become the first casualty."

"I'll remember," Peter promised.

"Good. I think now that Marjorie would like very much to see you."

The two men went down to the inn together. The lobby that was usually so quiet was the scene of considerable running about; two guests who had checked in from somewhere were on the point of departure, tables were being brought in, and the little maids seemed to be trying to accomplish several different things all at the same time.

Marjorie was in her room; she had just finished changing also and was wearing a work outfit that the inn had somehow managed to dredge up in a size large enough to fit her. "When I went into town last time with Hiroshi, I bought some work gloves," she said. "I thought that we just might need them. Here's yours."

Peter accepted them and tried them on. They fitted well enough and with them on his hands, he felt much better equipped to undertake manual labor. "Thanks," he declared. "That was a damn good idea. What are you going to do?"

"Whatever they will let me. I can help fill sandbags or look after kids. There'll be something."

"Look," Peter suggested. "There are some guests leaving. You could go into town with them and hole up there. In that way . . ."

She silenced him with a look far more eloquent than any words she could have used. At that moment he was fiercely proud of her, and thought of the all-but-useless female he had come so close to marrying. What a helluva lot of difference there was between them; it amounted to guts. Marjorie had them, and he felt possessive about her.

Miss Noda, the schoolteacher, came to the door with a message which Akitoshi translated. "All public transportation in the storm's path will stop tonight at six o'clock. There will be no buses or trains for perhaps two days or more."

Since that was a standard situation during typhoons, no one appeared unduly interested in the announcement. Outside the inn Peter heard a small car start up; the little engine sputtered into life for a few seconds and then began to retreat down the narrow roadway.

"Will there be enough food in the village?" he asked.

"Oh, yes," Kojima answered him. "The farmers have storehouses, so there will be plenty of rice and other things. We will all eat."

Peter went outside the inn to see what was going on. He looked first up into the sky and saw that while the sun was still shining brilliantly, a long narrow triangle of high clouds was beginning to move in, point first. It was like a wedge that was being driven from the west and while it was not ominous in itself, he sensed that it was a beginning of much more to follow.

In front of the inn a work party was being assembled. A large number of straw bags had already been piled up and some tools were being gathered together. Noda was there getting things organized; when he saw Peter he took a moment to smile and then pointed up the hill. Having answered the unasked question, he returned at once to the job at hand.

Two of the farmers were tying the empty bags into bundles, large and bulky ones that seemed much too big to be carried. While that thought was still in Peter's mind, one of the men took the straw rope across his shoulders and with some helping hands got one of the huge loads onto his back. He settled it into position, spoke a word to Noda, and then started toward the base of the path that led up the hill, on his way toward the irrigation lake and the canal network that fed water with measured care into the vital channels. Peter realized fully that they would need heavy reinforcement if they were to withstand the brutal hammering of a full-scale typhoon.

During the next half hour the rest of the men who were to work at the head of the irrigation system picked up their loads and began their climb, some carrying great bundles of empty straw bags, others heavy loads of digging tools that would be needed to do the job. During the preparations Peter was impressed with the fact that there was no discontent or complaining. No pep talks were needed, no charging the troops up for battle; these Japanese farmers knew that they were facing a severe challenge to their homes and means of livelihood, and they were responding with a united effort that was unstinting. It was one of the most intelligent things he had ever seen.

From the work sheds of the village more bags began to appear, brought in most cases by wheelbarrow. There was no question of whose property was which; all of the bags were taken to the north edge of the village where there was a raw sand and dirt bank that would provide suitable filling. No one had to be told the location; they all already knew.

As the bags arrived Noda began to organize things. He pointed out over the paddy fields and directed where the first of the filled bags were to be used. He delegated a lieutenant to remain in charge of the bag filling operation and sent for some additional tools. Peter took his own cue from that; he could not understand the Japanese, but he knew what Noda wanted. He returned to Midori's home and found a stout shovel in the toolroom. He took it and returned to the work area, where he found Akitoshi waiting.

"Where did they get all those bags?" he asked.

"They were made to hold the new rice crop."

"Will there be enough?"

"I think perhaps yes, there are many more that are still in the barns. When there is spare time in winter, then always more bags are made. It never stops while there is still straw."

More wheelbarrows had been brought and there were more people than there had been when Peter had left. Noda was continuing to set things up and this time Akitoshi explained what was going on.

"Some will fill bags for a while, some will take them out where they are needed, the rest will help to put them into place. Later we will make turns, with time to eat and to go to the toilet. Mr. Noda is now appointing two men to help the women prepare the houses to endure the typhoon. One is the son of the *yuryokusha*. He is not a farmer, but he is a good man with his hands."

"Noda knows what he is doing."

"I think so also; he is a very intelligent man. Everyone trusts him."

"That includes me," Peter said.

"Noda is now saying something else. He says that the typhoon is coming from far away, so the black woman cannot be blamed for it. I think, Peter, that he is wise to tell them that; some are still very superstitious. He also says now that if anyone is hurt, they are to come to the inn and the nurse will care for them."

"What nurse?"

"Everyone knows that Marjorie made well the knee of the maid who hurt herself, so he is calling her the nurse. It is very smart of him, I think."

Far overhead the advancing wedge of clouds cut into the edge of the sun and some of the bright sparkle of the rice paddies began to dim. The air had been almost completely still, but now the beginnings of a gentle breeze could be felt.

Noda ceased speaking and picked up a shovel. He handed it to the lieutenant he had appointed and then headed toward the rice paddies. The half dozen men who had not been assigned to the bag loading and moving detail followed him, Peter and Akitoshi included. By now the narrow dikes that separated the paddies were fully familiar to Peter and he walked along them with confidence. When the small party stopped at the end of the paddies that belonged to Mitamura Peter looked across and saw that in adjacent fields the men of the neighboring villages were already at work putting filled sandbags into position.

"If the wind is indeed very powerful, it can blow down the dikes," Akitoshi explained. "It can seize the paddy water and hurl it against the thin walls and smash them. That is why the bags are needed to make them stronger."

Noda was again speaking and Akitoshi translated. "Mr. Noda says that we will do the farthest paddies first while it is still not too hard to bring the wheelbarrows this far. Later, when the wind is stronger, there will not be so far to go."

Peter looked back toward the village and saw that several wheelbarrows were already approaching the point where he was standing. He checked the side of the mountain, but he could see no sign of the work party that had gone up there. He picked out Midori's house and saw that she had already pushed the storm panels into position; otherwise everything seemed quite normal. He turned when he heard Noda jump down into a deep paddy bed; that left five of them still standing on the dike.

Noda gave some brief further instructions and then pointed to Peter.

"He wants you to join with him in putting the bags into place," Akitoshi said. "He is giving you great face by choosing you to be the first. He says that you are very strong."

Peter kicked off his sandals and then without hesitation measured his distance and jumped well down into the paddy mud. As soon as he was in position, Noda looked up and gave the others some final orders.

Akitoshi bent over. "We are going to help bring the bags because the wheelbarrows cannot come this far. There is no place for them to turn. Mr. Noda will show you what to do."

As the artist turned away, Noda gave Peter an encouraging grin. Peter smiled back and held out his hand. For a moment the Japanese farmer did not understand, then he took it and pumped it once. At that moment Peter was genuinely proud that he was standing barefoot in thick mud, ready to work as a common laborer under the direction of a man for whom he had a genuine respect. In the back of his mind was the thought that if he reached the end of his rope, Noda San would find an honorable way to relieve him while he was still on his feet. But first, he resolved, he would give the utmost of which he was capable.

Very shortly the first of the sandbags arrived, carried on the shoulder of a stocky farmer who had been one of the party that had come out into the paddy area with them. As he passed it down Peter was surprised how heavy it was — more than a hundred pounds by his estimate. Then Noda took the greater part of the load and with Peter's help braced it hard against the wall of the irrigation channel. That done, he pointed where the next bag was to go.

Fifteen minutes later Peter was on top of the job; he had already learned how to ease the heavy bags down and help put them into place with a minimum of wasted effort. His breath was shorter than he would have liked, but he knew that he would soon be getting his second wind and his muscles were working smoothly. His mind was well attuned to the job at hand. Had he had the advantage of a Japanese education, he would have known that his *ki* was flowing.

He looked up when he had a moment and saw that the odd-shaped incoming cloud had split the sky into halves and that the sun was well behind it. Much of the blue had disappeared. The air was still hot and the freshening breeze seemed almost a blessing during the early stages of the work.

Chapter Fifteen

To MARJORIE SAUNDERS the first two hours of response to the typhoon warning was a period of almost complete frustration. She felt herself a part of the village, she wanted to work, she was ready and willing, but no one would give her anything to do. Most of the women were busy preparing their homes to withstand the expected storm, but the inn in no way required her help.

She took her work gloves and went to the place where the sandbags were being filled, but there was a full crew at work and when she indicated her willingness to lend a hand, she received quick bows in reply and then the men returned immediately to what they had been doing. If she had only been truly fluent in Japanese she could have expressed herself, but now her language limitation seemed to be insurmountably solid.

She was uncertain how much her rejection was based on the fact that she was a woman, how much on her inability to speak Japanese, and how much on the fact that she was black. She had been under the illusion, at least, that the people of the community had begun to accept her, but now her uselessness seemed to wash all of that gain away. In a thoroughly upset frame of mind she returned to the inn.

In the lobby she found the little maid Miyoko wrapping up a large package in a huge square of strong cloth. When the girl looked up and saw Marjorie she dared to smile; her knee was much better and she was convinced that no devil woman could have been so kind to her.

Marjorie determined to try her Japanese once more, limited as it was. *"Sore wa non desu ka?"* she asked.

Miyoko understood her question at once. *"Tabemono,"* she replied and then, with rare tact, knowing Marjorie's problems with her language, she pointed upward toward the hill.

Tabemono meant food, Marjorie knew that. The rest was easy, this was a meal that had been prepared for the men who were working up at the lake. At that moment a second maid appeared, also with a considerable package that she had already finished knotting up.

Without asking permission, Marjorie picked up Miyoko's large bundle and tested it for weight. It was surprisingly heavy, much more than she had expected, but she judged that it was not beyond her strength. Now she wanted very much to say something in Japanese but she simply didn't know the words — her language records had not prepared her for this situation.

The second maid continued uninterrupted with her work. She tied a heavy cloth band to her bundle and then, squatting down, passed the band across her forehead. When she stood up, the package was suspended in the middle of her back. Then she waited patiently for Miyoko to finish.

Marjorie looked again at the girl's knee and knew that there would still be some discomfort in it, but that was incidental. When the head strap had been attached, Marjorie waved Miyoko aside and then pointed to herself. At last, thank God, she had found something she could do.

Miyoko called out and the manager appear in a matter of seconds. When the situation was explained to him he was about to settle matters quickly when he recalled the stern injunction he had been given by Kojima Sensei that the black woman was to be treated with maximum courtesy at all times. Or else. In a way it was a blessing, because he desperately needed to keep his full staff on the job and sending two of the maids to carry the food up to the lake would handicap his efforts. The young man who usually did such chores was out filling sandbags.

He spoke a few quick words and then with gestures made certain that he understood what the black woman intended to do. Despite himself his heart warmed to her a little; this was the second time that her presence had been useful. He made a concession and personally helped to hoist the heavy package of food up onto Marjorie's back. As he adjusted the headband across her forehead he looked at her closely for the first time and discovered that she was rather nice. And willing to help — that had to be considered too. Quite suddenly, and to his own surprise, he liked her.

Miyoko bubbled into active speech. The manager listened and then granted her request: the second maid set down her burden and Miyoko, with a smile, picked it up in her place. Then with a polite gesture she waved Marjorie ahead to be the first through the door.

It was a moment to be remembered, and to be cherished. In one brief half minute all of Marjorie's accumulated frustration and dawning bitterness was swept away. When the manager had looked at her and had liked what he had seen, she had known it instantly. And little Miyoko, who had been terrified of her when she had treated the lacerated knee, had asked to accompany her, bad knee and all, on what would have to be a hard and taxing climb. The little maid was now her friend and despite the darkening sky overhead, God was indeed in His heaven and much was better in the world.

She reached back and found that by using her hands she could divide the weight of her load between her arms and the strap across her forehead. It was a good way to carry things, because if she needed to use her hands at any time, they could be free. Resolutely she turned toward the path that went up the hill and within a minute or two she had begun to climb. She was not afraid of the madman; at the lake there were many strong and able men who would block him from coming down onto the lower path. The burden on her back was indeed heavy, but if the devil himself had been perched on it, she was determined to carry it every inch of the way to where it had to go. And without complaining.

Behind her Miyoko was coming steadily, and she actually seemed to be happy.

When she had reach a point well above the village Marjorie paused for just a brief moment to look back. She saw the steady line of wheelbarrows and workers taking the sandbags out to the critical parts of the paddy system, but she could not pick out Peter. She thought of him working out there and fervently hoped that he would not overtax himself and possibly do himself physical injury. As she turned to continue her climb her heart was warm and the weight balanced in the middle of her back seemed lighter by half.

It took more than an hour to make the whole climb, because at some places it was necessary to go slowly and Marjorie was wise enough to pace herself. She remembered that it was a long way up to the lake and also there was Miyoko to think of, patiently bringing up the rear. Despite the fact that she was a good four inches shorter than Marjorie, and her load seemed to be equally great, the little maid climbed steadily and whenever Marjorie looked back to see how she was, she smiled.

At the end of forty-five minutes Marjorie admitted to herself that she was getting very tired. Her muscles were protesting so vigorously that if she had been alone she would have stopped for a few minutes to rest, but a determined, fierce pride kept her on her feet. She looked back once again to see if Miyoko wanted to rest, but when she lifted her eyebrows and gestured, her companion waved her right hand to and fro and smiled once more.

Any man who married one of these girls would get himself a dedicated worker, if nothing else. And there was a lot to be said for that. She knew a few women who were very appealing and who had no trouble attracting men, but with a typhoon coming they would be on the first train or whatever going out. It wouldn't be their affair. Miyoko was cast of better metal and she would stick when the going got tough. In pursuing these thoughts Marjorie kept herself entirely out of them; she continued climbing and, if anything, took pride in the fact that so far she had not been found wanting.

She heard the men working just before she reached the point where she could see them. Even by the sound she knew that the labor was heavy. There were no wheelbarrows up here; as she reached the clearing and approached the edge of the lake she saw that two of the men were filling bags, six more were carrying them, and two were packing them into position against the thin dikes. A great deal had already been done; they must have been working like beavers.

One of the men raised a shout when he saw the women coming. Two of the farmers who had just unloaded their sandbags came over to help. Stubbornly Marjorie continued on until she reached the spot where she knew that the food should be set down; then and only then she allowed them to take the heavy package off her back. As they were doing it Miyoko squatted down and slipped the headband over her own hair unassisted.

Quite suddenly Marjorie did not think that she could go another step. Her legs were shaking and the muscles in her calves began to knot painfully from the unaccustomed strains they had endured. But she did not sit down. Instead she turned to the large pack she had just carried up and began to untie it. As she did so, she wondered how she had managed. But she had, and it was a small triumph that she had earned.

When the cloth covering had been laid aside there were a number of containers and a stack of food trays all capped with close-fitting lids. When the last of the filled sandbags had been deposited, the men quit work and gathered around. They were smiling, all of them, and when Miyoko spoke to them, they all seemed to appreciate whatever it was that she said.

They sat in a circle and accepted the food that had been brought to them, saying things that Marjorie would have given a great deal to understand. They immediately offered her one of the trays, but she declined; she had not carried that heavy load all of the way up the long mountain pathway to eat some of it herself.

The amount of sandbagging that had already been done told her that the men had worked far harder than she. But at least she had done something: black, female, and all, she was part of the team and a little fragment of Mitamura now belonged to her.

By the patient way that Miyoko was waiting, she understood that they would have to take the empty containers and trays back with them; they would probably be needed again soon. She studied the sturdy farmers, all named either Noda or Taminaka, and hoped that someday, when she found her own man, he would be as dependable.

Fifteen minutes later, when she started down, it was very simple and easy. Miyoko had nested the dishes so that they took up very little space and their weight was nothing at all. They still split the load, but it took hardly half an hour for them to reach the upper edge of the village and from there it was only another five minutes to the inn. The work of sandbagging was still going on at the same steady pace, but the sky was visibly darker and the wind had gained enough to make the rice plants wave gently in long rippling curves, like a vast green surf searching for an invisible shore.

When Peter Storm had tried his hand at rice transplanting, the Nodas had not required his help in the preparation of their paddy and his two hours of inexperienced work had not accomplished a great deal on their behalf. He had created a certain challenge for himself and he had met it, but the element of anything essential had been entirely missing. As he labored now putting sandbags into position, he was acutely aware of the vital importance of what he was doing, with the result that both his mind and his body responded. He was tired, yes, but he had brushed fatigue aside and his well-loosened muscles were serving him efficiently and well. He knew it, and it gave him a fierce satisfaction. The spirit of adventure was in him and despite his heavy exertions, he was enjoying himself.

He had a genuine admiration for the sturdy, stocky farmers with whom he was working; they were not men who would be easily defeated by disaster. He liked every one of them and as they continued to work together, he felt closer to them than he ever had before. He was also secretly gratified to see how Akitoshi, who, like himself, represented the city-bred element in the working force, was standing up. For more than four hours the artist had been pushing a wheelbarrow part of the time and had been carrying the heavy sandbags on his shoulders in areas where the barrows could not go. He asked for no special consideration and accepted none. The respect that he commanded would have been visible to a blind man.

The afternoon was well advanced when Noda stopped work, looked up into the sky for a few seconds, and then turned to Peter. "*Tabe mashō,*" he said. To be sure that he had been understood, he pointed to his open mouth and then rubbed his stomach.

Peter nodded his agreement; he was more than willing to stop and eat. He was not conscious of being hungry, but he knew that if he did not stop and rest fairly soon, he would be done for and disgraced. Together with Noda he climbed out of the paddy and then rotated his shoulders to keep the muscles from cramping. He had thought of himself as being in good physical condition, but the painful truth was flooding through his body and once he had stopped work, fatigue began to seize hold of him.

Halfway back to the inn he encountered Akitoshi, who had another sandbag across his shoulders. "We're going to eat," Peter said. "Can you join us?"

"I will be glad to." Despite the fact that he had to be bone-tired too from the unaccustomed physical work, the artist's voice betrayed nothing. He was in complete command of himself. As he continued to walk with Noda toward the inn, Peter resolved that he wanted to keep Akitoshi Kojima for a friend for the rest of his life.

As he paused at the entrance to the inn to take off his shoes, he looked one more time at the changing pattern overhead. It was fully overcast and the wind, he noticed, was quite a bit stronger.

In the lobby a serving buffet had been set up so that the men could eat in shifts. Many of the wives were helping out and it was at once clear that the individual dishes had come from many different homes. There were mounds of steaming rice in covered plastic bowls, platters of seafood that had been carefully arranged to make them appear as attractive as possible, both green and black tea, plates of vegetables, and some items less easy to identify.

Midori was there. As soon as Peter came in she hurried over and looked into his face, reading how well he had stood up under the hard physical work. "You are all right?" she asked.

Peter smiled at her. "I'm just fine."

Together with Noda he sat down at one of the low tables that had been put in the lobby and was grateful not to have to do anything at all. One of the maids quickly poured tea for them, then Noda's wife was there with a filled plate she had prepared for him.

As she was setting it down Midori was at Peter's elbow, a plate and a pair of fresh chopsticks in her hands. She looked at him again and Peter felt a sudden surge he could not define; he knew only that as she bent to serve him she was at that moment his woman and even his weary body cried out for her. Not in an animal way, but he wanted her to be with him just so that he could look at her and drink in her presence.

A moment later she was gone and he missed her. Within a half minute she was back with a glass of cold water and what was more, it was a large glass. That in itself was an accomplishment, since small dishes and limited portions were the ordinary rule, with frequent replenishment expected. She had learned that when he wanted a drink of water he wanted a long one, taken without interruption.

She knelt beside him, split his chopsticks for him, and offered an encouraging smile. He knew then that he was very close to loving her.

One of the farm wives asked her something and there was general laughter. Midori replied and the laughter re-echoed. As she spoke, Akitoshi took his place with them at the table. "What was that all about?" Peter asked.

"Mrs. Taminaka saw how well Midori was taking care of you, so she asked if you rolled over in your sleep."

"And what did Midori say?"

"She said that she didn't know because her hearing wasn't that good."

Peter picked up his chopsticks and began to eat. As the nourishing food touched his palate he realized for the first time how hungry he was; he had been unaware of it before. He went through the entire plate without stopping and when he finally did, he realized that his whole body was aching. It was a good, clean hard ache, the result of honest labor, and because he knew that, it lost its power to annoy him. He would have loved to have soaked in the hot bath, but that was out of the question while so much still remained to be done.

When he had finished his meal he got to his feet and flexed his arms to loosen them up. As he was doing that, Noda spoke to Akitoshi, who translated. "Noda San says that you have done more than your share; it is time for you to rest."

It was a tempting invitation, but Peter steeled himself against it. His face was on the line and so, to a degree, was Midori's. "The job isn't finished," he answered. "Now that I've had something to eat, and some hot tea, I'm ready to go again."

There was a brief exchange in Japanese and then Akitoshi spoke again. "Noda San asks if you can use a wheelbarrow."

"Of course." He hadn't had his hands on one since he had been a boy, but that made little difference. Also, thank God, it was a drier job. "Let's go," he added.

He went out of the inn with Noda, but not before he had turned and thanked everyone for his meal. As he received a chorus of bows in return, he added, *"Arigato gozaimasu, Midori San."* He owed her thanks and he didn't care what any of them thought. As a matter of fact he had been most polite in thanking her so nicely and they thought that it was most considerate of him.

Even during the brief time that he had been in the inn, the wind had risen somewhat. It was warm and not a factor as yet in getting the necessary work done, but the flat calm of the early morning and the brilliant sunlight that had accompanied it were both long gone.

Despite the fact that he already had several hours of labor behind him, Peter found it good to be moving again and relubricating the muscles that had tightened up during his rest period. He attached himself to a wheelbarrow whose owner had gone in to eat and lined up to receive a sandbag load. Some of the larger barrows were hauling two, but when one had been slung up onto his, he was patted on the shoulder and pointed on his way.

It was a welcome change of work; the tension on his arms felt good and helped to relieve the incipient cramps that had been threatening for the past half hour. His legs were grateful to be moving on dry land and not constantly standing in paddy water and mud. He felt reasonably fresh and ready to go on for as long as was necessary.

The far end of the paddy area had been thoroughly reinforced so the distance he had to cover had been considerably shortened. He delivered his sandbag where it was needed alongside the main irrigation ditch and went back for another.

After an hour he realized that his body was at last beginning to protest the unaccustomed heavy work with increasing vehemence, and he had to take a fresh grip on his determination. He was unsure how much longer he would be able to go on. As he brought up his empty wheelbarrow for another load, he looked at the pile of empty bags waiting to be filled and saw that it was severely depleted. It was now a question which would occur first: the coming of darkness, which would effectively halt the work, or the last of the visible bags would be filled and put into position.

To keep himself going he calculated the probable number of trips he would still have to make before the job would be finished and resolved to check them off in his mind as they were completed. He was moving mechanically now, with a certain amount of will power continuously needed to keep him going at the same pace.

He made six more trips before he returned to find that the steady procession of wheelbarrows and human bearers had stopped; the last of the empty bags had been used up. Almost afraid to do so, Peter looked back over the paddy area in the dimming light and saw that only a short segment of the irrigation system remained unprotected.

Akitoshi, now clearly as tired as himself, came over. "How about a bath?" he asked.

The thought was ambrosian. "Hell, yes," he answered. He had

done his part now; he had lasted as long as the others, and he had helped to complete as far as possible an essential, emergency operation.

He heard sounds behind him and turned; the men who had been at work up at the lake were returning, their tools over their shoulders. They spoke with the other briefly, and advised Noda what they had accomplished. "They have finished," Akitoshi explained. "They did not have quite enough bags, but they piled dirt and stones until they had done the best that they could."

"They must be hungry." It was not a very intelligent remark, but Peter was too tired to think clearly.

"They were taken their lunch. Marjorie helped carry it up."

He had vaguely wondered what she had been doing, but the thought had never emerged into his clear consciousness. He was quietly proud to learn that she had been doing her share also. Now, perhaps, they would better understand that she was a human being too, and a damn good one, if he was any judge.

Peter took off his shoes and went back into the inn. The food buffet had been replenished and augmented; he was grateful that there was so much food to feed the hungry and tired men who would be coming in behind him. Midori was still there and their eyes met. He smiled at her and when she lowered her head slightly in acknowledgment, he felt a flow of sudden inner warmth.

Marjorie came in from the kitchen area carrying a platter. She had tied her hair up in a white cloth so she almost seemed to be one of the regular helpers, despite the fact that she was at least four inches taller than most of the other women.

When she had set down her load she came over to speak to him. "You must be dead," she said.

"I am tired," he admitted.

"Go get your bath; it's all ready and God knows you need it. Then I have a little surprise for you — I've made some potato salad and some other American dishes out of what they had. And there's lots of tomato soup."

He could have kissed her for that, but he was too bone-tired to consider the idea further. He limped into the room the inn kept for him and got out of his clothes. Every movement that he made brought a protest from his body, but the thought of the hot, relaxing bath dominated everything else. He decided that someday when he built his own home he would have a Japanese bath in it if nothing else.

He put on his *yukata* and without even bothering with slippers went to the bath room. He washed himself and then sought the sanctuary of the big tub.

Within three minutes the miracle of the hot water had begun to take effect. He was still excessively tired, but the stabbing thrusts of discomfort that had been coming from overtaxed muscles had stopped and he felt as though he had never been in better physical condition in his life. When Akitoshi came in, he lifted one hand in greeting and then just shut his eyes. The water was as hot as his body could endure, which made it all the more wonderful.

He stayed in the bath until he felt that it had done all that it could for him, then he dried himself and put on his *yukata* once more. He was ready to eat a horse, but he waited for Akitoshi, knowing that it would only be a minute or two.

When he entered the lobby with his friend it was comfortably full and he was greeted with a mass of bows. Noda came forward and patted him on the back, a considerable demonstration for a Japanese. A place was found for them at one of the temporary low tables and as soon as he had made himself as comfortable as he could, Marjorie put a bowl of tomato soup before him and gave another to Akitoshi.

He had only sipped a little of it when the grave and rather austere *yuryokusha* came over and dropped to his knees in the classical Japanese sitting position. Then he bowed to them both and spoke.

"He is offering his thanks to you on behalf of Mitamura for your great labors," Akitoshi said. "You had no home or fields to protect, but you worked very hard nonetheless."

"Please tell him that I had the homes and the fields of my friends to protect," Peter responded. "I am honored to have been permitted to participate."

"Before I translate that," Akitoshi told him, "for a *gaijin* new to this country you are learning very fast. Congratulations."

When he heard Peter's words put into Japanese, the doll maker bowed again and made a brief formal speech. "Mr. Taminaka asked me to tell you that the village of Mitamura is honored by your presence here," Akitoshi supplied.

Peter ate his fill and was richly satisfied. Marjorie's American dishes tasted unexpectedly good and he drank three bowls of her tomato soup.

When he was through he did not bother to dress again. He left his soiled work clothes just where he had taken them off, knowing that the inn would understand. He retied his obi about his waist, collected Midori, who had been at the inn most of the day, said good night to Marjorie, and headed for his *futon.*

As he walked with Midori the wind was gusting enough to whip his *yukata* about his legs, but it did not impede his progress. He was walking in Japanese dress through a Japanese village, with a Japanese young woman, and he felt perfectly at home. Even the straw sandals on his feet were entirely comfortable.

When they reached the house, Midori stood back a half step to allow him to open the panel. It was the first evidence he had seen in Japan of a woman expecting to be waited on and he obliged; he did not understand that she was allowing him to assume the role of master of the house. As he waited for her to go first, she motioned him ahead. That made a partial impression, but he was still too tired for his mental processes to function at their best.

He got out his own *futon* and spread it on the tatami matting, grateful for its thickness and for the promise of comfort that it held. He dropped a pillow into position, rested for a few minutes, and then went to the wardrobe for his pajamas. Normally he did not use them, but he had been carefully putting them on each night while he had been living in Midori's house.

When he turned back he discovered her standing in the opened panel that led to the kitchen area; in her hands she had a tea service.

Tea! He had drunk enough of it to float a good-sized ship since he had arrived in Mitamura, but apparently it was only the beginning. He wondered what it would be like if he really enjoyed the stuff; perhaps in time he would. He dropped to his weary knees and accepted a cup from her hands. As the warm liquid ran down the inside of his throat, it did carry its own message of peace and contentment.

When he had finished, she motioned for him to lie down. Apparently she was simply indicating that he was to rest; in response he pointed to his pajamas. To his surprise she shook her head and for one mad moment he wondered what she had in mind. If this was, at last, her consent to their lovemaking, she had chosen a time when he was so physically exhausted he could hardly be expected to respond properly to her. But despite his fatigue, his mind sent an electric current through his body.

Doing exactly as she had asked he lay down, waiting for her to make the next move. Silently she knelt beside him and her soft hair brushed against his face. Then he felt her cool fingers begin to work the muscles at the base of his neck.

After some minutes she was expertly massaging the muscles of his upper right arm, and it brought him relief that was Olympian. "*Arigato,*" he murmured, his face buried in his pillow.

"You are welcome," she answered, and her fingers kept up their merciful work.

Within the next two minutes he was asleep.

Chapter Sixteen

T HE VILLAGE OF MITAMURA was able to go to bed fairly early that night. The last preparations had been made to secure against the coming violent winds, the hot baths had been taken in the clustered farmhouses, and the *futons* had been spread out for well-deserved rest. By nine practically all of the lights had been put out and only at the inn were there any continuing signs of life.

Most of the food that had been put out as a community effort had been eaten. An unexpected success had been scored by Marjorie's American offerings: the tomato soup had been short-lived and the potato salad had also found favor. She had had to modify the recipe somewhat to suit the ingredients she had had available, but the result, when she had tasted it, had met with her full approval. She had put it out with some pride and the last of it had been eaten by the innkeeper himself, who declared it delicious.

After the remaining food had been stored as well as it could be without any refrigeration, and the lobby had been restored to order, Marjorie shed her things, slipped into a *yukata*, and sought the bath.

She had finished washing and was in the water when the manager appeared and asked if his presence would be objectionable.

"*Yoko irrashimashita,*" Marjorie replied, making him welcome.

After he had washed himself and entered the tub, he leaned back on his elbows and admitted to himself that while he was still disturbed by the color of her skin, he could not deny that his companion was a fine figure of a woman. Her body was magnificently shaped; her *chichi* were much fuller and better than those of most Japanese girls, and her long legs were splendid. If she had been either *hakojin* or Japanese, she would have been devastating. As it was, the manager was grateful that the very hot water was sure to protect him against any awkwardly visible embarrassment.

He tried to talk with her and to a limited degree he succeeded. He did not know a single word in English, but with very elementary Japanese and some gestures, he communicated. He managed to thank her for her work. While he was about it, with signs he thanked her for fixing Miyoko's knee. Marjorie smiled at him in return. Once more he realized that, skin or no skin, this was some woman. He tried to think of her as very deeply suntanned, but then discarded that artifice as unworkable. She was *shuroi* and that was it, but he had never seen a better formed woman in his life.

When she returned to her room, Marjorie was in a particularly relaxed frame of mind. She had put in a hard day, but it had brought its rewards. She was completely aware of the admiration she had received in the bath and she was definitely proud of it. Without her clothes on anyone could see that she was indeed black all over, but the inn manager, who had been so carefully draining the bath water each time after she had used it, would probably have different thoughts now. She brushed her hair for some time, looked into her mirror without fear, and knew that given time, she could conquer any obstacle that nature or man chose to put before her.

She sensed that there was going to be a tap on her door before she heard it, and she knew that it was Akitoshi.

When she slid the panel open he bowed to her. "May I come in?" he asked.

"Of course."

"I'm not interrupting your writing?"

"You can interrupt me any time you like." She turned and looked at him. "I thought you would be asleep, you worked so hard today."

He shrugged his shoulders. "It is easy when there are many others working too. It is like being part of a parade."

"Did you get the job finished?"

"Almost. There were not quite enough bags, but the important things have been done. Tomorrow, perhaps, they may be able to do a little more if the storm has not yet come."

As he finished speaking an exceptionally strong gust hit the side of the building and the room shook enough for it to be felt.

"I wouldn't count on it," Marjorie said. She knew that he had not come to discuss the day's work; but it was possible that he just wanted her company. She hoped that might be the case.

"How are you feeling?" he asked her.

"All right."

He seemed to hesitate for a bare moment. "I have finished my picture of you," he told her. "You can see it if you would like."

"Now?"

"Whenever you choose."

She pulled her *yukata* a little more securely around her body and tightened the obi that held it in position. It was not a protective gesture; she had nothing to fear from the man before her, but now that she could see his painting of her, she was unaccountably disturbed. Images of Dorian Gray came to her and she had to thrust them aside. He had told her that it was not a conventional portrait — he had even warned her that she might not like it.

Suddenly she felt as though some diabolical force had pulled her limbs all out of position so that she was elongated like an El Greco, or as wildly distorted as some of the things she had seen in the Museum of Modern Art.

She went into his room not caring whether anyone saw her or

not. In one corner there was an easel set up and a painting of considerable size was resting on it. There was a cloth thrown over its face so that only the smallest lower corner was visible. It was rich with yellow color, but that was all she could tell.

"When you see something, if you want a picture of it just that way, it is best to use a camera," Akitoshi said. "It will see everything and forget nothing. A painting is something else: it is what the artist himself sees. It is like a song: the music is the same, but it will sound differently if different people sing it."

"I understand," Marjorie told him. She hoped to heaven that she really did.

"You will forgive me if you do not like it?"

"I promise." She made a quick mental resolve to keep her word on that, no matter what.

Akitoshi walked over and carefully took the cloth off the front of the painting. Marjorie looked at it, studied it, and felt her knees go weak. She had thought of many possibilities, but not what confronted her now.

She was there, standing just as she had posed for him in the middle of the rice paddies, the sheaf of straw in her arms. He had transferred her to canvas with astonishing skill, but at the same time, she thought, he had made her much more attractive than she actually was. He had infused her with youth, beauty, even radiance, but also with dignity. Never in her most potent dreams had she ever imagined that she could look like that.

But there was more. In the upper right third of the canvas there was another figure, this one a classical Japanese beauty in full kimono, her black hair swept up in an elaborate formal arrangement crowned by a sprig of cherry blossoms. The face that looked out was delicately Japanese, a very pale ivory complexion with open, inviting, intelligent eyes. It was the portrait of a court beauty from the days of old Edo, but it was also, unmistakably, a portrait of Marjorie — Marjorie as she would have been if she had been born here in this ancient, tradition-filled land.

From the other side of the picture a blond, Caucasian girl looked toward her with a frank openness that also spoke of high intelligence, breeding, and something far more profound than mere good looks. It was the face of a gifted and confident young woman who had a great deal to offer and who would receive a great deal in return. The world lay before her and she was ready to take possession of her share of it — and possibly more.

It was then, for the first time, that Marjorie knew exactly how she would have looked if she had been born a member of the white majority in her own country — for the face, despite the subtle alteration, was still hers and it could be no one else's.

As she stood, looking at the astonishing three-way portrait, she realized something else. The Japanese beauty was an exquisite creature, and the blond, blue-eyed girl was also stunningly attractive, but the central figure dominated the picture. It came to her that her own true appearance, as she really was, completely superseded the other two realizations of what she might have been like had the circumstances of her birth been otherwise.

As she continued to study the picture, she realized that the two side portraits were done in slightly more subdued colors so that they blended a little into the background and thereby suggested an aura of unreality, but the way that she stood in the center, an American Negro girl on a Japanese farm in the early summer, made her heart beat a little faster. Without knowing why or how, she suddenly wanted to give thanks that she was as she was.

In a matter of a few seconds, the picture had become part of her life.

When the tears began to come into her eyes, Akitoshi quickly took her hands and turned her away from his creation. "I have hurt you?" he asked.

She pressed her lips tightly together and then shook her head. Impulsively, because she had to, she reached for him and pillowed her head on his shoulder. Her body shook for a second or two, then a renewed attack by the wind made the whole room respond.

She could not speak, she did not want to move, she simply stood there and held onto the man who had his arms around her now and who understood. Understood more profoundly than she thought that anyone who did not share her heritage ever could.

She did not want to stand any longer. She let her knees unlock as she felt his strong arms ease her gently down onto the tatami floor. She sat, supported by his own body beside hers, and let it all flow out. When she at last recovered herself, she knew that she had to say something to him, or he might misunderstand terribly.

She intended to say something about the picture, but instead her mind forced her to say the real thing that was within her, for nothing else would come out.

She did not look at him as she shaped her words. "Ever since I was a very little girl, and knew that I was different, I've wondered why. And wished, and wished, so many, many times, that it might have been different. I've been fortunate, my father's seen to that, but despite him there have been times . . . times even when I wanted to kill myself. And I asked God why he had done this to me, and why the world wouldn't take me as I am and just let me be me."

She stopped and wiped her eyes with the sleeve of her *yukata.* When she went on, she was a little calmer. "Here in Mitamura it all came back — they called me the devil woman, I know about that. I didn't despise them because they're Japanese; they were just people to me and I wanted to be just a person to them, only they wouldn't let me. They changed the bath water after me as though I had made it filthy. If it hadn't been for Peter, and the embarrassment I would have caused him, I would have fled from this place, and from Japan, and from all of the dreams that I had about it."

She was almost out of breath. For a few seconds she remained quiet and still, leaning against him and not even being aware of it.

She swallowed and recovered her voice. "Now," she said, "you've made me proud to be black. I have been before, in a way, or I thought that I was, but deep in my heart I wasn't that sure. Now you've shown me. I want to be the girl in the middle of that picture — I don't want to be anyone else."

She looked up at him. "It's wonderful," she said. "I think you're a genius."

"Many people," he told her, "hate Japanese."

A gust stronger than any that had come before shook the building, and with it came the sudden sound of rain. For a moment the lights faltered. "Turn them off, will you?" she asked.

He got up and obliged. When he came back the room was not dark; the translucent panels admitted enough light to outline all that it contained. He sat down beside her again. "I did not want to upset you," he said.

She put a finger across his lips to silence him and then just sat very still.

Presently she spoke again. "If I was the Japanese girl, the one you painted, then I would try very hard . . . to make you like me."

"You've already done that," he told her. "Made me like you, I mean."

The room shook again from the force of the mounting wind, and the sounds of the rain grew stronger.

"Enough?" she asked.

The people of the inn had been through many storms before, but this one was going to be the worst that had come for years. They lay in their *futons*, resting while they could, in the expectation that the following day might call for their utmost exertions. In such weather no incoming guests could be expected; if any did arrive, there was a bell they could ring. The lobby was shut tight; the storm doors were in place and all that could be done had been done.

The inn had gone to bed, to be shaken in its sleep every few minutes by a fresh assault from the ever increasing wind and its accompanying rain.

In the front guest room, which was the best that the inn had to offer, a woman lay very still in the arms of a man and in the creaking timbers that had been put into place more than a century before they heard the timeless music of their own private Eden.

When Peter awoke in the morning it was because the floor on which he was lying was shaking every few seconds and the sound of the wind outside was like a demented banshee. He sat up, wondering how he had managed to sleep at all under such conditions. Then he remembered his promise to be sure that Midori's house would be protected as fully as possible against the storm; he was suddenly filled with the guilty knowledge that he had done nothing whatever to help her.

He got into his clothes as quickly as he could. He kicked his feet into slippers, opened the panel, and strode across the small vacant room into the kitchen area.

Midori was there and he saw in a glance that she was frightened. She came to him at once, concern etched on her face. "Peta, you all right?"

"Yes, of course," he answered. "How is the house? What can I do?"

"House I think all right. I made everything fix. But wind very big.

"I know. Is it always this bad?"

"No, Peta, first time this big I remember. I worry some."

She had a right to. Because the situation was urgent, and also because he had failed completely so far to do anything at all to help protect her home, he began an immediate inspection. The construction of the house was elementary; there was a central supporting post that was well set into position, but there were no cross members at all. The danger in that was immediately apparent to him; if anything happened to the roof, then the whole house would collapse.

As he studied the low thatched pyramid, it seemed to him to be vulnerable. Even as he was looking at it he saw it shake under the impact of a fresh gust. If the wind grew very much stronger, then it would only be a matter of time.

That called for action and he resolved to take it. "Midori," he said. "It isn't safe for you here. I think the inn would be better."

"No, Peta, I cannot go. I must be . . . *rusuban.*"

"What's that?"

"When family go away, maybe house catch fire. So always one person stay to make sure safe. Called *rusuban.*"

"That's no excuse to risk your neck. And the house isn't going to catch fire in all this rain. I'm going outside to see how bad this really is."

She was almost terrified. "No, Peta, no!" Must not open door. If do, wind come in, blow house down!"

As the structure shook once more under the impact of a new assault of wind and driving rain, he could see the truth of that. The house had originally been built so that, to a degree at least, it would shed the wind. But if its outer shell was broken, then the blasts could come inside and lift off the straw roof in a matter of seconds.

The storm panels were old and dried out, so that in many places there were cracks that admitted considerable light. Peter went to one of them on the south side and peered through, trying to measure the force of the wind and see what damage, if any, had already been caused in the village.

The sky was an angry mass of boiling clouds wrapped in sheets of heavy rain. There was no hint of relief to come; if anything the typhoon seemed to be gaining in strength, so that the whole of Mitamura might well be swept away. He could not see enough to be sure if any damage had been done to buildings, but some of the dike walls in the paddy area seemed to have been blown down in the small section that had not been sandbagged. The rice plants themselves were lying almost horizontal to the ground as the wind tore at them mercilessly.

A small outbuilding rolled into the middle of the road and remained there for a few seconds, then it was lifted bodily and flung over the edge into the nearest paddy. Peter had had no previous experience with typhoons, but he knew that this one was of killer intensity, and growing worse. Any idea of getting Midori safely to the inn had to be abandoned; they would never be able to stay on their feet in the raging blasts that were now almost continuous in their unabated fury.

He calmed down and thought carefully for a minute or two. If he had been free, there was little that he could have done to have prepared the house any further. Two men had been delegated to help wherever necessary and undoubtedly they had done everything possible.

What was pertinent now was a plan to be followed if and when the house came down about them. He looked up at the roof construction once more and decided that such a contingency was not only possible, but likely. As he reached that decision the house shook again with a force that almost threw him off his feet; the walls creaked violently and for a second or two he thought that disaster had already overtaken them. As soon as the surging gust had passed, he wasted no more time. He took hold of Midori, not mattering how, and hurried her into the kitchen area. If the house tipped over, then the flooring would almost certainly go with it. In the kitchen there was no floor, which gave a small measure of added safety.

"No fire," he ordered.

"No fire, Peta, not make. I know better."

"Good."

The safest possible place, he decided, was at the edge of the flooring where he usually sat to take his meals. If the roof came down, the raised flooring would protect them; if the whole house went, they would have a good chance not to go with it. It was not entirely satisfactory, but it was the best plan available to him at that moment.

"Wait," he told Midori.

He went the few steps back to his room and gathered up his *futon;* with it he returned to the kitchen and spread it on the earthen floor next to the protective edge of the raised section. Without ceremony he planted Midori on it and indicated that she should lie down. He did not stop to consider the niceties; there was not time for that.

When he went for her *futon* he found that, despite the storm, she had carefully put it away. He pulled it out of the cabinet and took it to the kitchen. As he made the trip another intense blast shook the house and one of the *fusuma* panels buckled, hesitated, and then fell out of its grooves onto the floor.

Peter put the *futon* down end to end against his own and asked, "How long will the storm last?"

"Maybe two days. Not before this big. I not know." She was frightened, but she still kept herself under control very well.

"How about food? Have you things that don't need to be cooked?"

"Have some, Peta. Not very good, but we can eat."

As she looked up at him with her complete trust, Peter understood that at that moment she was regarding him as the head of the household. He was grateful for that, simply because it made it easier for him to take care of her in whatever way might be necessary.

He lay down on her *futon* so that they were head to head and he could talk to her above the howling of the wind and the constant beating of the rain. "Midori, listen carefully. The wind may blow this house away, you understand?"

"Yes — understand."

"If that happens, we will go to the inn. It is built against the hill and will be the safest place. But we won't try to walk, the wind is too strong."

"Maybe house fall on us, Peta."

"If it does, lie still and I'll dig you out; one way or another. Now, if the house starts to go, take hold of my hands and hang on, do you understand? Like this." He demonstrated what he meant.

"All right, Peta, I will do."

"Then we will crawl to the inn. We will stay on the ground. It will be hard, but it will be much safer."

"Maybe inn blow away too."

"That's possible, but it's in a safer spot. Also, it's a stronger building, I think."

"Yes, very well maked."

"Now — one more thing. If the wind eases up any, so that we can make a dash for it, we will go to the inn anyway. Never mind about the house. Is that clear?"

"What is 'dash'?"

"Dash means to run — to go as fast as we can."

"You say, Peta, I go."

There was a loud wrenching sound and an almost explosive protest from tortured timbers that were being taxed to the limit of their strength. Peter was fully prepared to see the house go; he seized Midori's hands once more and looked into her searching eyes. He read the fright there and the fact that he was her best and only hope. At that moment he was surgingly glad that he was here in this village, sent by some divine and benevolent authority to protect her.

There was one thing more he could do: raising his body, he swung himself around until he was close beside her. In that way he could shield her with his own body if things came falling down. He had already written the house off in his mind; saving their lives was the important thing now.

From somewhere outside he heard a fierce, thunderous crash — something had fallen, but he did not know what. "Hang on, Midori," he told her. "I'll take care of you."

"I know, Peta."

The words were very simple, but she had put something into them that made him react in spite of himself. He knew that he was fully responsible for the woman who, for reasons of protection, lay so close to him with her arm across his shoulder.

He could think of nothing further to do. It would be hopeless to try to reinforce the house in any way; he had no materials, and no way to use them if he did. He reviewed in his mind everything he knew about the house and the land immediately around it, but he could not think of anything better to do, or any safer place they could go.

He put his arm under her head so that she could use it as a pillow. Then, as his mind subsided, he allowed himself to admire her. She was a tremendously appealing person and something about her was intensely warm and magnetic.

"Peta."

"Yes, Midori?"

"Thank you, take care of me."

As her lips formed the words she was at that moment very precious to him. He kissed her. "I'm glad I could," he said.

He found more satisfaction in that than he had on those occasions when he had been in bed with a woman. Few of the girls he had made love to had really mattered to him; it had usually been a case of a welcome mutual enjoyment. With Midori it was something totally different, and he wanted it to be that way.

Another surging blast of wind tore at the house and very nearly lifted it off its foundation, but the old farmhouse that had already endured so much refused to yield. It groaned and held, but it had been a perilously close thing. If the storm grew more violent still, it would have no additional strength with which to resist.

In the house of the *yuryokusha* there was a calm that was unnatural. While the violence of the storm raged outside, and the building itself shook frequently and heavily from the fierce buffeting it was taking, the *yuryokusha* himself sat in the middle of the floor of his principal room, a symbolic closed fan held in his hands, saying and doing nothing. Clad in his black, at-home kimono, he was, like Dr. Watson, a fixed point in a changing age.

There was no tea before him only because it was impossible to prepare any. No fire could be safely started, for the gale threatened to take the house at any moment and under such conditions fire could take hold and spread despite the heavy rain. Nowhere in Mitamura was there a fire of any kind and probably none would be started until the storm was well passed. To attempt to work was out of the question, so the doll maker sat in formal decorum, a Japanese gentleman steeped in the traditions of his country and observing them. If he was to be called this day to face his ancestors, he was fully prepared to make the transition properly.

Because it was his duty, as well as the correct thing to do, his son sat with him, somewhat behind him and to the side, dressed as his father was as a mark of respect and admiration. There was nothing whatever either of them could do to abate the howling fury of the typhoon that ripped and tugged at the foundation of their home, the artistic tradition that they upheld, and their very lives, so they sat in the way that only a Japanese can and gave no outward signs of any kind.

In a corner of the room little Setsuko Taminaka was terrified.

Too many pieces fitted together in her mind and she did not like the picture that they formed. The fact that she was in danger, and that both her home and her life were threatened, was something that she knew, but it was not her principal concern at that moment. She knew her father much better than he suspected and as she crouched in a corner, taking what solace she could from the friendly *fusuma* panels behind her, she all but read his mind.

Typhoons were nothing new to Mitamura — they came at the rate of fifteen to thirty each year — but almost all of them were small ones that only lasted a short time and never did any serious damage. Never before, as far as she knew, had there been a storm like this one.

The life of the village had been undisturbed until Sutoramu Sensei had arrived, with Majōri. Then there had been many serious discussions, because the black girl was a terribly evil omen. So bad that her own father, whose manners were a model of perfection, had broken the rules of hospitality in order to protect his family from her presence.

Setsuko, too, knew the secret of the crazy man on the mountain. She understood perfectly that he had been a good man, one with a wife and a home, when the *kokujin* soldier from America had done something so terrible to his wife that he had run screaming up the mountain toward the temple and he had never come down again. This dreadful thing had weighed on her father's mind ever since it had happened, first because he was the *yuryokusha* of the village, second because the crazy man was the first son of his younger brother. His second son had married the city girl from the wrong direction and he was now dead.

Setsuko had never seen the crazy man in his frightful condition, but she understood why her perfect father could not, at first, welcome another *kokujin* to his home.

Later, after Majōri had done good things, he had proven his

greatness by humbling himself before her. Now, Setsuko knew, he was totally convinced that in doing so he had committed the one great error of his life, for this terrible, lashing, violent gale was the work of demons, it could be nothing else, and the black devil woman was here to direct them.

Because he had made such a terrible mistake he was sitting, waiting to receive his punishment, and so was her brother, because whenever a family member commits a wrong, the blame is shared equally by all of the others. It was a rule as inexorable as the one that holds the captain of a ship at sea totally responsible for everything that happens on board, regardless of his own personal involvement.

She too was responsible for what her father had done, and she knew it acutely. Much more than the others, because at the meeting she had dared to speak in Majōri's behalf. Only one thing did not fit into the total picture: she still believed that Majōri was a good person. The storm, therefore, was not her fault.

But her father would never believe that.

As she sat, realizing the terrible thoughts that were going through his mind, she did some thinking of her own. If she could stop the storm; if she could make it pass away without doing any more damage, and if the sun would come out once more and nourish the rice paddies, then the whole thing might be forgotten and Majōri would no longer be called the devil woman.

There was one avenue open to her, simple and direct, that she knew held great promise: she could pray to the Lord Buddha. She would not be able to see Him in his glory listening to her from Nirvana, but He would hear; she had been taught that personally by her father, therefore it was a truth beyond all question.

Only because she had a most important and pressing duty to perform, she left her father's presence very quietly and slipped into the corner of her home that was reserved for worship. There she sat down, arranged her skirt around her, put her hands together, and began her earnest supplication.

She did not expect that it would be a simple thing: life was not so well ordered that it was only necessary to speak once to Lord Buddha about any problems to have them resolved immediately. The Enlightened One looked into the hearts of men and women and tested them, therefore it would be necessary to petition Him with great sincerity and conviction. Any immediate results were seldom to be expected.

It was early in the afternoon when she began her vigil; it was almost two hours later when the miracle occurred.

She was still sitting as she had been when she had begun, immune to the pains in her legs from their having been folded under her for so long. It was the only suitable position from which to address the Blessed One and having seen her duty, she had never faltered.

Her concentration was broken only when she became aware of a change outside, a change so dramatic that it forced itself into her consciousness.

The wind was stopping, and with it the slashing rain. Not gradually over a period of hours, but with a suddenness that was startling. The house ceased shaking. The howling noise subsided so swiftly that it almost left an echo where it had been.

Bowing her head to the tatami mat on which she sat, Setsuko first gave fervent thanks; then she excused herself to go and witness the wondrous thing that had been granted. She had never questioned the supreme authority and all-encompassing goodness of the Enlightened One, but never before in her short life had she ever seen them demonstrated in so totally dramatic a manner.

She knew that during a storm it was absolutely forbidden to open one of the *amado* even a crack, but the storm was over; she could hear it.

Very cautiously she slid one of the storm doors open the merest crack and peered outside.

The trees were barely moving. The wind was no more than a pleasant summer breeze and the rain had ceased entirely.

She opened the panel wider and looked up into the sky. She saw a great round opening in the clouds and while the sun was still covered, its brilliance irradiated the rich blue circle of heaven that stood revealed.

In utter and profound gratitude Setsuko fell to her knees, covered her face with her hands, and poured out her heart. When she had done her utmost to express her boundless thanks, she opened the panel halfway and welcomed the miracle into her home.

Her mind continued to work. Many people who prayed never saw the results of their petitions, but to her had been granted the unutterable blessing of being allowed to behold, with her own eyes, the power of Divinity.

To see it even better, she slipped outside. Although it was no longer necessary, she carefully closed the storm door behind her.

The air was soft and warm. Little still puddles and the wet ground were all that remained of the almost torrential rain and the wind was a caress against the side of her face. She looked up again at the great round hole in the sky and joy infused her whole being. Now they would all know that Majōri was good, because if she had been a devil woman, the Lord Buddha would not have so dramatically blessed the village where Majōri was.

Then she knew what she was called upon to do. For great blessings, great thanks should be given. She had already spoken twice from within her home, but there was a vastly better way for her to show the depth of her gratitude.

She did not need to tell her father; having seen the miracle himself, he would understand immediately. Feeling more depth of emotion that she had ever known in her life, she turned resolutely toward the base of the long pathway that led far up the mountain to the temple that crowned its summit.

Chapter Seventeen

When the wind began to abate, Peter listened intently to determine what was happening. After a minute or two he was certain that the gale was rapidly dying. It was falling off with a suddenness that meant a heaven-sent opportunity if he read it correctly.

For another three minutes he continued to lie still. He knew that if his guess was right he would have enough time, but if he was by any chance wrong, this was his chance to find out. When he was certain, he was ready to take immediate action.

"Midori," he said carefully. "We're going to the inn. We cannot wait; we must go now."

"What has happen, Peta?"

"It's the eye of the hurricane. Right in the middle of hurricanes, or typhoons, there is a hole. While it is passing, everything is calm and still. Then the storm hits again full blast; that's usually the worst time."

The explanation in English was not entirely clear to her, but she had no opportunity to think about it further. Peter pulled her to her feet and faced her toward the outside. "Stay with me," he ordered. "We should have plenty of time, but if we get caught in the open, it could be very serious."

"All right, Peta." At that moment she would have gone with him anywhere.

He slid a panel open and took her out into the deceptively mild calm. He closed the panel behind him and gave it an extra push to seat it securely, then he took her hand and led her down the sloping path toward the inn.

In five minutes they arrived. Peter took quick, powerful satisfaction when he saw that the *ryokan* was standing as solidly as ever; it would be the best sanctuary for Midori and himself. Also Marjorie would be all right. And Akitoshi.

The door was heavily secured, but when he pounded on it, it was opened almost at once. The manager was there with Akitoshi right behind him.

"Peter!" the artist welcomed him. "We've been so worried about you both. I was coming to see if you were all right."

Peter ushered Midori in ahead of him. "It was a near thing," he said. "Two or three times I thought the house was going. How was it here?"

"Not quite that bad; this place is very solidly built. You certainly did the right thing to come here. Did you see any damage?"

"To be honest, I didn't look too hard; I concentrated entirely on getting here. I was very concerned for Midori."

Marjorie appeared from Kojima's room. "Oh, thank God," she said. "You don't know how worried I've been."

"You're all right?"

"Yes. We took a pretty bad shaking here, but we're in the lee of the hill and that helped a lot. The worst is still coming, isn't it?"

"Yes, but only the first couple of hours should be at maximum force. I'm not a hurricane expert, but I understand that's how it is."

Midori addressed the manager in Japanese and obviously received a full assurance from him. "She is apologizing for leaving her home," Akitoshi explained, "but she said that you are giving the orders. That was not an excuse, she only means that she was obedient."

"We would have been lunatics to have stayed there. If it gets any worse, there may not be a house left standing."

"That's why they have been watching the door, Peter. This is the only place that's any more secure. I don't know why they all aren't coming now."

At that moment there was a pounding on the door and the manager opened it as quickly as he was able. The *yuryokusha* stood outside like a man in his death agonies. He came into the lobby with every muscle in his body tense and his face tight with anguish. He spoke rapidly in a voice that was hardly his own.

"He is asking if his daughter is here," Akitoshi supplied quickly and quietly. "She has disappeared from his house."

"Setsuko?" Marjorie exploded.

"Yes, Setsuko."

"Oh, my God!"

She stopped to allow the doll maker to supply what details he could. As soon as the eye of the storm had come he had begun an inspection of his house and workshop; it was then that he had discovered that Setsuko was missing. He had at first assumed that she had hidden herself somewhere in fright and he had searched the work shed.

"She wouldn't do that," Marjorie said.

The *yuryokusha* finished his brief account. When the search had failed, they had gone outside and called, but there had been no answer. They had thought it possible that she had come to the inn, possibly to see her friend Majōri. As he spoke those last words the doll maker carefully looked away. Marjorie did not understand the Japanese, but she recognized her own name, and knew. She turned and almost ran from the room.

Akitoshi glanced at his watch, then asked one or two quick questions. No, there was no other place she would have been likely to visit. The inn was the only place open and she definitely would not have gone to visit another child.

The artist spoke rapidly in Japanese. "I will look for her; she cannot have gone far."

Peter thrust out an arm and intercepted him. "Tell Taminaka San that I'm going to look for his daughter. Is there any rope here?"

"Rope?"

"Yes, I may need it if the eye passes. It would be hell out there."

Before his question could be answered, Marjorie reappeared. In an astonishingly short time she had changed into a pair of slacks and she was tying her hair up in a headcloth. She did not pause, but almost ran across the lobby and pulled the door open.

"Wait!" Peter barked.

Akitoshi ran after her and caught her a step or two outside the door. "Go back inside," he commanded. "Peter and I will find her."

Marjorie shook her head violently. "We all will; it's her only chance."

Akitoshi knew that short of using force he could not stop her. The eye could last for another half hour and that should do it, so he left her alone. He began to run down the road toward the other side of the village, calling her name. He knew that he could cover the entire *mura* in ten minutes; he hoped he would find her before then.

Peter was close behind him. When he saw which way Akitoshi had gone, he swung toward the paddy area. The Taminakas did not own any fields, but he reasoned that she might have wanted to find out how well the vital crop had withstood the storm. He assumed that she would not understand the eye and might have thought that the typhoon had already passed.

After ten minutes of frantic searching he had not found her. He had called out constantly, and his chest was knotted in pain from his exertion. The one good thing was the fact that he had not covered a high-probability area; Akitoshi had a far better chance.

As he ran back toward the inn he found his second wind and

physically felt much better. One quick look into the lobby told him that Akitoshi and the little girl were not there, and he did not see Marjorie. He ran back outside, desperate now that the time was growing so short.

Akitoshi came running down the path from the upper part of the village. He threw out his arms, hands up in inquiry, and Peter shook his head.

"Check the houses," Akitoshi yelled. "Just say her name, they'll understand."

Peter saw the wisdom of that immediately; if she was not anywhere outside, then someone must have seen her and taken her in. It would have been the only sensible thing to do. His breath short once more, he ran up to the first house in the lower row and pounded on the panel.

Marjorie Saunders had one enormous advantage — she had once been a little girl. She thought first of Midori's house; Setsuko could well have gone there to see Peter, possibly to advise him and Midori to go down to the inn. She was quite intelligent enough to think of that.

Midori's house was tightly closed, which was to be expected. Marjorie pulled a storm door back, then the shoji panel, and went inside. Two minutes later she knew that the house, and the toilet room, were empty. She had called out loudly and there had been no response.

At that juncture she stopped and thought. The men were in the streets of the village; if she was there, they would find her. If one of the other families had taken her in, she was at least relatively safe. But if neither of these possibilities was correct, what then?

One fact stood out in Marjorie's mind: Setsuko Taminaka was not an ordinary little girl. She possessed an extraordinary intelligence that verged on genius, so what would such a remarkably gifted child be most likely to do?

Definitely she would not have just wandered off to play. But being eight years old, she very likely would not know what the eye of a typhoon was. She *had* gone outside, but where?

Where would an amazingly intelligent little girl go if she had been deceived into thinking that the typhoon was over? To visit friends? No. To go to the inn? Yes, but she wasn't there. *Where else, for God's sake?*

God!

She could have thought that the storm was over and gone to give thanks. A wild, absurd possibility, but she had done *something* unusual, and she did possess that penetrating mind.

The Taminakas were strict traditionalists; they went to the temple regularly. And Setsuko went with them, she had learned that during her interviewing.

But the temple, God help her, was high up on top of the hill and there was no way to get there before the storm would return with all of its blasting, raging fury.

Marjorie came out of the house and looked toward the inn to see if there were any indications at all. She saw Akitoshi going down the path at a run, and then throwing out his arms in a gesture of failure.

She did not hesitate, because Setsuko was only a little child, for all of her intellectual ability, and there could not be too much strength in her small body.

Marjorie followed the path toward the mountain until she saw the footprints. For a bare moment she considered going back for help, but that would consume far too much of the remaining precious time. She knew the risk she was taking, and she knew what else might await her on the mountain, but she began steadily to climb. Because Setsuko Taminaka was her friend.

She did some thinking about God herself as she started up the long hill. Perhaps under the thick trees the violence of the winds, when they returned, would be lessened. She did not try to call out;

Setsuko would have stuck to the path, so she saved her own breath for climbing, and went on.

As she worked her way upward, she thought again about the painting that Akitoshi had made of her. She looked down at her dark-skinned hands, as she had so many tens of thousands of times before in her life, but that simple action had lost its power to hurt her. Because they could have been the hands of a Japanese beauty tightly wrapped in a multilayered kimono. Or they could have been the hands of a Caucasian with some sort of European ancestry, but in neither case would they have been hands that were any more capable, or able to serve her in any better way.

A quick, sharp blast of wind hit the side of her face and gave her a first warning. On the chance that she might already have come far enough, and while she could still be heard, she stopped, gathered breath, and then called out as loudly as she could. She did it once more and then listened, but she heard nothing.

She looked up into the sky and saw that the great round hole was very nearly gone. Clouds were coming in like a tidal wave; there was no longer any hope of getting back to the inn before the typhoon unleashed its full, frightful power.

She climbed as long as she could until the first mighty blast howled down upon her and almost threw her off her feet. The second was right behind it and more powerful still; she just had time to throw herself under the trees before a torrent of rain burst all around her and with it the mounting fury of the typhoon that was far more terrible than she had dreamed. For a few moments she lay completely still on the ground, already soaked to the skin, and let the howl of the storm rage over her while she measured her ability to survive.

She had been right about one thing: the trees did offer some slight protection, but they were already waving violently and at any moment one or more of them could come down on top of her. She was so terrified she had to strain to keep from voiding her bladder. The wind was now a raging gale, but its most terrible blows came in the form of blasting gusts that hit like monstrous sledgehammers. To some degree she could sense when they were imminent; the trees ahead gave warning. The slashing rain was pounding her body mercilessly. She tried to ignore that and concentrate on the real danger — the wind. When a gust passed she got to her feet and climbed upward until she saw the next one coming. She clung to a small tree while it passed and at once resolved never to do that again; its force almost tore the skin off her face. When it had passed she climbed again, then threw herself down on the sodden ground when the next blast was almost upon her.

Her eyes watered until she could hardly see. Her breath fought against the confinement of her body and cramped the walls of her chest. Her mind refused to think of anything but how many feet upward she could go until she would have to lie flat, clutching at whatever she could with her fingers, until the worst was over.

Her world became the trees around her, the sleeting rain, the pitch of the ground ahead, and the all-surrounding terror of the gale; the gale with its ripping, tearing, slashing winds and incessant howling that sought to split the very earth apart.

She went on by force of determination, and because her mind did not allow her to think of anything else. Like a cornered animal trapped by an immensely more powerful adversary, she fought back with total intensity and her utmost strength, and each time that she moved a few feet ahead, she scored another victory.

Time ceased for her as she battled the raging typhoon. It almost stopped forever when a tall tree directly before her gave up its life in an agony of splintering wood and came wavering down very nearly on top of her. Only the tree she was under saved her; its heavy branches intercepted the massive falling trunk and deflected it a few feet away. The ground shook when it landed; the shock of the impact so close to her gave Marjorie a sharp, sudden seizure that told her to give up — to do anything to get out of the inferno of blasting, killing winds, drenching rain, and ear-splitting shrieking sound.

She did not give up because she could not; there was no choice given to her. Through her pain and fear she was dimly aware that the upward slope of the ground had eased off; looking sideways, she saw that she had reached the level of the lake.

It came to her then that she would go on and on as long as she could and then, when she could go no farther, the end would come. And with it peace and contentment: no more battles to fight, no more shame and dishonor heaped upon her simply because of the accident of her birth. She did not fear or dread it; it would come sometime and now was as good a time as any. But she would not give up and just lie where she was; it was her fate and duty to keep going as long as she could, just as the trapped animal will fight to the death. She was a human animal and she could do no less.

She remembered the horror of the madman who was somewhere up on this mountain, perhaps just a few feet from where she lay —watching her. But the poor demented creature would be as much a victim of the killer typhoon as herself. It horrified her to think of that vacant mind trying to fight back against elements it could not comprehend, its own raging fury vastly outmatched by the unrelenting hostility of the storm. The added risk was meaningless to her, because she had no strength left even to think about it.

The trees thinned out somewhat and the typhoon tore at her with such demonic fury that normally she never could have withstood it. She kept on only because her mind was now made up and what she had to do lay before her. It would not be much longer.

She tried to get to her feet once more when the lashing winds seemed to abate for just a few seconds. She struggled up and in her desperation tried to run, but the next surging blast caught her and threw her to the ground so violently she almost fell directly onto the body she had not seen when it had been five feet in front of her.

Total shock overwhelmed her and her mind nearly gave way as she collapsed across the tattered figure that was curled up almost in fetal position. Raising herself with her arms she forced herself to look; then for the first time she saw what had been the head. Her body rebelled and she vomited with such force that she had to gasp for breath. Pure raw instinct kept her breathing until her mind cleared and she was able to regain something of her sanity.

She knew that it was a corpse — and she knew who it was —but she could do nothing about it. As her dulled mind fought to regain full control, a large rock, almost a boulder, came bounding down the mountainside. That told her what had happened; she looked and saw the great stone that had come to rest in a small hollow below and to her left. It had hit him and had killed him instantly — probably without his ever knowing.

Because she was human, Marjorie was suddenly very sorry for him and her tears flowed like a small child's. He had once been a good man who had been frightfully wronged and now, in death, his peace had been restored. It seemed to her that she should pray for him; it was the thing she had been taught as a little girl and now, so close to the end of her own rope, compassion flooded through her. Her lips moved, but they made no sound and her mind formed no coherent words.

The most violent gust that the storm had as yet unleashed seized her and threatened to lift her bodily off the ground. She felt herself beginning to go; in desperation her fingers locked around the arm of the corpse and she held on in pure frenzy. The terrible wind threw an almost solid wall of water against her and forced her back. The corpse came with her, turning onto its back until it faced upward, unseeing, toward the sky and from the protective hollow that it had formed, Setsuko let out a startled cry.

For almost a quarter of a minute Marjorie shut her eyes and tried to believe. She knew that the driving demons of the storm had almost possessed her, but the fact that she felt sharp pain where she had just fallen told her that she was still alive and in possession of her own body. She opened her eyes and reached out across the cadaver with both her arms to seize her little friend. "Are you all right?" she gasped.

In the midst of that terrible, blinding, terrifying gale she did not realize that the child spoke a different language and could not understand her. But she did know when she saw fresh tears on the rain-soaked face and heard the voice of hope in one word, *"Majōri!"*

She gathered Setsuko to herself and held her as closely as a mother could, and the love that surged between them knew no barriers whatever.

Her strength came back like fire into her limbs and the typhoon that tore at her body seemed to be raging the fury of defeat. She could turn back now, from death into life, and she could bring back Setsuko with her. She locked the cold, drenched child in her arms, waited for a moment until she could move, and then struggled to her feet. For a few yards she ran with surging joy, her burden unfelt, aware that a great unspoken prayer had been answered.

She could not talk to Setsuko; what little Japanese she knew was useless, but with signs she could make herself understood. Despite the awful terror she had just known, the little girl trusted her and understood immediately what she was being told to do. That was a great help. Setsuko was still terrified, but she looked at Marjorie as she might have looked at a Bodhisattva: a living saint sent from Nirvana to help her in her time of greatest need.

Because of that Marjorie ceased to feel the pain that had permeated her body, and the blackness that had clouded her mind was exorcised. When the next terrible gust came she fell on her side with Setsuko still tight in her arms and waited, her ears all but dumb from the unrelenting howling of the blasting wind and the tearing of timber that created a cacophony all around her.

The storm was eternal, it would never relent, it would fight on with its overwhelming power to the end of creation, but when it would pause for a few seconds to reorganize its fury, there would be a chance to reach the base of a strong tree twenty feet away that would give some shelter.

Marjorie waited, but the typhoon maintained its awesome anger and when it threatened a new crescendo of intensity it had never reached before, she began to crawl. Foot by foot she made her way, enduring the hammering of the wind as it almost ripped the rain-soaked remnants of her clothing from her back, until she reached the shelter of the tree.

It was then that she realized it was beginning to grow dark. Much of it was the storm, but the sun was leaving the sky and when it was finally gone, it would be almost impossible for her to go on.

She raised her head to study the place where they were. It was a very slight hollow, now filled with water, but the tree was a strong one and not likely to go. There was only one thing she could do: stay where she was and take care of Setsuko. The typhoon seemed to be gaining, but she blocked that out of her mind. She maneuvered her body as close to the tree as she could so as to form a pocket of protection for Setsuko, and resolved to wait. The last of her strength had been drained from her body and very little daylight remained. Exhaustion was beginning to overwhelm her.

She had just made her decision when she felt a fresh force against her body compelling her to turn over. Because she had to, she fought back desperately against this new horror until she looked up and saw the face of Peter.

Chapter Eighteen

THE ATMOSPHERE INSIDE the inn was almost as heavy as the violence of the typhoon that raged outside. For as long as the false calm in the eye of the great storm had lasted there had been constant hope; at any moment one of the men could have returned with Setsuko, or it had been quite possible that she might have come in on her own. But as soon as the first sharp gusts returned, everything drastically changed. The *yuryokusha* himself made for the door and the manager had physically to restrain him.

"Sensei," he pleaded, "do not attempt it! There are two strong men out there, and they are very resourceful. Your courage is superb, but they will do all that is possible. We must wait for her here."

"The black woman is out there too. I believe that she is a witch."

"Sensei, with the greatest respect, it cannot be. I know, I thought that way myself before she began to live here. She is black in the same way that Watanabe San in the next village cannot walk — it is a physical misfortune, but no more."

The doll maker shook his head. "I would give much to believe that," he declared.

"I can give you the proof. She has done good, and it is impossible for a demon to do that. She is skilled with medicines. When Miyoko cut her knee open, Majōri repaired it so well that it is now almost completely cured."

That point carried some weight because Miyoko was the *yuryokusha's* wife's niece.

"Also, yesterday she carried one of the lunch packs up to the men who were working at the lake and it weighed more than twenty-five kilos. No one got sick."

The inn, sturdy as it was, shook under the impact of a massive blast and the doll maker turned pale. "Setsuko cannot live out there in this," he declared.

The manager came to him. "I know, Sensei, but think of this: it is now most likely that one of the families saw her and has taken her in. It is the only reasonable explanation. I am now most concerned for those who have gone to look for her: Kojima Sensei, Sutōramu San, and Majōri. They may be out in this holocaust and I fear for their lives. They have no protection except for a rope that Sutōramu San took with him. It was very intelligent of him, I think."

The older man thought very carefully. Then he seated himself once more, as though to prepare himself to accept the disaster that fate had thrust upon him. "It is my fault," he declared. "I did not explain to her the way that a typhoon can sometimes stop in the very middle. She did not disobey me; she thought that it was all over."

"I believe that that last part is true," the manager said.

"When I next go up to the temple, I will ask to be forgiven for my incompetence. I believe that it has cost my daughter her life, and she was a beautiful child. I can never atone for what I have done."

Because they were old friends, the manager put his hand on the *yuryokusha's* shoulder and gently massaged the muscles. "You blame yourself far too much," he declared. "There is one more thing I must say to you: when Majōri learned that Setsuko was missing, you saw how quickly, and with what determination, she went to look for her. She has put herself in great danger doing that.

I believe that Setsuko is in one of the houses; most likely the men found her there and they are presently with her. Tomorrow morning, or perhaps much sooner, they will bring her here."

Without turning his head or moving his body, Taminaka San spoke the terrible thought that had been on his mind. "While I was sitting with my son, Setsuko left us and went to the shrine room. It has occurred to me that when the storm apparently stopped, she may have tried to go to the temple. She is very devout; we have raised her that way. It is a long walk for her even in good weather. She would not know that the storm would return."

The manager could not think of anything to say because if the *yuryokusha* was right, then almost certainly he was also right that he had lost his daughter. And he would not be able to have another; his wife was past the time of bearing children. "There is a very good chance that she is in one of the houses," he offered.

"I do not think so. If she was, they would let me know. There are ways."

Miyoko came in bearing a tray. By some means the kitchen staff had managed to prepare tea. She dropped to her knees in a proper manner and set out the service. Then, when she looked up, Taminaka San saw that there were tears in her eyes. "Is there any news?" she dared to ask.

"We have heard nothing." He picked up his cup of tea, held it in his palm for a moment, and slowly revolved it to show regard for his host by admiring its design. Then, carefully, he drank. "Thank you," he said.

Midori came into the lobby. Unable to endure the tension that had been racking her, she had retired to one of the rooms in back and there she too had petitioned the Lord Buddha for His mercy. Out of conscience she had prayed for Setsuko first, because she was young and weak; then she had most fervently implored protection for Peter. She herself would have gone out to search, but the manager had restrained her. "There are enough," he had said.

"They will find her." At the time he had sincerely believed it himself.

As she sat down on the floor Midori did not ask for any news; she could read clearly the faces of the men, who had all but forgotten that she existed. "May I have the honor to prepare food for you?" she asked.

The manager relaxed a little and remembered that she was by far the best cook in Mitamura. If anyone could produce a satisfactory meal without a fire, she would be the one. Also it would give her something to do, and that she clearly needed. "Please," he replied.

Midori bowed and left quietly, her face concealing the emotions that were boiling within her.

As it grew dark in the inn, the fury of the outside gale did not seem to abate. Every few seconds the building continued to shake to its foundations and echoed with the fearful sounds of the storm. One of the maids appeared with candles. She set down a basin of water and put the candle holder in the middle. In that way, if the candle were to be blown or knocked over, the water would extinguish it. She lit the lobby as best she could and then silently withdrew.

After half an hour Midori reappeared with Miyoko, who was carrying a tray. Carefully she set out what she had prepared. "I have been able to provide some hot soup," she said. "I could not steam the rice, but I have made some *sushi* and vegetables. I hope that they will give you strength."

"I ask that you join us," the doll maker invited.

"I will eat when you have finished."

That was a proper reply and he appreciated her for it. This was a woman of breeding and good manners; he did not believe the rumors that were circulating concerning her and Sutoramu San. The clatter of old women seldom held much meaning.

He was raising the bowl of soup to his lips when a pounding

came on the outside door. The manager leapt forward and had it open within a few seconds.

Akitoshi was there. Despite his youth and strength, he had been savagely battered. There was blood over much of his rain-soaked face and his clothing had been almost torn from his body. He was visibly at the point of total exhaustion; the manager seized him and called out for immediate help. The *yuryokusha* was already there to untie the rope that was around his waist, then he took Kojima's other arm to help him inside. Midori came forward quickly, her hand in front of her lips, an urgent question on her face.

Only the heavy shelter that had been built around the entrance kept the furious gale from tearing the door off its hinges and blasting into the lobby.

Two maids and the young man who normally worked at the inn came running to give their support. As they did so, Marjorie appeared in the doorway. She seemed dazed: her clothing was in shreds, she was drenched in rain, and she was bleeding from many different places on her body. She was on her feet, but she did not appear to know where she was.

Miyoko reached her first, threw her arms around her in support, and began to comfort her in rapid Japanese. The other maid came to help as the young man unknotted the rope that was secured around her waist. As soon as they had her free, Miyoko ran for a *futon*, spread it out, and helped her down onto the lobby floor.

At the door Midori cried out; the others turned quickly to see Peter there, resting against the jamb as he fought for breath, and holding Setsuko in his arms.

The lobby was suddenly alive with action. Many hands helped Peter inside. Swiftly the door was closed behind him and secured while the desperately anxious doll maker bent over, trying to see his daughter. He attempted to take her away, but Peter's arms were locked around her in a grip that would not be broken.

Still standing, Peter breathed deeply for a full two minutes, all but unaware that Midori had thrown her arms around him and was crying on his shoulder. As he began to recover himself, she bent down and carefully removed what was left of his shoes for him. The manager undid the rope and waited to see what else he could do.

Slowly Peter looked around him. He shook his head as if to clear it, then, quite calmly and unemotionally, he set Setsuko down.

As she stood there, blinking to force the excess water out of her eyes, the *yuryokusha* knew for the first time that his daughter was still alive. He spoke her name and waited, as though he was afraid to move.

Setsuko saw him and then began to realize where she was. She came forward a few timid steps, dropped respectfully to her knees, and bowed before her father.

The doll maker swept her up into his arms; he was a different man as he cradled her and spoke softly into her ear. Peter continued to stand, reorienting himself and getting his normal breath back into his lungs. Then he realized that Midori had her arms locked around him and that she was crying.

As gently as he could he released her, then he looked into her face and tried to smile. As soon as he had done that he dropped to one knee, bent over Marjorie, and asked, "How are you?"

She was lying on her stomach to protect her bleeding back, her head in her arms. "Just don't ask me for the next dance," she answered.

Akitoshi slowly got to his feet, his face still a mask of bleeding. He allowed Miyoko to take off what remained of his shirt without giving the matter any thought. He looked at the *yuryokusha* and said in Japanese, "I hope that she is all right."

The older man lowered his head. "I owe you my life and all that I have."

"You owe me nothing; I had the smallest part. For the saving of your daughter, it is Marjorie that you have to thank."

The doll maker did not seem to grasp that, his mind was intent on his next question. "Did Setsuko try to go up to the temple?"

"Yes, Taminaka San, she did. In some way Marjorie reasoned that out and went up the mountain after her. Alone."

"Did she know . . . the thing we have all kept from everyone?"

"Yes, she did. But that did not deter her."

"And after the typhoon had come back?"

"Yes, in the face of its full, terrible fury. It was an act of the utmost raw courage; I have never known anything like it in my life."

The *yuryokusha* bowed his head.

"Storm San and I searched the village until we knew definitely that Setsuko was not here," Kojima continued. "We were aware that the only other place she could have gone was up the mountain toward the temple. We tied ourselves together with the rope and attempted to follow. Storm San is a man of great physical strength and intense determination, but it was all that he could do, on his hands and knees, to withstand the terrible winds. I succeeded only because of his support and help. He is utterly fearless. I cannot possibly understand how Marjorie alone ever made her way so far up the mountain; it was a superhuman achievement."

"But where was Setsuko?"

"Somewhere above the lake. It was a very long way."

"She was on the path?"

"I do not know. You must understand, Sensei, that it was Marjorie who found her; she is the one who went highest and recovered your daughter. The blessing of Buddha must have guided her every inch of the way."

The old man began silently to shake. "Go on," he said softly.

"We were already above the lake when we found them. Marjorie had Setsuko, and was attempting to bring her down off the mountain under conditions impossible to imagine. She had been crawling forward on the ground, somehow holding your daughter in her arms. That is why she is so badly lacerated. The storm at that time was terrible; I do not know how either of them survived, for we barely did ourselves, and we are men."

Kojima let some seconds pass in silence, then he spoke as gently as he could. "Your nephew was also out in the storm. While trying to save your daughter, he was hit by a great stone rolling down the mountain. He protected her with his own body. I have the honor to tell you that despite his affliction, he died the death of a hero. At his last moment he rose to the highest tradition of the samurai; I bow with greatest respect before his memory."

The *yuryokusha*'s eyes filled with tears. "Can this be true?" he asked.

Akitoshi bowed. "It is indeed true, sensei. His body was close to where we found Marjorie and your daughter. Marjorie was tortured almost out of her mind by the frightful storm, but in her daze she asked us to help him. Even though she must have known that he was dead."

The *yuryokusha* looked up and asked a perfectly serious and deeply felt question. "Could she be a reincarnation of a Japanese?"

"It is very likely, sensei; some great heroine of the past. And your nephew: when the supreme test came, I believe that his mind returned so that he might rise to the greatest heights that a Japanese samurai can achieve. He gave his life in defense of the innocent."

He did not really believe that, but the words were words of comfort to a man who have been constantly pained by dreadful knowledge for a long time. He looked into the face of the man who for all of his life had lived by, and believed in, the deep-seated traditions of Japan, and hoped that his fiction, by the blessing of Buddha, might not be fiction at all. To speak well of the dead was never wrong.

As Akitoshi ended his account, Miyoko knelt beside him and

held out a small tray with tea. Complete gentleman that he was, he bowed his thanks and then waited for Taminaka Sensei to be given a fresh cup.

The *yuryokusha* himself felt the urgent need for the strengthening beverage. Nevertheless he waited, and then asked with a voice that he could hardly control why Peter and Majōri had not yet been served.

The inn did the very best that it could under the circumstances and gave a very good account of itself. A way was devised in the kitchen to heat a limited quantity of water. The bath could not be considered, but basins were prepared and rushed in for medicinal use. Of those who had been out in the fury of the storm, little Setsuko appeared to be in the best condition; all that she really appeared to require was the total comfort and reassurance of her father's arms. She had some abrasions and both of her knees were raw, but she seemed immune to the discomfort. Safe and forgiven, the horror she had so recently been through was beginning to lose its power to terrify her.

She told her father how she had believed that her prayers had been answered and that she had not willingly disobeyed him in going outside. She had gone to give thanks to the Lord Buddha and had loved the beautiful calm He had sent until the sudden return of the full force of the frightful typhoon had engulfed her in a torrent of slamming winds and the screams of the demons that had created that awful weapon of destruction.

She had seen the wild man and he had seen her. He had come lurching at her and even the storm had not been able to stop him. When he had seized hold of her it had been the most frightful moment of her life, but then he had tried to protect her. He had lain down on the ground and had wrapped his body around hers so that the awful wind was kept away. She had been frightened and she had kept her head down and her eyes closed, so she had not seen the boulder that had come bounding down. She had known when it had hit him, but he had not even cried out, he simply lay very still after that. She had been terrified of the frightful storm and she had not dared to move. She did not know how long she had lain there until Lord Buddha had sent Majōri to save her.

She looked up at her father, wide-eyed, to see if her true account was being believed. She was immensely reassured when her father nodded gravely, accepting everything that had been told him so far.

Immediately she launched into the rest of her account.

When Majōri had come, the demons had unleashed their wildest fury, but they had not been able to destroy her, because Lord Buddha had blessed her and given her part of His own strength. With Majōri she had started back and it had been terrible until Peta had come with Kojima Sensei and they had tied themselves all together and Kojima Sensei had told her in Japanese that it was going to be all right now and together they had started back down the mountain, but because the wind was so terrible and the demons so furious they had had to crawl on their hands and knees most of the time and she did not know how long it had been because it had turned all dark, but Peta San had carried her and Kojima Sensei had supported Majōri until at last they had reached the top of the village and then she had known that they were going to be safe because Lord Buddha had helped them all of the way and her only mistake had been in thinking too soon that the typhoon was over. Now she was hungry.

Her father put her down at her request so that she could go and look after Majōri. Her resilience was astonishing as she almost ran into Marjorie's room to watch gravely as Miyoko bathed her friend's back very gently in warm water to take away the dirt and all of the dried blood. None of the color came off, but Setsuko had not expected that it would. She did not care, that was Majōri's complexion and she did not see that it made any real difference.

As Peter Storm lay on the *futon* in the room that the inn had provided for him, he was quite content to do nothing and to let Midori take care of him. He felt the welcome warmth of the hot water she used to clean his abrasions and reveled in the touch of her gentle fingers as she carefully massaged the muscles of his arms and legs. It had almost been worth going out into the storm to have an aftermath like this.

After more than an hour of her ministrations, he sat up and put his arms into the *yukata* that she held for him. A little unsteadily he got to his feet and made his way into the lobby to see how the others were doing. He found the *yuryokusha* there. The older man came and stood before him, then he bowed, very calmly and very low. No words could be spoken and none were necessary. As best he could, Peter bowed in return and then, not certain if it was the right thing to do or not, he held out his hand.

Understanding that this was the way of Western etiquette, Taminaka San took it and despite the aversion to physical contact that was part of his culture, he was glad to feel the warmth of the man to whom he owed so much.

Food had been set out and was waiting. With swift skill Midori prepared a plate for Peter, arranging each portion so that it would be part of an attractive-appearing whole. Peter ate, and was refreshed. When he had finished he spoke briefly with Akitoshi, who had just come to take his own dinner, and then went in to see how Marjorie was doing.

She was lying very quietly on her *futon*, a half-finished bowl of soup beside her. Miyoko was still close beside her, attending to her needs. She obviously needed rest more than anything else, so he left her alone.

When he returned to his own room, two *futons* had been spread out on the floor. If that was the way that the inn wanted to do things, he had no objection. Helen of Troy would have been no enticement to him that night. Since he had no pajamas there, he crawled into the *futon*, *yukata* and all, pounded the pillow into the desired shape, and resigned from all human concerns for the next twelve hours.

When at last the great typhoon had ceased venting its fury at Mitamura and the neighboring countryside, and had moved out over the sea, the farmers of the village emerged from their homes and began to assess the damage that had been done. The rice crop had been terribly battered, but the stalks had still been supple enough to allow a considerable percentage of them to survive. There was a loss, but due to the intensive sandbagging, most of the paddy walls were intact and the crop that remained was sufficient to insure against economic disaster.

In bright summer sunlight the work of reconstruction began. Midori's house, like the others, still stood substantially unharmed; the men who had built it so many years ago had known a great deal about typhoons and they had employed their knowledge successfully. Bruised and sore, Marjorie was back on the job, most often sitting before her typewriter preparing her notes and turning out copy for Peter to review and revise.

The work of removing all of the sandbags was a massive task, but the pressure of time had been relieved and within three days it had been done. The farm wives had been in the paddies during almost all of the daylight hours, straightening plants that had fallen over, splitting clusters to fill the gaps that had been torn in the neat rows, and cleaning up the broken stalks that were beyond saving.

Life in Mitamura returned rapidly to an even keel with one notable change: wherever Marjorie went, when she left her writing to pick up some alternate task, she was made welcome. The people of the village no longer considered her to be *kokujin*, or *hakojin* either, for that matter: they considered her to be Japanese. Clearly she had been that in a previous incarnation, and she would return again.

Peter had very nearly completed his work and was close to returning home. He had written to Archer Bancroft about the suggestion that Akitoshi had made and had received back a prompt and enthusiastic reply that was very like the man who had sent it. "In case you do not already know, and I presume that you do," Peter read to Marjorie from the letter, "Kojima is widely regarded as one of the truly outstanding young artists of Japan. His work is currently showing in Rome, where it is receiving an excellent reception. I think it is your extreme good fortune to have fallen in with him."

Marjorie looked up at him then in a very significant way. "I'll second that," she said.

Peter was not surprised; disregarding differences in origin they were well matched — he the sensitive, brilliantly talented artist; she the woman with full appreciation of his gifts and with a great deal to add to them of her own. She was one hell of a person and whoever did marry her would have himself a fantastic wife.

When Akitoshi returned to the inn with his equipment, he took Peter aside. "I have some news for you," he said. "While my English is not very good, I have read what Marjorie has written about your work here and I think that it is very good. My publisher friend will like it, I am sure, if your foundation will permit."

"It will," Peter assured him. "Bancroft took care of that. There is no problem at all."

"Excellent. I am most happy. Now, Peter, tonight the men of the village are going to have a party. Here at the inn, in celebration of the passing of the typhoon and the fact that its destruction was not as great as was expected. You have been invited."

"Then I'll come," Peter said.

"Good. You will have a fine time and you will get very drunk."

"I'll certainly have a good time. About getting drunk . . ."

Akitoshi raised a hand to stop him. "At a party like this, everyone gets drunk. It is expected of you. If you do not feel that way, then it will be necessary for you to pretend to, do you understand?"

"In other words, I get drunk regardless."

"That is correct. If you know any improper songs, prepare to sing them. They will not understand the words, but as long as they know that it is . . . how do you say . . . sexy, they will be delighted."

"I can't sing," Peter declared.

"Tonight you will sing. Everyone will sing."

"How about Marjorie?"

"She will have dinner at Midori's house. Also invited are Miyoko and Setsuko. It will be what you call a chicken party."

"Hen party," Peter corrected.

"Of course, my poor English again. At this party, Peter, you will be welcomed as a member of this village. No one will say this formally, but the meaning will be there."

"I'm honored."

"Fine. After the party, you can stay here or go home and sleep with Midori."

"You mean in her house."

"My English is not that bad, Peter. I observed how she cared for you after the storm. She is in love with you."

"Toshi, for her sake let me explain that I have not been sleeping with her."

Akitoshi showed a slight evidence of impatience. "Peter, for the sake of our friendship, which I so highly value, stop being an American and become sensible. Also you should know that the *yuryokusha* is planning to marry her off; he has been checking with all of the neighboring villages that are in the correct directions. Her present condition is unnatural and also she cannot survive indefinitely with no satisfactory income. So do the honorable thing and sleep with her while you can."

"It's an attractive thought," Peter admitted.

"I am glad that you are coming to your senses. Now tonight remember one thing: it would be best if you become Japanese at the party. I am sure you can accomplish it now."

Peter turned that advice over in his mind as he walked outside and once more looked over the rice paddies, glinting in the sun as the standing water between the stalks reflected back its brilliance. He did love the village of Mitamura; he knew every house in it now, and most of the people. There were other communities close by, because there is almost no such thing as privacy in Japan, but Mitamura managed to live its own life nevertheless.

So they were going to take him in as a citizen, even if very informally. That was good, because he returned the compliment in full. He regretted that he would not be here to take part in the harvest. He wanted to experience the reward for so much hard work when the grain was at last gathered in. He had helped to plant it and to protect it, and part of it, it seemed, was indirectly his.

His life had expanded here to a whole new set of dimensions. He felt himself a part of a different culture. He had learned a great deal about the growing of rice. He had made what he hoped would be a lifetime friend in Akitoshi. He had cast off many of the academic confinements that too much living on a campus had instilled. He had acquired a profound and deep regard for Marjorie, and he was not ashamed of the word love. God, what a woman she was!

And Midori . . . Midori with her gentleness, her understanding, her courage, and, yes, her beauty. Akitoshi had said that she was in love with him. Possibly that was so because she had been so lonely until he had come. Then he remembered her face, and the way that she had looked at him as they had lain together on the kitchen floor while the awful typhoon had raged over their heads. She had been terribly frightened, but there hadn't been a whimper out of her.

Peter looked up into the sky and prayed. "Thank you, God," he said, "for bringing me here."

Then he set out on the errand he had to do.

Chapter Nineteen

Accustomed as they were to adapting themselves to meet a wide variety of circumstances and requirements, the staff of the inn had shifted panels so as to provide a single large room where most of the male population of the village could be seated on cushions around a single, large composite table. Four maids were assigned to provide service and were put into working kimonos for the occasion. An ample supply of food was prepared and a substantial quantity of sake was readied for heating.

Not long after the last of the daylight had faded from the sky the farmers began to arrive, each one entering the lobby as though the inn were a place where he had never been before. Every one of the guests had had his evening bath and had put on his suit, complete with collar and tie, in order to complete the illusion that the workaday world of Mitamura was far removed from the forthcoming event.

Within half an hour all of the men had come and had been shown to their places by the kimono-clad waitresses, who, in at least two instances, were their daughters. Peter and Akitoshi joined the party when they felt that the time was appropriate and sat down with a proper spirit of camaraderie to share in the festivities.

The food was brought in with a suitable amount of ceremonial bustle and activity, the manager of the inn personally directing where certain of the dishes were to be placed. It was to a considerable degree play-acting, but all of the participants appeared to be enjoying it to the fullest. When the meal had been been well begun, a stocky woman who resided two villages away appeared carrying a samisen. She seated herself at one end of the room, tuned her three-stringed instrument, and then began to play — plunking the dry-sounding notes with a spade-shaped device held in her right hand.

Conversation picked up as soon as the music began and continued at a higher level thereafter. By common unexpressed consent, the omnipresent subject of the rice crop was for this one evening set aside in favor of other topics. Although Akitoshi did not attempt to translate everything that was being passed down the long table, Peter was able to sense much of it and to the best of his abilities, he joined in the proceedings.

The samisen player continued to pluck away, a fixed smile frozen on her face, while she professed not to hear anything that was being said. As the tiny sake cups were filled and refilled, the mood continued to build. Peter tried the warm rice wine and thought it mild, unaware that it was one of the most deceptively potent drinks in the world. It did loosen him up considerably, and as he continued to eat, he reflected that if he got nothing else out of his Japanese experience, he had definitely learned to eat with chopsticks. He handled them expertly now, not even aware of the way he was manipulating them.

His newly acquired skill was noted and commented upon, accompanied by much laughter. As he looked at the ruddy-faced men around him, Peter felt that he had earned his place with them. They could not teach his classes, but when it came to rice farming, they were true professionals worthy of his respect. When the waitresses had withdrawn, the conversation became more earthy and the laughter was frequent. From across the table a broad-shouldered grinning farmer put a question to Peter in Japanese. At once the entire table erupted in fresh laughter.

"He is asking if it is true that your penis is twice as big as Japanese men," Akitoshi translated. Then, in Japanese, he announced Peter's answer. A fresh burst of laughing followed and someone raised a toast.

"What did you tell them?" Peter asked.

"I said that you were three times the size of Japanese men and that if they didn't believe it, they should ask their wives."

Peter himself laughed heartily and responded to the toast. He held his hands ten inches apart and even the samisen player burst out in gold-toothed laughter.

Akitoshi then announced his decision to paint all of the unmarried girls of the village together in the nude, the picture to be hung in the prefecture capitol.

Someone far down the table loudly suggested that to make his work easier, he should paint only the virgins. And, of course, he would be best qualified to state who was eligible.

In that case, Akitoshi responded, his picture would have to be a landscape.

Across from Peter a farmer got to his feet. His face was almost rectangular and so weatherbeaten that his eyes seemed to be mere slits on each side of his small nose. He tottered slightly, then, after composing himself, he began to sing.

His song was pitched high up on the scale, so much so that the tessitura was almost in the falsetto range, but the tones he produced conjured up the Japan of the olden days so that even Peter understood and felt their meaning. The samisen player joined him immediately, supporting and supplementing the timeless melody that was full of augmented seconds and some intervals unknown to Western notation. He sang for almost five minutes and when he had finished, he was greeted by enthusiastic applause.

Another farmer arose, unbidden, drank an additional cup of

sake, and began a *nagaota*, the almost tuneless song form of Japan that carries its message through nuances and intervals. It went on for more than ten minutes and although he had never heard a song like it, Peter understood that it was a far more refined composition than it sounded. At times the singer seemed to be wailing, but the sharp punctuation of the samisen gave it added body and strength. It was a mood piece as evocative as Ravel's *Le Gibet*, and created much of the same atmosphere.

It came to Peter then that he had a new facet to his mission — to discover what the ancient culture of Japan had to contribute to the rest of the world. There was so much of it: the martial arts with their philosophy and severe discipline, Kabuki and the Noh play, the music, the literature, even the ability to extract three full tons of rice from a single acre of paddy land during one growing season.

The *nagaota* singer finished to applause and a toast for his efforts. Akitoshi then stood up, closed his eyes, and began to sing of the rain in the streets of old Edo. Despite the entirely foreign nature of his song, Peter knew at once that he was a very good singer; the strange intervals and sliding tones were beginning to make sense to him.

He listened intently until Akitoshi had finished, then he joined in the applause with sincere enthusiasm. His friend was forced to do an encore. When the room was again quiet, he began a very simple melody that was magnetic in its appeal; as the artist sang of the moon shining on a ruined castle a whole new mood took over the party. The samisen once more underlined the melody and as he listened, Peter knew that he was in love — with Japan.

When Akitoshi sat down to enthusiastic applause, Peter grasped his hand. "Wonderful!" he said.

"It is a very simple thing, Peter, but very beautiful. *Kojo no tsuki*. I will teach it to you if you would like."

Someone down the table shouted something. "It is now your turn to sing," Akitoshi told Peter.

"I told you, I can't."

"Stand up and sing. And remember to be a little drunk. You must."

Peter arose, feeling at that moment that he was absurdly tall. The only song for which he knew all the words was "Home on the Range." As a boy he had had a favorite record of it by John Charles Thomas that he had played almost to destruction. Fortunately it called for only a limited range and if he was compelled to perform, then that would have to be it.

He began as best he could, highly conscious of his vocal limitations, but after the first three or four bars he sensed that they made little difference. His confidence grew, and so did his rendition of the familiar cowboy song. As he paused a moment to draw breath, he realized that the samisen player was accompanying him. He looked quickly at her and received a wide, gap-toothed smile in return. She knew it!

Abandoning caution he delivered the second verse with style and verve; when he sat down the applause told him that he was the hit of the evening.

Akitoshi shook his arm. "More!" he demanded. "They insist on it."

Peter stood up again and remembered that he did know one more song. It had never been recorded as far as he knew, but it *was* widely known in its own field. And none of the farmers gathered around understood any English.

He drained a cup of sake in one swallow and thus lubricated, he began in a lusty voice: "Now minstrels sing of an English king who lived so long ago . . ."

The samisen player was compelled to wait and listen, but two bars into the second verse she was with him and accompanied his song the rest of the way through.

Peter received an ovation. It was repeated after Akitoshi explained in Japanese that it was the most famous ribald song in the English language. He capped that climax by announcing that it was grossly disrespectful to the highest level of distant authority. At that the enthusiastic villagers stopped applauding and cheered.

Peter slept in the inn that night. He was not at all sure that he would be able to reach Midori's house under his own power, and he would not trust himself if he did get there. Through long experience and admirable foresight, the inn had laid out a *futon* for him and had made all the other preparations. Peter undressed in a half-conscious state and blissfully went to sleep.

When Marjorie returned from her evening out, she looked in on him and read the truth with sure instinct. She tucked him in and then, without his knowing it, gave him a good-night kiss.

She also checked on Akitoshi and found that the artist had a formidable ability to hold his liquor; he was awake when she came in and he sat up to welcome her. "Where are you going to sleep tonight?" he asked.

"Where do you want me to?"

He pointed to the second *futon* that the inn, also with the aid of long experience and admirable foresight, had already provided beside his own.

As Marjorie Saunders sat, the pain in her legs was excruciating. But despite her acute discomfort, she was totally determined that she would not reveal that fact by any outward sign. The Japanese could sit on the floor with their feet folded under them apparently for hours, but they started at a very young age. Her own feet refused to bend backward far enough to lie perfectly flat on the tatami mat and her knees were totally unaccustomed to the sharp bend that she was demanding of them now. As she suffered, she wondered whether the fact that so many Japanese girls had relatively short legs, and frequently crooked ones, was a direct result of hundreds of hours of sitting in what was to her a thoroughly unnatural position.

As she sat now, Marjorie's back was straight and her hands rested properly on her knees. She felt that by making a supreme effort she could endure it for another three or possibly four minutes, after that she would have to have some relief.

Across from her the *yuryokusha* sat in the same manner, apparently with complete comfort, but he had noticed the unavoidable perspiration that stood out on her brow. To Marjorie's right little Setsuko sat with a happy smile on her face and remained properly still. Opposite her, and completing the foursome, Hiroshi was so stiffly formal that Marjorie thought it a trifle comic. But no one else did, so she rejected the improper thought.

The *yuryokusha* spoke and Hiroshi translated. "Taminaka San asks if you would be more comfortable sitting another way. He realizes that your manners are beautiful, but he thinks that you are in pain."

"He is right," Marjorie acknowledged. "Don't tell him that, but ask if I may have his permission to change."

When the translation had been made the doll maker nodded his head and called out a command. Seconds later a pillow was brought in and offered to Marjorie. She could hardly get up; her legs were already cramped. After a few moments she did manage to move into a new position, with her legs beside her, that was like the balm of Gilead; it was hardly comfortable, but it was not agonizing. She bowed her thanks for her host's consideration and then waited while the tea was brought in and served. She accepted her cup quietly, but within her a fierce flame of satisfaction burned brightly and warmed her whole being.

Again the *yuryokusha* spoke and Hiroshi obliged. "Taminaka San expresses to you his great pleasure that you are honoring his home."

"Tell him that it is a lovely home and that I am glad to be here."

Turning to his dignified host, Hiroshi translated. "Miss Saunders San states that the great honor is entirely hers and that she will never forget that so humble a person as herself has been permitted to sit in your presence."

The doll maker lifted his tea cup as a sign of approval. Despite the fact that she came from a foreign country noted for its extreme crudity, and that she was *kokujin,* the young woman before him obviously had excellent instincts and breeding. He now accepted the fact that her father was a famous and skilled physician. He had misjudged her.

Proudly Setsuko raised her own cup, basking in her father's approval of her friend. She gave inward thanks that Majōri had known exactly the right thing to say, but it was no more than she had expected of her.

The tea was consumed in relative silence. Marjorie drank hers still wishing that she could have a little lemon and sugar, but knowing that such additions were unthinkable under the circumstances, even if they had been available. She still had not come to like tea, but she had read somewhere that the Tibetans drank a minimum of at least thirty cups a day, all flavored with rancid yak butter, and at least she had not had to face up to that.

When she had finished, her host set his cup down and clapped his hands in a manner that revealed his authority in his own home. His son appeared carrying in his hands a doll masterpiece. It was a samurai warrior, much larger and more splendid that the usual product of the *yuryokusha's* studio, and detailed to an almost unbelievable degree. When it was carefully set onto the tatami mat, Marjorie was fascinated. It was the most magnificent creation of its kind that she had ever seen; it almost breathed life and the whole of the culture and tradition of Japan was encased in its twenty inches of height.

She bent toward it and spoke. This time as Hiroshi put her words into Japanese, he had no need to improve them. "Miss Saunders states that it is so magnificent, it could only have come from your hand."

The *yuryokusha*, the master craftsman who had been formally proclaimed a living treasure of Japan, bowed. "It is a poor effort that I made some years ago. I have kept it until now because, with all of its limitations, it is the best that I have ever done."

When that had been translated, Marjorie replied quite simply and accurately. "It is a priceless masterpiece," she said.

"I ask now," the *yuryokusha* stated formally, "that you accept it as an unworthy small remembrance from myself in appreciation for what you did for my daughter."

Marjorie was beginning to get into form; she bowed as low as her position would permit. "I am totally unworthy to receive it," she said.

Beaming, Hiroshi translated that verbatim.

"It is yours, and with it please accept my everlasting gratitude."

Hiroshi was enormously impressed to see a man of such stature humble himself this way before a female, but it could be considered another indication of his greatness.

Still maintaining the same state of formality that the occasion called for, Marjorie spoke once more. "Since it is of such incomparable value, may I have the benefit of your guidance on how to pack it? I will carry it in my own hands back to America, but I want it to have the maximum protection. My father will be overwhelmed when he sees it."

When the translation had been done, the son spoke for the first time. "I will pack it for you. It is my father's finest effort."

"It must be — and it will forever be my proudest possession."

Ten minutes later Marjorie left the house of the doll maker with proper ceremony and turned to walk back down to the inn. She had left the superb doll behind her to be packed, but in imagination she held it in her hands and her heart overflowed. She suddenly loved all of humanity; most of all, the people of Mitamura.

Her whole being was singing as she neared the inn; the song grew brighter when she saw that Akitoshi was waiting for her. "You have been to the house of the *yuryokusha*," he said.

"Yes! And he gave me a magnificent doll; it must be this high." She showed him with her hands.

"I know the one you mean. It is his masterpiece; he has kept it himself for many years."

"Toshi, it was far too much for him to give me; is there any way . . ."

Kojima shook his head before she had finished. "No, Marjorie, you must accept. And because it is a gift to thank you for saving his daughter, nothing should be offered in return. It is yours. Keep it and treasure it — it is very valuable."

"I know."

It seemed to her that the sun had never shone in the sky with such clear brilliance. She felt that she would like to stay outside where her spirit would have all the room that it needed to expand and grow, but when he asked if she would come inside, she complied gladly.

He led the way to his room. "Peter now has one of my paintings," he began, "the one that the Nodas gave him of their daughter. He has been kind enough to say that he intends to keep it always. The picture that I did of you is far less worthy than Tamanaka San's magnificent warrior doll, but I did it with the thought that it should be yours."

She drew breath to speak, but he silenced her with a gesture. "You have already given me so much, it is far too little to offer in return. But if it would not be too much bother to take it home . . ."

"Bother!" At first she was overjoyed, but then something else forced itself into her mind and she knew that she would not be able just to push it aside. "Let's talk," she invited.

"All right." He dropped two cushions onto the tatamis and sat down on one of them, his legs crossed in front of him.

A little self-consciously, Marjorie took the other. She folded her hands in her lap and this time tried hard to forget what color they were. "The last time that we slept together, you said some very kind things to me."

Akitoshi nodded. "I know. And I meant them."

"Toshi, in a few days we'll be leaving Mitamura, because our work will be finished. But this village is a part of me now; I've got friends here I'll never forget. Someday I'm coming back."

"Everybody will be happy to know that."

"If so, it's because of you."

He searched her face in honest bewilderment. "I don't understand," he told her.

"Because you accepted me as a person when no one else here would. If you hadn't, it would have been impossible for me to have stayed and worked here."

He reached out and took her hand. "Marjorie, please . . ."

"Let me finish." She looked directly at him, face to face. "I've met quite a few men in my life, men of different backgrounds, but of all of them, there isn't one who even comes close to you. I don't think that there's a girl anywhere you couldn't have if you really wanted her."

Akitoshi laughed. "Marjorie, that's ridiculous! In the first place, many people don't like Japanese, some even hate us. Millions think that we're subhumans because our eyes are different."

That made her angry. "Did you ever really look at yourself? In the first place, you're damn good-looking. That's only on the surface, but it's still important to a lot of people. You've got a fantastic talent, and you know how to use it. But those aren't the big things.

When it comes to the basics that make a man a man, you're on top of the pile, and I don't mean sex."

"You're imagining things," he told her.

She ignored that. "The way you carried those sandbags, hour after hour; the way you and Peter came up the mountain after Setsuko and me. All the things you did for me. No wonder I wanted to go to bed with you! Not just for sex, but because I wanted to feel that for a little while, at least, I was part of you. Now do you understand?"

"Have you considered the fact that you have been far from home, and perhaps lonely?"

She looked at him with fresh pride in her face. "I'm quite old enough to know my own mind. I tend to be very selective, I'm made that way, but you knew that you weren't the first."

"Of course not, but it makes no difference."

"Thank you. Now, will you forget your Japanese customs and manners for a few moments?"

"If you want me to."

For a few seconds she dropped her head so that he couldn't look into her eyes, because the tears were very close. Her throat constricted at the thought that it was almost over when it had really only just begun. And what barriers there were between them — barriers that had no right to be between a man and a woman — had been put there by other people, prim in their smugness, who didn't even know that the barriers existed — or how she felt.

"You can make of this whatever you want," she said, "but in plain, unadulterated English . . . dammit, can't you see that I'm in love with you!"

She was infinitely glad when he took her in his strong arms and pressed her body against his; it was the thing she wanted most in the whole world and nothing — nobody — had been able to prevent it.

When he started to speak, she laid a finger across his lips. Then she spoke to him, very softly, because his ear was so close to her lips. "More than anything else in my life, I wish I could take you home with me and shout before the world: look, here is my husband! Or else stay here in Japan, and be your wife. That's how I feel, and I don't care if I'm not supposed to say so."

Then, deliberately she placed her hands against his chest and gently pushed him away. "Toshi, I can't have it, and I know it. I just wanted to tell you how I feel — that's all."

He kept his hands locked behind her waist so that the contact between them was not broken. "You said that you're old enough to know your own mind. Well, so am I. And I make quite a good living."

She reached out and put her palms against the side of his face. "You were wonderful — the way that you backed me up here, but in your career, a *kokujin* wife would ruin you. Hiroshi told me all about your family: how important your people are. If I became your wife, I know that they would be very good and kind to me, for your sake, but I would know all the time how hard it would be for them."

A maid interrupted them; she came in with tea and bean cakes that the manager had sent with his compliments. She set the refreshments out carefully on the low table and then ventured to smile before she withdrew. After she had gone, Akitoshi closed the inner shoji so that they would not be disturbed.

Automatically Marjorie played hostess. She poured the tea and served the cakes with just the right touch of Japanese formality. The break was good for her; by the time they were sipping the tea, some of the tension had run out of her, but she was not ready to drop the subject. "Toshi, have you ever been in my country?" she asked.

"No, not yet. But I hope to soon."

"Good. I'd like to have you meet my father. And my mother,

too, of course, but that's dangerous because she has me completely outclassed and she looks about twenty-five."

"I would expect her to be a lovely person."

"You won't be disappointed."

Akitoshi pulled her down onto their cushions once more, then he hitched his over so that they were side by side. "Tell me, do you think that your father would accept me?" he asked. "So many people don't like Japanese."

She took that seriously. "Of course he will!" She took his hand once more. "Naturally he prefers my friends to be . . . from our own social group, but whoever I bring around is always welcome." She became a little more intense. "Understand, Toshi, all he really wants is to be sure that I don't get hurt. With you, that would be impossible."

"I'm glad," he said. He stretched out and then pulled her down with him. She came willingly, glad to lie beside him and share the wonderful thing they had in common. She felt his presence through every inch of her body and it was fulfillment; she would have been content to stay that way forever. They might be social misfits in the eyes of some of her countrymen, but at that moment they were a man and a woman.

Akitoshi slid his arm under her pillow and thereby took possession of her. "What are you afraid of?" he asked.

"I know a girl. She's intelligent, very attractive, and has a terrific personality. But her father was an American black G.I. Her mother is Japanese. She doesn't belong anywhere."

"I understand," Akitoshi said. "The *ainoko* have a very hard time. But it will not always be that way."

He saw that she was beginning to cry; he wiped her eyes dry and then kissed her gently on the lids. "Let's start at the beginning," he proposed. "We are going to remain very close friends if nothing more. Do you agree?"

"If we don't, I'll cry my eyes out."

"Then we're friends — say a little more than that."

"A lot more."

"Absolutely. Now you go back to America and in a little while, perhaps the images you have of Japan will begin to dim. Things sometimes work that way. And I will go back to Tokyo . . ." he quirked a half smile ". . . and the captivating Japanese girls. Some of them are quite fascinating."

"I know!"

"That will please both of our families; at least for the time being."

She seized hold of him, because they were long past the point of pretense, and when he responded with his own strong arms, the world reshaped itself.

"Toshi . . . Toshi . . . what will happen if we do this and then all we do is lie awake at night and think of each other?"

"I will come to America; there is a gallery in New York that has been pressing me for some time."

"Do!"

"I'll come. Meantime, while we're waiting for the world to catch up with us, if I buy a nice private island someplace, will you come and live on it with me?"

"Yes!"

He released her and got to his feet. "For the moment," he said, "just for the moment, I'll settle for that. The bath will be ready by now — coming?"

Marjorie got up and smoothed her clothing. "When I get home, the first thing I'm going to ask Dad for will be a Japanese bath in our house. It's the greatest thing since sliced bread."

He looked at her in mock disapproval. "Just to keep things straight," he declared, "the Japanese bath was invented a few centuries before sliced bread. You Americans, you have some funny ideas sometimes."

She put her arms around him once more. "I want to relax," she said, "and maybe dream a little."

His hand stroked her hair and enjoyed it. "Good. I'll meet you in five minutes."

Chapter Twenty

Peter Storm checked the sides of his suitcase to be sure that nothing was caught between the edges, closed it securely, and fastened the latches. When that was done he picked it up, hefted it, and set it down again on the tatami mat. He turned to Midori. "I have been very happy, here in your home," he said.

She bowed her head in reply. "Thank you, Peta."

Once more he looked around the small room that had been his home for the past several weeks. He had grown used to it. It was very simple and plain, but he had become attached to it none the less.

"May I go to the shrine?" he asked.

She was surprised by the request, but stepped to the north side of the room and slid back the panel. Ducking his head, Peter entered and stood before the little altar that Midori so faithfully maintained in her home. From his wallet he took out a ¥10,000 note and placed it with the other offerings. "For protection of this house during the great storm," he said.

Beside him Midori bowed her head once more. If he had offered her the extra money she would have refused, but an offering made in that manner was something else entirely. It would remain on the altar for several days as a symbol of his gratitude, then by default it would become hers. She could not refuse his tribute to the forces that had protected her home and it would be a great added help to her. Particularly now that he was leaving.

Peter led the way back into his own room, then he turned toward her. "You understand why I am moving to the inn. I must work with Marjorie very closely for the last two or three days — to be sure that we have everything that we need. I will see you again before we go."

"I understand, Peta."

"Good." Then he did the thing he had been waiting weeks for the right moment to make possible: he held out his arms halfway, not demanding, but inviting. Midori hesitated a small moment, then she came forward a half step. That was all that he needed; he gathered her in, held her, stroked her soft black hair, and looked down into her upturned, totally Japanese, completely appealing face. Then he kissed her.

Since they were entirely alone, he continued to hold her, simply letting the physical contact between them express some of the feelings that overflowed within him. Then he became aware that she was responding, tightening her own arms around his own body. He drew a great surging joy from that; he wanted kiss her again and he did. As he pressed his firm lips onto hers, he tried to tell her silently how he felt. The touch of her body was like magic to him, but he was wise enough not to ruin the wonderful moment; he released her and stepped backward, the better to look at her.

"If I come back to Mitamura, may I stay with you again?" he asked.

She smiled a little. "I lose face if you not."

"Then I will."

He slid open the outside panel and saw that the porter from the inn was coming. He set his suitcase out on the ground, checked once more that he had left nothing behind him, and then went outside for the last time. He turned and bowed. *"Iroiro ōsawani narimashita,"* he said.

This time Midori bowed very formally and replied in Japanese while her head was still down. He did not understand the words, but he knew their meaning. Then he waited for the porter. He could have carried his suitcase down to the inn very well himself, but he had been in Japan long enough to know not to break someone else's rice bowl.

He knew the path so well now that every little turn that it took was familiar to him; he knew all of the soft spots and the places where a root protruded. It was indeed like home to him.

When he reached the inn, Marjorie was in her room working at her typewriter. Peter took a few minutes to install himself in the room that had been provided for him, unpacking only those things that he would need for the next day or two. It was all strictly business now, and that was the way he wanted it.

When he had finished he went to Marjorie's room, piled some cushions on the tatami, and sat down with a thick stack of his accumulated notes.

If the inn personnel had had any curiosity concerning what was going on behind the closed panels of the *kokujin* girl's room, the steady clatter of the typewriter would have answered their questions. At noon Miyoko took them their lunch and dutifully reported back how hard they were working. It was a surprise to some that there was so much to report about simple little Mitamura, a community just like so many thousands of other villages and hamlets that were crowded together across the countryside of Japan. They did not consider themselves important at all, and they did not understand why anyone else would think any differently. People grew rice all over the world and it was the same backbreaking job everywhere, with the same risks and the same hope for a small profit if the crop was successful.

Hideko Watanabe, née Noda, had prepared dinner for guests, using her new oven and had created a mild sensation. A small delegation from the next village called on Peter with an invitation: when he had completed his studies in Mitamura, he would be welcome to repeat the process in their community if he so desired. There was no avarice in that; they had simply received word that he was a good man and they would be glad to assist him and his unusual wife.

Miss Noda, the schoolteacher, invited Marjorie to visit her classroom and teach English. The children had acquired a whole new desire to learn the language, inspired in part by Setsuko Taminaka who already could tell the time in the incredibly difficult tongue.

The inn was very hopeful that the publication of Peter's book, with the wonderful pictures by Kojima Sensei, would bring an influx of new visitors to see the village. Almost all of the traditional business had come from occasional transients and visitors who had come to see relatives in Mitamura or other nearby villages. Also the inn hoped that Kojima Sensei would not forget to include a picture of their very fine bath — the best for miles around.

The *yuryokusha*'s son had packed the splendid doll with great care and had delivered it personally to the inn. He had stopped to see the picture of Marjorie painted by Kojima and thought it wonderful. It was also his opinion that Marjorie had been Japanese in a previous incarnation; the signs and indications were all there.

It was all work for Peter and Marjorie now. They could have done much of it at home, but it flowed better on the scene and questions kept cropping up that could best be answered in Mitamura itself. Peter checked the calendar and allowed three more days; after that they would have to return home as promptly as possible. He was stretching it a bit even at that, but somehow writing about Mitamura in Mitamura had much to recommend it.

When the first hard day's work had been completed and it was time to think of the bath and dinner, Peter wondered where Akitoshi had been. When the artist returned, he did not have very much to say; he mentioned only that he had been visiting some of the neighboring villages in the company of Taminaka San, the doll maker. He seemed reticent and Peter did not press him for any further explanation.

On the evening of the second day after Peter had moved to the inn, Taminaka San, the *yuryokusha*, emerged from his home clad in his most formal black kimono. He was joined by two of his closest friends, older men who had been in the village for a long time, and together they went through the proper ritual of greeting. In his hands he carried a thin packet carefully wrapped in white paper. When the necessary preliminaries had been completed, he led the way for a short distance and then gravely stopped before the door of Midori's house.

According to custom, he opened the panel slightly and announced himself through the opening. When Midori appeared in response, she looked once quickly at the men gathered before her door and her heart dropped with a leaden impact.

She knew her obligation and there was no possible way to avoid it. She at once invited them in with full ceremony, apologizing for the unworthiness of her home, for its lack of good order, and for her own wretched appearance. Actually her small house was immaculate and while she had not been expecting visitors, she had hoped that Peter might come to see her. The simple *yukata* that she had on was, therefore, fresh and clean.

Her manners were perfect; the *yuryokusha* seated himself and assured her that since no call had been anticipated, her appearance was entirely satisfactory. Bowing with great respect, Midori begged permission to leave her guests long enough to prepare tea. When she had departed to perform that essential task, her guests remained sitting quietly, not even talking among themselves.

As she boiled the water, Midori tried desperately to think clearly, for she was certain that she was unexpectedly confronted by a momentous decision that she would have to make. Two months earlier it might have been easier, but now she had allowed herself to dream, and that was one of the most dangerous things that she could do.

She set out her best tea things and prepared everything very carefully. When she was ready, she carried a tray in to her guests with her face devoid of any emotion. Dropping to her knees, she placed the tea service on the low table and offered refreshment to each of the three men from that position. She did not presume to take anything herself; it was not her place to do that.

The *yuryokusha* accepted the tea and after waiting until his companions had been properly served, he raised the cup to his lips. Midori sat silently before him, waiting patiently to be informed why she had been paid this signal honor, and pretending that she had not already guessed.

When he was ready, Taminaka San spoke to her in the formal manner that the occasion demanded. "All of us here grieve with you over the tragic loss of your husband. By living alone as you have, maintaining his farm to the best of your ability, you have shown great respect for his memory. For this I would like to commend you."

Midori bowed her head to the floor in acknowledgement, but properly remained silent.

The *yuryokusha* continued. "You have now observed a most proper and suitable period of mourning, doing everything that was expected of you. Because we all have confidence in your good character, and being aware of your circumstances, we have permitted the American, Sutoramu San, to live here in your house for these past several weeks under conditions that might have been subject to some criticism. I must now ask you a question before I can go any further. Before I do, I wish to assure you that your answer will be kept as a secret of honor by each of us here; it will never under any circumstances be repeated to anyone. Have you, during the visit of your *gaijin* guest, still chosen to uphold the honor of your late husband?"

For one mad instant she wondered if she could escape what was inevitably coming by lying. It would destroy her reputation, but it could save her. At the same moment she realized that such a lie would also destroy the face and the honor of the man who had respected her so completely. Only one thing was possible: because she had been directly addressed, she replied truthfully with the fewest possible words. "Yes, I have."

"You are not then, possibly, expecting a child?"

"It cannot be."

The doll maker opened his fan and used it: a sign that her answers had been satisfactory. "Then there is no reason why an honorable man, true to the traditions of Japan, should not address himself to you?"

She could give only one answer. "No, sir, there is not."

"Then I inform you that I am here as *nakado*, to arrange a marriage for you. I bring you this very good news in the hope that it will warm your heart."

Midori bowed again.

"It has long been obvious that you cannot operate this farm alone; despite the fact that it is very small, it requires a man's hand. I have had this in mind for some time, but for reasons which I need not detail, it has not been an easy task to find a suitable match for you. Also the problem has been somewhat complicated by the fact that a man has been living here in this house for some weeks. I have taken it upon myself to vouch for your good character and proper behavior during this period."

"You overwhelm me with your kindness."

"We all realize that you must have a fresh source of income; you cannot continue indefinitely as you are. Your paying guest has provided a most generous temporary solution, but he is now about to leave. I have, therefore, been in communication with the proper people in certain nearby villages. In doing so, I have most carefully considered the matter of direction. I have been fully aware of the fact that you are not, due to your upbringing, an ideal farm wife, but against this I have cited the fact that you were a good wife to Taminaka San, may the Blessed One liberate him from all future suffering."

"You do me far too much honor."

"You are also a very good cook, and that too is in your favor."

The *yuryokusha* took time to finish his tea and declined the formal offer of a second cup. Then he continued. "A man has been suggested to me and I have investigated him. He has good farming skills. He is intelligent and hard-working. He has no bad habits. Because his appearance is not all that it might be, and because he did not inherit a farm of his own, he is without a wife. Those he has worked for speak well of him. Although he has not yet been shown a picture of you, because I did not have one to present, he is willing to accept you as his bride."

Carefully unwrapping the small white packet that he had laid on the mat before him, Taminaka San spread out the paper and revealed a face-down photograph. Then he straightened himself once more. "There is presently no one to inherit your farm. You cannot adopt a son, or possibly bear one, without a husband. I therefore bring to you the joyous opportunity to enter into an honorable marriage and end the unnatural state that you are now in."

Midori placed her hands on the mat before her and bowed until her forehead touched the straw. By the exercise of the greatest willpower that she could command, she kept her face impassive as etiquette required. "I cannot express the gratitude that overflows my heart," she stated formally. "I was unaware that you were doing me the very great honor of concerning yourself with my welfare. It is far beyond my poor ability to repay you."

She was trapped, and there was nothing whatever that she could do.

The *yuryokusha* returned her bow to the degree that was required and then with the end of his closed fan he pushed the picture toward her.

It was her fate and she could not escape it; the deep-seated traditions of Japan were inviolate and denied her any choice whatsoever. She was a widowed, unfortunate woman and therefore she would have to take what was offered; even the privilege of being alone if she wished was denied to her. Her dream, her precious dream, was snatched from her and crushed into the dust. But the discipline in which she had been reared supported her and helped her in her moment of greatest, bitterest need.

She placed her hands on the picture, turned it over, and saw the face of Peter Storm.

The overwhelming shock froze her body; she could not move a muscle. Her throat locked tight and she could hardly breathe. She tried to look up but she could not, because her eyes were suddenly overflowing with tears. Her body began to shake and she could not control it. She was utterly disgracing herself, but she was immune to the dishonor.

And then the wings came and lifted her up, raising her desperate and wonderful dream from the dust into which it had crumbled, and filling her with such life and stunning realization that her whole body turned to joy. Her spirit soared into the infinite glory of the sky and even there it could not find enough room.

She was still grasping for reality when the *yuryokusha* spoke once more. "In acceptance of my advice, he has left your house and is now living at the inn. Your place of residence is therefore almost exactly northwest of his, the most propitious possible direction. You could perhaps find him there now, if you so desire."

When she heard that she dared to look up, despite the disgrace of her tears, and to her utter amazement, the *yuryokusha* was gently smiling. With his folded fan he indicated the panel that led to the outside.

"Go," he said.

It was unthinkable to leave her guests; the prohibition was so strong that for a few seconds she could not move. Then the doll maker held out his hand to assist her. She took it as she had to and with that slight physical contact reality flooded into her; she got to her feet, bowed quickly to excuse herself, and pulled the panel wide.

Never before in her life had she ever run down the path to the lower level of the village and the inn, but even in the straw zoris that she had automatically slipped onto her feet, she managed. Her eyes were wide and wet and a great sense of disbelief surrounded her. It held her so completely that she did not see Peter waiting for her until she was almost upon him. He held out his arms and she fled into them.

"You want me?" she cried, "You really want *me?*"

"That's the general idea," Peter answered.

Her body shook with sobs as he held her. It was a good sign and he let her get it out of her system. All of the feelings and love for her that had been building up within him for so many weeks found their expression in the simple fact that she was in his arms and he knew that she belonged to him. There was no other woman anywhere else in the world; she was the only one possible. And every second that she was in his arms that knowledge grew and expanded until she was his whole life and she always would be, forever and ever, amen.

When she began to show signs of recovery he produced a handkerchief. She used it to wipe her eyes and then the top part of her face. She swallowed twice, very hard, and then looked up at him, still unbelieving.

All of her limitations began to parade themselves before her eyes to torment her. The very first one mocked her.

"Englishu terrible," she confessed.

"Cooking good," he responded, smiling at her.

Another memory forced itself upon her, and she could not escape its impact. She looked up into Peter's face for a long moment before she spoke again. "Peta, I have been marry, you know."

"I know, but what of it?"

"Peta, how you say Englishu — I used."

He held her as tightly as he could so that she could not see his face for a few seconds; it would be disastrous if she thought that he was laughing at her. Then he put a finger under her chin and lifted her head so that he could look into the lovely face that was now an integral part of himself. "So am I, a little," he admitted.

"You marry?"

"No. Just friends."

That seemed to satisfy her completely, so when he detected a remaining shadow in her features, he knew that it was something else. "Peta, maybe priest not like, not want to marry us."

That one was easy, but she was very serious and he answered her that way. "Midori, if he doesn't, he'll be looking for work."

That was enough conversation. He could tell her later about the warm congratulations he had received from Archer Bancroft and the cordial welcome that awaited her on the campus where he worked. He had so many things ahead of him. It would be more than a week, at the least, before he could leave Japan. Details flung themselves into his mind. Midori would need many things; Marjorie had promised to help with that. He would have to go to the embassy and make the necessary arrangements there. There would undoubtedly be other legal formalities. Thank God, both Marjorie and Akitoshi were on hand to take their respective parts in setting up what he fervently hoped would be a simple wedding.

But it would all work out. He was living in a new and different world; from now on he would no longer be alone. It had not bothered him too much in the past, he had plenty of friends, but now when he came home at the end of the academic day there would not be cold empty rooms, but companionship and love. And the little things too: such as having his dinner ready and waiting for him, and someone truly wonderful to share it with him.

The *yuryokusha* had agreed to handle the matter of the farm. It was odd, calling it that, it was so small. That would call for a gift, of course; he would have to send something suitable from America.

There was so much involved in this business of taking a wife. But the dazzling rewards were so great, he could not even begin to count them.

"Come on," he said to Midori. "We've got an awful lot to do."

GREAT BOOKS

E-BOOKS

AUDIOBOOKS

& MORE

Visit us today

www.speakingvolumes.us

Made in the USA
San Bernardino, CA
27 March 2019